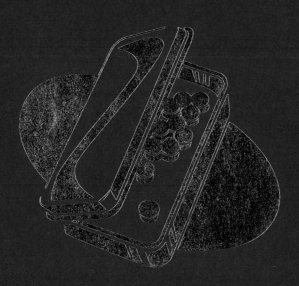

THE OCTOPUS ON MY HEAD

Also by Jim Nisbet

Novels

The Gourmet (1981; reprinted as The Damned Don't Die, 1986)
Lethal Injection (1987)
Death Puppet (1989)
Ulysses' Dog (French pub. only, 1993)
Prelude to a Scream (1997)
The Price of the Ticket (2003)
The Syracuse Codex (2005)
Dark Companion (2006)

Poetry

Poems for a Lady (1979)
Gnachos for Bishop Berkeley (1980)
Morpho (with Alastair Johnston, 1982)
Small Apt (with photos by Shelly Vogel, 1982)
Across the Tasman Sea (1997)

Nonfiction

Laminating the Conic Frustum (1991)

Recordings

The Visitor (1984)

This one's for Erno

MORT · 2007

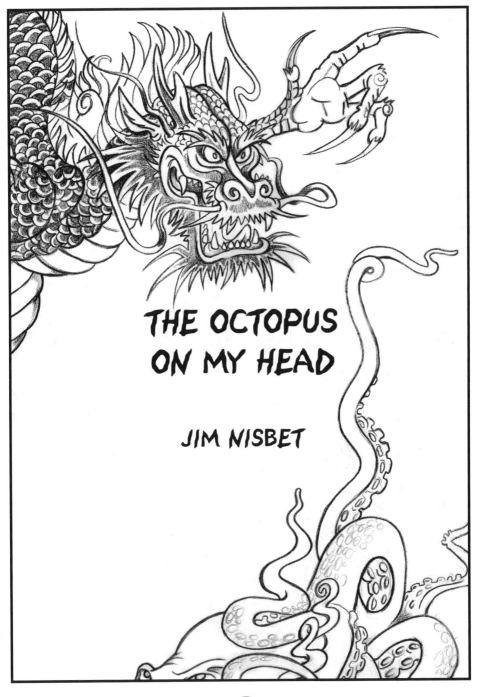

THE OCTOPUS
ON MY HEAD

JIM NISBET

20 07

The Octopus on My Head copyright © 2007
by Jim Nisbet. All rights reserved.

FIRST EDITION
Published July 2007

Dustjacket and interior artwork
by Carol Collier.

ISBN 978-0-939767-57-1

Dennis McMillan Publications
4460 N. Hacienda del Sol (Guest House)
Tucson, Arizona 85718
Tel. (520)-529-6636
email: dennismcmillan@aol.com
website: http://www.dennismcmillan.com

...un noy, pensif parfois descend...
[...sometimes, a drowned man pensively descends...]

— Arthur Rimbaud, *Le Bateau Ivre*

THE OCTOPUS ON MY HEAD

One

Ivy Pruitt had a little pad over a garage in Oakland, up one story by an outside flight of stairs on the back of the building. Its landing overlooked the biggest cemetery in town.

I went to see Ivy because I thought he might be ready to play again, and I wanted to be around when it happened. I don't know why I thought he might be ready for a change and in any case Ivy was always a lot of trouble, but there I was. There was Ivy, too, smoking heroin.

His studio apartment had a lot of potential. He'd sweet-talked his nonagenarian landlord into something like six months of free rent in exchange for which Ivy would run errands at his, Ivy's, convenience. Ivy wore clean clothes when he couldn't afford cigarettes, and though he never cooked or entertained, he cleaned house compulsively, so, except for the redolence of burnt tarball, the apartment looked exactly as it must have looked when he moved in. Freshly painted, gleamingly porcelained, sparklingly windowed, brightly scoured, damply mopped, and barely furnished at all, there were a mattress on the floor of the streetside room and a card table flanked by a pair of aluminum lawn chairs in the kitchen. Add the bathroom, and that was it. Sizewise it was about the same as my place in San Francisco, except Ivy's wasn't a dump and cost half as much. He moved the chairs

1

around as occasion demanded, but I'm sure that often he just stood, leaning against the stove, on the nod like a sleeping horse. Most of the time he was alone. I saw no television, no stereo, not even a radio, and there wasn't a sign of a musical instrument.

Even the bathroom remained immaculate, as if dispossessed, just like the kitchen, for a junky doesn't have much use for either end of alimentation. But the kitchen had a southern exposure which flooded it with sunlight, and it's always sunny in Oakland. So despite its otherwise sordid and solitary employment, the room seemed, at two in the afternoon, almost oppressively cheerful. And it was to this room that Ivy repaired, after cursory amenities at the door, as inevitably drawn to the stove as a comet to its epicenter. Among the few appliances in sight—a refrigerator, a hot water heater, a toaster with a thrift-shop price tag—the stove retained an incomparable utility.

At that time I had never seen tar heroin, let alone chased the dragon; but Ivy Pruitt soon reduced these cultural deprivations to a pair of quaint artifacts.

The stove was gas-fired. Ivy produced a tarball from a black cylindrical film can and rolled it around between his flattened palms, much as an artist kneads a gum eraser before applying it to a sketch. When the ball was quite round and about three-eighths of an inch in diameter, he fired up a front burner, and, with a casualness that belied considerable dexterity, he juggled the ball between the flat blades of two table knives, one in each hand, whose violet patinas betrayed them as well-inured to this particular sortie of etiquette. He twirled the tar in and out of the blue flame and brought it to a seethe without combustion, with the prowess of a sushi chef partitioning snapper. He talked the whole time, too.

"Now listen, Curly, you don't want to overheat this stuff or it turns to shit. The dragon escapes. The dragon doesn't cotton to being trapped in small adhesive balls for months at a time, so he's always laying for a chance to beat the rap. Although the

2

cocksucker shouldn't complain. Most sentient beings remain trapped for entire lifetimes. Not the dragon. The dragon chafes if he goes six months beyond the poppy harvest. Did I ever tell you what Lavinia used to say about letting me fuck her in the ass?"

The inevitability of such 'confidences' between 'men' being yet another uninteresting aspect of both concepts, I said no, emphatically. What's more, I added, I was hoping to get through the day without hearing a word about Lavinia.

He ignored me. "'Trying to get that joint of yours into my asshole is like trying to put God back into the peyote button. It's not going to happen.'"

"Hey," I said, impressed, "that might be the best definition of entropy I've ever heard."

Without averting his eyes from his task Ivy said, "Oh, we knew a thing or two about entropy, Lavinia and I did. Ivy, she always said, that joint of yours is too little for heaven and too big for hell. So," he wagged his head from side to side, as if adjusting his spine, "Me and my joint spent a couple years in purgatory, tending toward chaos the whole time." He grinned into the flame and uttered, "Heat death," as if it were an invocation, with uncommon relish.

Abruptly the ball of heroin sublimated noiselessly into a wraith of redolent blue smoke, uncoiling its mortality up and off the two blades only to encounter the descending numinous rapacity of Ivy's flared nostrils, these cued by some inscrutable signal from the alembic, and into which the serpent disappeared entirely, with great sinuosity, whipping into its proper lair like a newlywed moray eel home for supper.

Ivy kept his lips and eyes shut tight while he continued to inhale deeply through his nose. If he'd been embracing the keydesk as he deployed the passacaglia at the end of Bach's Toccata and Cantata in B Minor on the big organ at Grace Cathedral in front of a thousand people, he wouldn't have appeared more concentrated, or more transported. After a pause he laid the two knives crosswise over a saucer in the middle of the stove top—maybe the only plate in the house, but quite as if a meal had been finished and wanted only a discreet waiter to quickly remove the remains and, with equal discretion, to hesitate in the bringing of the check in order to permit his customer the languid pleasure of a lingering surfeit. Under the saucer lay a quarter page of folded newspaper. The headline read, "Animal Feminization Reported Spreading."

Ivy produced a long and smokeless exhale, like a pearl diver gone to sixty feet and back. He watched the air for perceptible wisps; none appeared and none, of course, meant an efficient intoxication. He sighed contentedly. His eyelids drooped and lifted; their pupils had become little black suns with no planets to warm. He half-smiled abruptly.

"Taste?"

A signal hospitality. And who was I to decline it?

Ivy had yet to extinguish the flame, but with that cavalier *Weltanschauung* of the junkie—that if he's high all's right with the world, and that therefore, if the world is not high too, it should be —he mistook my acceptance of his generosity by the light of his own familiarity with the ritual, an oversight which would require a second generosity, slightly begrudged. For it was but a wink later that, by my unschooled hand, the flame had carbonized the proffered gift into an irretrievable pollutant of the kitchen's hygienic atmosphere, consumed in the flash that comes of too rapid an application of the heat; leaving my nose spiraling after an acrid vapor as coy as it was inert, much as the air pushed by the advancing swatter seems only to abet the escape of the fly.

Recognizing his misjudgment Ivy rolled up a second, punitively smaller dose, administered it with the doting efficiency of Proust's mother fumigating her son's asthma, and I got high.

We stepped out the kitchen door to a whitewashed landing barely big enough to contain two people standing. Dazzling,

4

parched and peeled by its remorseless southern exposure, the little porch presented to us, blinking happily behind our shades, a grand and silent expanse of tombstones and lawn, sepulchres and cypress trees, lavender and obelisks, mourning doves and solarized granite. The vast cemetery stretched south and west from a moss-flocked wall at the back of the narrow yard, almost directly below us, to the freeway nearly a mile distant, and swept east up the hill to our left, perhaps another half mile, all the way to an asphalt apron surmounted by the looming Mormon Tabernacle. This necropolis appeared to cover everything as far as the squinting eye could see; but it extended, in fact, only so far as its pixilating vaults, rolling over the crown of a hillock and out of sight, engaged and lost a quick skirmish with the fierce rays of the meridian sun; there, as if redoubled one for one they seemed to stagger in a blur all the way to the twinkling expanse of the San Francisco Bay, some six or seven miles away.

The sight put me in mind of Paul Valery's poem, *The Cemetery by the Sea*, or *Le Cimetière Marin*, as it's properly called.

"French," Ivy sniffed, cosseting his high against the intrusion of thought.

"May I spare you the opacity of a foreign language, not to mention its music?"

Indolent, he shrugged. I was indolent too, but I like the poem. A modest if liberal decantation of a few lines came readily to mind.

> This tranquil roof, where doves parade,
> among murmuring pines and tombs...

"Murmuring," Ivy agreed. "Play soft."

> ...The judgment of noon consigns the sea
> To fire—the sea, every day renewed!
> What recompense, after deadly meditation,
> This prolonged regard of godlike tranquility...

"With apologies to the original," I added, "it's a very nice meditation on life and death. I prefer it to Thomas Gray's *Elegy Written in a Country Churchyard.*"

Ivy's eyebrows raised above his sunglasses. "If you think of God at all, do you think of Him as tranquil?"

"It's plural, in the French. But if we're talking about one god at a time, and if it's a male god, well . . . I suppose His tranquility would depend upon whether or not He is comfortably ensconced in His peyote button."

Ivy smiled.

We gazed over this silence, basking in as thorough a serenity as might be hoped for, tranquil as lunchtime on a week day in a blue-collar neighborhood.

After a while I noticed a large smokestack of whitewashed bricks at the top of the block, about a hundred yards up the hill from us, beyond which a tall Monterey pine appeared to undulate in the heat waves emanating from the smudged mouth of the chimney. Invisible vapors caused the boughs of the tree to dance more languidly and erratically than they otherwise might, even were there a breeze. I asked what it was.

"That's our local columbarium."

"We're watching a cremation?"

"Some hapless mortal coil, oxidizing to ashes," Ivy confirmed. He made a curt motion of his hand, and not without a certain delectation. "Even as we reflect on the meaning of existence."

Lofting from some cornice among the tombs a pigeon appeared to jump a foot as it flew between the top of the stack and the background pine, only to resume its direct flight once past it.

"The gift of serenity," Ivy suggested.

"They say," I ventured, "that only teeth remain among the ashes."

Ivy grimaced. "There's your recompense, no matter how much meditation is applied." His emphasis on the two nouns made it clear that he rendered little credence to either concept.

6

"No doubt," I suggested, "some enterprising type has long since invented a tooth rake?"

"A simple gravel screen would do," Ivy nodded. "But the real deal is to send a man to hell with his teeth intact. The better to gnash with, once he gets there. Same thing he did with them here," he added softly.

"I hadn't thought of it that way," I admitted.

Ivy's own smoke-yellowed teeth contrasted nicely with the glint of his tinted lenses. "To gnash," he spread his hands, "is to live."

"That sounds somewhat . . . monaural."

"It's all figured out ahead of time."

"Ivy," I queried him, "do you stipulate predestination?"

"Not in the micro." He shook his head and drew himself up, as if with effort. "Certainly not. The paths vary. But in the macro it cooks down to the same thing for everybody." He passed a hand, palm down, over the view. "Is it conceivable that, out of ten thousand stones, *It's all bullshit* isn't chiseled into at least one of them?"

There were a lot of stones out there.

Ivy turned his head to one side, still surveying the necropolis. "You'd think a guy with an octopus tattooed on his head had best readily agree with that." He chuckled.

I chuckled, too. "So you would think."

I kept my eyes on the cemetery, though. After a decent interval I said, "But, in all seriousness, what about music?"

Ivy turned his dark glasses towards me, plainly astonished.

I asked again. "Come on, Ivy. You think music is bullshit, too?"

He laughed pretty hard this time. It wasn't the chuffing whinny of a juvenile stoner, either; rather it was the delighted outburst of a man who, if he's seen everything, now finds himself genuinely amused. But it was also the mild, unfueled percussion of the junky, whose ergonomic can only fully deploy itself upon the

7

one thing, not on delight *per se*. Finally, it seemed the laugh of a man who doesn't lately do much laughing.

Ivy shook his head, smiling. "Go find me some jumper cables. I'm fixin' to fibrillate."

I had taken only a little coffee that morning, thinking Ivy and I might go for a late breakfast. So when I puked over the railing, there wasn't much to it. Bile, mostly.

That's when Ivy really began to laugh.

"I've missed you, Curly," he said affectionately, when he could make himself understood. "Where the hell you been?"

Two

After she left Ivy Pruitt, Lavinia got herself a girlfriend. Girlfriend had been paroled from the California Institute for Women—California's "joint for the jointless," as Ivy called it—less than six months before she was shotgunned by a terrified convenience store owner she was trying to stick up with an air rifle.

Lavinia hired a lawyer who failed to clear the girlfriend's name. But, via subversion of the discovery process, a dub of the pertinent ten minutes of videotape from the store's surveillance camera made it into San Francisco's underground rave scene, with a sound track that sounded like two forklifts fighting over a fifty-five gallon drum full of ecstasy. The clip was deemed danceable, and Lavinia found herself the here-and-now spokeswoman for the deceased ex-girlfriend, an authentic wild-blue-yonder countercultural antiheroine ("...a woman protagonist," Ivy sententiously reminded me, quoting from a review of the 'performance' on a website called KlubXeen.com, downloaded and printed at his local branch of the Oakland Public Library, "as in a play or book, characterized by a lack of traditional heroic qualities."); from which fifteen minutes of notoriety Lavinia entrepreneured herself to the persona of Auntie, heroin dealer to the hipoisie.

I professed shock.

Ivy shrugged. "A girl does what she knows best. What Lavinia did was talk a Mexican tarball wholesaler into a franchise."

I professed incredulity.

9

"Want to experience entrepreneurial zeal at its most pristine?" Ivy extended an open palm. "Gimme ten bucks."

I professed uncertainty.

"Look at it this way," Ivy suggested. "It's the same price as the latest stupid Hollywood movie targeting a demographic you know nothing about, less the cost of parking and popcorn, but the taste it leaves in your mouth lasts longer."

I frowned.

"A soon-to-be-forgotten movie."

I forked over the ten bucks.

"Now we need a phone." He held out the other hand.

I looked at Ivy over the tops of my sunglasses. "You don't have a phone?"

"I don't have a phone."

"But Ivy, they're giving phones away."

"Who is?"

"The Providers, I think they're called."

Ivy dismissed them with a gesture.

"Not to Ivy Pruitt," I surmised. "Ivy Pruitt can't get credit."

"True story," Ivy affirmed. "I don't regret a thing."

I handed him my phone.

He dialed a number. "It's being forwarded." We both heard the three beeps of a pager. "What's the number for this thing?"

I told him.

Ivy tapped it into the keypad and rang off.

"That's it?"

He draped his forearms over the peeling 2x6 that served as the deck's bannister. "Give it a minute."

The heat waves had ceased to issue from the brick chimney. A raven perched on its rim and looked into it. A hearse drove out of the columbarium's parking lot, doglegged around the northwest corner of the vast cemetery, at the top of Cardoza Street, and disappeared.

At that corner, in front of the cemetery's high stone wall, stood

10

a fire department callbox. About five feet high and a very sun-faded red, its column was festooned with heart-shaped Mylar balloons and plastic leis. Two flower pots, each sprouting a red, dessicated poinsetta, stood at its foot, the whole pediment encircled by empty pony bottles, shoulder to shoulder like the posts of a stockade. The balloons, too, were past their prime. Though still listlessly aloft, each was obviously helium-deprived and softening. The strings that tethered them to the post were slack catenaries in the windless afternoon. One, violet and silver, bore scarlet letters outlined in gold glitter that spelled, WE MISS YOU. Wilted metallic fronds, dangling off the fluted post, must have been balloons which had expired completely.

"It's a memorial," Ivy explained. "A kid was gunned down on that corner two weeks ago."

"For what?"

Ivy shook his head. "Gang turf, a bad dope deal, a mistake—who knows? His mother had moved him and herself out of here a few months beforehand, trying to head it off. She went all the way to Vallejo. But the boy got on the bus every day and came back, just like a commuter. He commuted to hang out." Ivy gestured around us. "It was the only world he knew."

"How old was he?"

"Seventeen."

"Young."

Ivy shook his head. "Not if you're black and male. He was the third kid in as many months to be murdered within a couple of blocks of here. A fourth victim was an older woman, also African American, who got caught in a crossfire. Thirty rounds in less than a minute. She was climbing the steps to her porch and never knew what hit her. Even though it was broad daylight, nobody else got a scratch, nobody saw it of course, and nobody got caught either. Not only that but she happened to be the same lady who had embarrassed the city into picking up the refrigerators and TVs and couches off the sidewalks around here and

11

towing away all the dead and stolen cars. It took her two or three years. She harangued them into it with petitions, confrontational public meetings and hearings, and by calling the newspapers and who knows what else—the kind of involvement with city hall and the community that nobody else wants to get into. The irony is troubling." He pointed the phone's antenna. "That punk up there might easily have been party to her death. He might just as easily been in the wrong place at the wrong time, just like her. See those bottles? Jack Daniels, Bombay Sapphire, Couvoisier—quality is important. The fellas drink a toast to the dead seventeen-year-old, leave the empty at the foot of the memorial, and go get shot themselves."

My phone rang.

Ivy studied it, chose a button, then tilted the phone so we could both listen.

"Auntie," said a woman's voice.

"Ivy."

"What's up, train wreck?"

"A ten."

"Wow," she whistled, "ten bucks. You get a job or something?"

"I'll never sink that low again."

"So just how low are you sinking? Skip that. I don't want to know. Just tell me where you're doing it."

"My crib. Where else?"

"We don't keep records, you fucking idiot."

"2733-1/2 Cardoza. Stairs up the back."

"Fifteen minutes."

"I'll wait here."

Ivy handed over the phone. "When they get here, hang back in plain sight. I'll do the talking."

We watched the cemetery for a while. Not far from the stone wall at the back of Ivy's yard a squirrel humped along the chamfered top of a catafalque of black granite flecked with pink.

12

When it reached a corner, it stood up to gnaw an acorn between its front paws, watching us the while.

I tried again. "You never think about playing music?"

Ivy didn't look at me. His hair had gone gray since I'd last seen him, but he still wore it in a pony tail, pulled neatly back. "Shit," was all he said.

In ten minutes they appeared at the foot of the stairs—two Mexicans, one of them a kid. The older one sized us up, then let the younger one precede him up the stairs and follow us into the kitchen. Once inside he pushed the door to behind him, not closing it, and held out his hand. Ivy laid the two fives across it. The younger kid spat a green penny balloon with a knot in its neck onto the palm of his own hand and passed it to Ivy, saliva and all. Ivy closed his fist around it, and the Mexicans left without a word.

"Home delivery," I marveled. "Are we strung out yet?"

"Speak for yourself."

"I am speaking for myself. That's just too damned easy."

"It is that," Ivy agreed. "The hard part's the money."

"Oh," I said. "You want I should iron the bills first?"

Ivy almost smiled. "It just makes up for the shit you wasted."

"So whose dope is it?"

"Ours, of course."

"How *simpatico*." I followed him to the stove. "What's with the kid?"

Ivy rinsed the balloon and his hands at the sink. "The kid carries the dope; the older guy handles the money."

"He's not sixteen," I surmised.

"True story." He patted dry the balloon and his hands on the folded newspaper. "They get busted, which they will, the kid is under age with no papers: no matter what they charge him with, he just gets deported. The older guy's clean, so he walks. Six weeks later the kid's back in the country and back in business."

"Nobody gets hurt," I concluded, "except the greater society."

13

"Jesus Christ, Curly, you are about as square as the corner in a 3-4-5 triangle."

"Oh, man. You really know how to hurt a guy."

Ivy bit the knot off the balloon and turned it inside out over his thumb. A lump of paste that looked like a quarter-inch of brown crayon dropped onto his palm. "Voilà." He rested his eyes on it. "One ten-dollar tarball." And, just then, I glimpsed Ivy Pruitt's solitude. With whom he was sharing these arcana was, perhaps, immaterial. Whether they were reprehensible didn't matter. He was showing me what he was doing, what it felt like, and how it worked. It seemed to me that he hadn't shared anything with anybody in a long time; equally obvious, he had only the one deal left to share. This brief glimpse was a reduction and a condensate, diminished and perversely so, of the kind of conjoint moment that people can discover when they play music together. And a glimpse was all it was. Ivy's solitude winked briefly through his savor of this moment of his addiction like a bit of glass tumbling over the muddy bed of a fast-moving stream. Then it was gone.

I was wasting my time.

"It sure enough looks like one," I said, blinking. Ivy might have caught the tone of my voice, but he didn't look up. All I could think to say was, "How's the weight?"

"Excellent," he replied, and the day resumed its pace. "She hates me, but she's always generous."

"It has nothing to do with keeping you strung out and grateful, I suppose?"

"Customer satisfaction, you mean?" Ivy held the tarball up to the light. "Who's strung out?" he said happily.

"SUV owners," I suggested, "on foreign oil."

"True story."

"So the older guy doesn't pack any heat?"

"Why should he?"

"Guys like you get desperate?"

"That'd be pretty desperate," Ivy said, "not to mention short-sighted and dumb. It could happen, of course. It has happened. But this racket is strictly word of mouth. If I took those two kids off for ten bucks, Lavinia would either have to cover for me or tell her Mexican wholesaler where the missing ten bucks went. If the former, she would then cut me off, and I'd soon be jonesing. If the latter, not only would I be cut off, her *jefe* would have me mainlined with acetone or battery acid or something equally difficult to metabolize. So you see," he smiled, "it's a matter of trust."

"My my my," I said, "here we ain't been on the road but two months and it's already Tennessee."

"Nowhere near it. But thanks for the ten bucks."

"You're welcome. I don't know why I'm such a soft touch."

"Sure you do." Ivy looked at me frankly. "I gave you a job in my band when nobody else would so much as give you an audition."

"So I'm sentimental."

"No way," he said with quiet conviction. "You're stupid."

I nodded toward the tarball. "Not that stupid."

"What do you mean, not that stupid? Where was your head an hour ago, while the rest of you was smoking heroin in this very opium den?"

"Good question. The answer is, it was being curious."

Ivy said impatiently, "Why did you come over here, again?" He lit the flame and adjusted its height.

"Something to do with music."

Ivy snorted. "Music." He took up the two discolored table knives and drummed a tattoo on the metal stove top between the burners, most of two four-bar marching figures called a *cadence* and *roll-off*. "You're the only motherfucker I know who's had the same telephone number for ten years."

"Twelve. How else are club owners and booking agents and record companies and gossip columnists going to find me?"

15

Ivy made as if to smash his fist onto the stove top but pulled the punch about a centimeter short and just touched it with the side of his hand. "Who in the fuck," he said measuredly, "wants to be found?"

"Not the lost, certainly," I answered, with some acid. "But, on the other hand, it seems to me that staying lost has got something to do with denying a certain responsibility that comes along with staying alive."

Ivy stared straight ahead. "It's true."

"Especially if you have talent," I added sententiously. "What's true?"

"There's no such thing as a free lunch."

"That's right. Now that you've got my ten bucks, you still have to talk to me."

"Says who?"

"Nobody. As a matter of fact, you could just make yourself unpleasant until I leave."

"I got a better idea. Why don't you and me split this tarball fifty-fifty and see what we got to say for ourselves afterwards?"

So there it was. If I got stoned enough, I would miss my gig, maybe make no music at all that day, maybe get fired in the bargain. Then maybe we would smoke up my pitiful bank account and my car, too. Maybe even my guitars. Ivy was interested in that. While the whole endowment might only get the two of us into next month, to Ivy that might well have looked like a protracted future.

"Seventy-five/twenty-five would be a more than generous split," I said carefully. "Biased your way. I'm not all that interested in getting so fucked up I can't drive or work or think or, for that matter, continue to talk to you. All of which I'm interested in doing," I added stubbornly.

"Me? I can talk to anybody about anything at any time, fucked up or not. Worth talking to," he cocked an eye my way, "or not."

16

"Yeah, sure. You get loaded and talk. It's different with me. I don't know about heroin, but all I want to do when I'm loaded on most other things is come down enough to get back to work. I don't want to talk to anybody, I don't want to fuck, I don't want to eat. All I want to do is work. Think of me as boring."

"No problem." Ivy made a minute adjustment to the height of the flame. "When you say work, you mean play."

"When I say play, I mean work."

"Work or play or none of the above, you're talking misanthropy. So, now what's the difference between you and me?"

Ivy was getting under my skin. "There's a big difference," I said, annoyed. "If I'm too loaded to communicate with the outside world, I'm doing something wrong."

"Which reminds me," he said. "Can you delete that number from your phone's memory?"

"Huh? Yeah. Sure."

"Do it."

"What's the—"

"Just do it."

"It'll be the last one." I retrieved the cellphone from its holster and paged through the calls. "Area Code 510?"

"Let's see."

I showed him.

"That's it."

As I was about to delete it, he said, "Show me how you do that?"

I showed him.

"Cool. Now. Where were we?"

I indicated the flame. "We were discussing misanthropy."

He watched it flicker. "So we were." He reinitiated the cadence with the knife blades on the stove top, then lost interest. "It's different with me, Curly."

"I know that, Ivy."

He persisted. "Smoking this shit is one thing. Who cares

17

what happens to me? Shut up," he snapped, before I could say anything. "I hated that life. The music sucked, the gigs sucked, dragging the kit from bar to studio and back to another bar sucked, and the money sucked, too. At this point, you know it better than I do."

"It still sucks," I agreed.

"So why do it?" He held one knife vertical, like a baton. "Don't answer that."

"Why not do it," I said anyway, "is more like the question."

"That's not an answer. Good. Non-answers are what I want to hear."

"You were good, Ivy," I countered hopelessly. "Better than good."

"And you're completely mediocre, Curly. How can you stand it?"

I enumerated three fingers. "It's all I've got, it beats a day job, and you haven't heard me play in ten years."

"I don't need to," Ivy said softly, as if kindly.

That really pissed me off, but I let it pass. People can change and I had, but they don't have to, too, and Ivy hadn't. Ivy had made up his mind about all this stuff a long time ago.

"As to the day job, who knows?" When he proudly smiled, I realized that a slight sibilance in his speech came not from loss of control due to the drug but because his teeth, not merely going, were mostly gone. "I don't."

"I do. I've had plenty of them."

"That's true. You were a Xerox clerk at an accounting firm, or something, when I first met you."

"Law firm. Before I quit, they promoted me to proofreader."

Without betraying a particle of curiosity Ivy said, "What's that mean?"

"They give you documents and you proofread them. Not even copy-edit them, just proofread for spelling errors and punctuation. That's it. Each line in the document is numbered. They run to scores and even hundreds of pages. It's all legalese; you couldn't copy-edit it if you tried. . . . How'd we get into this?"

"In discussing how low I've sunk, we were casting about for a standard of comparison."

"Fuck you, Pruitt. I'm the one who came up with ten bucks without stealing a radio."

"Who the hell said anything about stealing radios?"

"You know what I mean, you ingenuous sack of shit."

"Ingenuous?" Ivy drew himself up to his full height. "I've been called a lot of things, Curly, but nobody, and I mean not a single person, ever, has called me ingenuous."

"I'm charmed and castigated."

"Throw in mediocre and you got a hit tune."

"Let me make an entry in my diary," I retorted.

But Ivy's attention had been drawn back to his tarball, which had been languishing on the saucer. He picked it up between the blades of the two knives as handily as an egret employs its bill to pluck a tick off the hump of a Brahma bull.

"How are you making it, anyway?" I looked around the kitchen. "Your gas bill must be enormous."

"Every day," Ivy said, rolling the drug in the flame, "I get an old friend to feel sorry for me." Abruptly he wheeled and held the fuming tarball directly under my nose.

"Son of a b—"

"You know all those sixteenth notes you hate to practice, Curly? The thing about this shit you're gonna like is it makes it feel like you got a whole bar to play each one of them."

"But you don't have a whole bar, man, you—"

"We're gonna do it all, Curly," he declared. "Breathe deep."

I was just about to pass out when Ivy abruptly removed the apparatus from beneath my nose and positioned it under his own.

"Mmmm. . . ," he groaned, without opening his mouth. Thirty seconds later he laughed the peculiar, powerless laugh of the

19

heroinated, exhaling not a wisp of smoke. "One part for you and two parts for me—wouldn't you say?"

As I was coughing little clouds like a preteen cigarette smoker, the room began to fill with uniformed police officers.

Three

Says here in the paper," said a guy sitting against the cold tile wall to my left, "that a tumor in your asshole can rupture your colon."

"I got your tumor," said the guy sitting against the wall to my right. When I turned to look at him he looked me back and said, "I got yours, too, motherfucker."

"It don't say asshole in the *Chronicle*," said a third guy, lying on his back on the padded floor against the opposite wall with his arm over his eyes. "The *Chronicle* is a family newspaper."

"That's true," the guy with the paper confirmed. "I was translating for the benefit of the rectally challenged."

"Probably says chocolate highway," said the guy on the floor. "¡Aieee! ¡No más! ¡No más por favor!" he begged enthusiastically.

"Nope," said the guy to my left, folding his newspaper. "Guess again."

"Oh, no," said a fourth voice. "Don't get them—"

"Bung hole," said the guy with his arm over his eyes.

"Anus," said the guy to my left.

"Tropical paradise."

"Quiver for the fun gun."

"Birth control."

The guy on the floor folded his hands behind his head, keeping his eyes closed, and said, "Sphincter Concerto."

"*Culo*," countered the guy to my left, but it took him a second to come up with it.

"Real sex," came the immediate reply.

"Unreal sex," came the fierce response.

"*L'usine de gaz.*"

"Waiting for martyrdom."

"Mortar for the pestle."

"Better than camel."

"The priest's retreat."

"Greek vacation."

"Nether lips. . . ."

"Watkins!"

"Cecum of devotion."

"Curly Watkins in here?"

"Perineal fiesta."

"Yo," said I.

"The astomatous solution. . . ."

When the turnkey opened the door, two or three men stepped forward.

"Prolapsed rectum."

"Not a chance," said the turnkey, shooing them back. "Get out here, Watkins."

"Cyclops on toast. . . ."

The door banged shut.

"Pirate's delight."

"Prostatic epiphany. . . ."

"¡Aieee! ¡No más! ¡No más por favor!"

Long story short, since Ivy and I had smoked the evidence, I walked.

They had some paraphernalia to test, but the rate of crime is sky high in Oakland, the rate of real crime that is, murder and whatnot. I was far too small a fry to prosecute. Besides, those were Ivy's table knives, not mine. Not to mention, Ivy had a record, and I didn't.

All the numbers in my cell phone checked out, as the one club owner, four or five musicians, and nine or ten take-out restaurants listed in its memory now had reason to know; a persistent cop with a yen for acting called every one of them and tried to score dope from whomever answered. I'm sorry I missed out on that aspect of the investigation, but as the years went by, I heard about these calls. Most of them, anyway. The "Curly said you'd hook me up" bit put two or three people off me for good. Ah, well. Push comes to shove, you can never tell what's going to break up a relationship.

The instrument case in the trunk of my car was clean, too, although how they figured that out without destroying the guitar inside it makes for an interesting question. Sort of. My record was so clean it was hard for the cops to believe I was in the music business. Statute of limitations, I assured them. And besides, who called it a business? Not like crime is a business. One of the cops said he played a little cornet now and then. Cool, I said, did you bring your ax? He blushed and said no. Good, I said with certainty, and the other cops in the room got a laugh at his expense. Maybe they'd heard him play. But he was a sport about it.

Meanwhile, the computer had turned up some prior beef Ivy had run out on in San Francisco, so they shipped him across the bridge and called it a day. That, plus the fact that as Ivy and I came out of his apartment in handcuffs, a squad car pulled up with the two Mexicans in back, which made it a pretty good haul. Why keep the consumer when you've got his connection? That's a good question, but we're not here to debate the Broken Window Theory; we're here to celebrate our freedom by claiming our Honda from the police garage.

Unfortunately, towing a Honda Civic backwards does something to the transmission, which costs about $250 to fix. I rode with the second tow truck over the Bay Bridge to the Unocal on Market at Duboce where Jim Zhong, who runs the place, was cool, as usual, about my Honda dangling off a hook again. He'd keep it on his lot and repair it as soon as I could pay for it. More than a square deal.

So it was late by the time I had trudged back to the one hundred block of Haight Street. In spite of everything I still had time to grab a jacket and take a bus to work, when but whom should I find chain-smoking on my front steps but Ms. Lavinia Hahn—"Auntie" herself.

"Hi, Curly," she chirped, her eyes as miotic as they were bright.

"Oh, no," I said, with feeling.

She dropped her cigarette to the pavement with several of its brethren and crushed it beneath the sole of her boot. "What's the matter, Curly? Blood sugar down?"

"How'd you know?"

"I used to own a massage parlor." She stood up and smoothed her skirt. "Can I come in?"

"What if I say no?"

"I'll tie you up and make you watch my video until you say Auntie."

"Auntie." I gathered the mail in the front hall and led her up the stairs. Three flights later I opened the apartment door and stepped aside. "If you need to shoot up, the bathroom's on the right."

"I'm cool," she said, brushing by me, trailing the by now unmistakable odor of combusted tarball. Once you've indentified the smell, you begin to notice it often.

"I always thought so."

"Besides," she said, appraising the apartment without bothering to conceal her disdain, "I don't carry weight when I'm working."

Wearily I closed the door and stood the guitar case against

24

the wall in the modest entryway. "What brings you to Hayes Valley?"

"You, of course." She breezed through the living/dining/sitting/practice room and set about checking her makeup in a mirror that overhung the kitchen sink.

"You, of course," I parroted. I noticed a blinking light on the answering machine and pushed the Play button. "I hear that video of yours is all the rage."

"Rave," she said past the tip of a lipstick. "Rage is for people who drive cars too big to park."

"Curly," growled the answering machine, "you asshole." It was the voice of Padraic Mousaief, who owned a coffee house way out Judah, almost to the beach. "Today this guy calls me to score for dope and says you told him I can hook him up? What the fuck? Not only that, he had to be a cop. You think this is funny? Do you have any idea what it means to be an immigrant in this country?"

"You know what my uncle and eleven of his sons do for a living in the Bekaa Valley?" I muttered unhappily.

"Although," Lavinia observed, "Talking back to your answering machine is symtomatic of rage, too."

"I think," Padraic continued, "is best you are canceled tonight and from now on, at least until you come to me with an open heart and explain to me why it is I should not deny employment to a man who peddles dope."

"Who doesn't cut me in," I added. "Goodbye."

"Goodbye," said Padraic. Three beeps indicated that there were no more messages, and the machine turned itself off.

"Why is it," I said to the wall, "that nobody calls a cell phone with bad news? What if I had gone straight from jail to my gig, instead of coming home to freshen up first?"

"They learned it from Hollywood," Lavinia said from under an eyeliner brush. "You know what the second hardest answer to get in Hollywood is?"

25

"No," I said, browsing through the mail for something that was going to get me out of this fix.

"That's right. Very good."

"Flyers, postcards, and performance calendars from every bar or club or coffee house I've ever played in—wait. Here's one from a street corner I used to play on." I culled the two phone bills—two phones, right?—and dropped the rest of the mail into the trash. "What's very good?"

"Your answer. It was correct."

"I need a drink."

"What," Lavinia pursed her lips at the mirror, "no blowjob?"

I shook my head sadly. "I can't get it up."

"You really know how to make a girl feel attractive, Curly. You send me, though. And how."

"Not far enough, evidently."

"Don't be so paranoid, Curly. I won't bite it off."

"Why not? Because your teeth are still in a jar next to the coffin you sleep in?"

Not to be outdone Lavinia hissed like, presumably, a vampire; like, presumably, she would know.

"I could have been a bag man," I said morosely, "or a stock broker. Numbers come naturally to me. I've counted sheep into the millions. But no. I had to become a bohemian. Not only that, I had to become a musician, too. My star must be an asterisk. Where's my beret?"

"You followed your bliss," Lavinia suggested.

"I wish she followed me once in a while." I squeezed past Lavinia into the kitchenette, covered a glass of ice with three ounces of vodka, and toasted her face in the mirror. "I never drink when I work." I took a big swallow. "Hard alcohol, I mean."

"Then take it easy, Curly. I came here for a favor."

I perched on a countertop and watched her in the mirror. Lavinia was under forty, no longer looked it, yet still managed to remain attractive. While her complexion had the grayish pallor of freshly hung drywall, the bluish blush and mauve eyeliner and dusky rose lip-gloss she deployed only enhanced it. The considerable money she spent on facials and mud baths in Calistoga only served to leave her skin with the unwrinkled sheen of a glazed doughnut. The net effect was an artificiality, which, if *à la mode*, so belied her eyebrows that they looked applied rather than expertly shaped. The traffic-vest orange of her hair only accentuated the impression that her hairline wasn't a line at all, but a seam. For all the time she spent applying cosmetics, I might as well have been mooting existentialism with a clown in the green room.

Yet, and yet, Lavinia's carriage, her self-possession, her intelligence, and our erstwhile friendship, which predated her two disastrous years with Ivy Pruitt by five or six more years, disposed me favorably towards her.

"Ivy sent me."

"Ivy's in jail."

"They gave him a phone call."

"You'd think they'd learn."

"Guy's got rights."

"Lavinia?"

"Curly?"

"How many times has Ivy been in the pokey?"

She permitted herself a little smile. "How many lesbians can dance on the head of a pin, Curly?"

"But aren't there theoretical limits? What happened to three strikes?"

"Curly, don't quote me, but you really got to fuck up to get three strikes laid on you." Her eyes caught mine in the mirror. "It's like getting busted for dope."

"How's that?" I sighed, feigning interest.

She turned around and stabbed at the floor with a 1963 Buick Riviera Purple eyeliner brush for emphasis. "You've got to try *really hard* to get busted for dope in Oakland," she said with mock

27

earnestness. "Almost as hard as in San Francisco." She started laughing.

"No doubt my expression is caught between a smirk and a grimace," I said ruefully.

"That little nocturnal mammal of your spirit spiked on the thorn of the moment by the shrike of your dignity." Lavinia tried to smile, but her lower lip was slack.

"The leer of the sensualist," I said quietly.

"The fuck you say." She turned back to the mirror.

"That fact is, Lavinia, I need the job, I'm a very straight boy these days, and I'm decidedly uncomfortable with the position into which Ivy seems to have landed me with a mere flick of a couple of table knives. I'm more than uncomfortable. I'm annoyed and cornered. That dalliance cost me a job and some auto repairs, not to mention ten bucks, and I'm not exactly flush." I took a sip of vodka. "More like flushed. Or about to be."

"It cost you a job." Lavinia continued with her makeup. "I've heard about that job."

I couldn't help myself: "You saw that review in the *Bay Guardian?* About my gig at the Caffeine Machine?"

"Heard about it," Lavinia said. "I also heard it pays you forty-five dollars a night."

I nodded. "And all the coffee I can drink." Of course she hadn't seen the review.

"Coffee keeps you awake."

"Water, then."

"Bottled water?'

"Hetch Hetchy; the freshest municipal water in the world. Plus a meal."

"Tap water." Lavinia fluttered her eyelashes at the rust-flecked mirror as if it were a camera.

"Yeah? So? It was a job. J-O-B. You remember what that is? Three nights a week, all year round, and whatever charts I felt

28

like playing, they didn't mind." I rattled the ice in my glass. "I was getting paid to practice."

"With that and rent control," Lavinia observed accurately, "a guy could tread tap water for the rest of his life."

"Fuck you very much," I said politely. I tried for another bracing swallow of vodka, only to get an ice cube against the incisors. I looked at the glass. It looked at me. "My vessel is drained of its essence."

"Did I sleep through another blowjob?" Lavinia asked sincerely.

I had made another cocktail and resettled onto the countertop, sitting on my hands, watching my boots swing back and forth, silently mulling the atonal œuvre of Arnold Schönberg note by note, when Lavinia said to the mirror, "There's more."

"Always." I blinked. "More what?"

"About you, silly, in that coffee house."

"No. There isn't."

"That's it. Exactly."

I stopped waving my feet. "What are you talking about?"

"You. In that coffee house. You were wasting your time there."

I set my heels loudly on the floor and paced to the back door and opened it. There I saw a broom whose straws were worn to a nub, a mop with a head like a nuked Medusa, a hot water heater with rust-stained rags knotted around its pipe joints, and an amazingly bad copy of Picasso's *Three Musicians*, painted onto a piece of plywood, that had been nailed sideways over a hole that once was a window. "You know," I said to the closet, "Ivy hasn't heard me play a note in ten years." I turned and paced back to the sink, hands in back pockets. "You know?"

Lavinia paused the reconstruction of her face. "I know," she said to my reflection in the mirror. "I didn't hear it from him."

I smiled in spite of myself, and shook my head. "I read an article about Sonny Rollins in the *Guardian* once. Right off the

29

bat it said that while he's never recorded a classic album, he's a pretty good saxophone player." I studied the glass of vodka. "What the fuck does *The San Francisco Bay Guardian* know about music, anyway?" I took a stiff swallow. "Is that self-deprecating enough?"

"Less than nothing," she said. "But hey, I didn't come here to tell you about your lousy life, or to hear about it, either. You're hard enough on yourself. And, I must say, when I heard about that review, I thought it was so great I'd crawl over broken glass to bring you marzipan if I thought it would ease your travail through this vale of tears."

"Marzipan?" I said. "Really?"

She smiled sweetly. "That review said you were great, despite the circumstances—streetcars and espresso machines and cellphones in the background, and whatnot."

"Special circumstances is life," I said, scrubbing my face with one hand. "And everybody gets the death-penalty. Thank you so much. I think."

"You're welcome. So." She began placing makeup tools into her purse. "That's that." She closed the purse a snap and turned to face me. "How do I look?"

"Animatronic."

"Wow, cool. Pornographic Hintai is all the rage, on today's Internet."

"You've put on weight, too. How is it possible?"

She blushed as only a 'toon can, who knows she rarely eats anything more substantial than a blue-screen carrot smoothie.

"No offense," I insisted. "For a girl who's five-foot-five, you carry ninety-seven pounds like it's natural. Plus the clothes help. Your legs look long, your hips look slim, your bosom looks shapely. " I framed her between squared forefingers and thumbs: "For a junky who hasn't slept or eaten in—how many years?" I moved the frame to one side. She shrugged. I looked through the frame again. "Sleek as the nose cone on a Studebaker. How do you do it? You got a trust fund?"

"I have a career."

"Dealing dope is a career?"

She arched a cold eyebrow. "I can afford my insomnia."

"What's to afford? We know you don't eat. As to rent—how many square feet can a coffin take up, anyway?"

"Fifteen hundred. On Grizzly Peak."

Do I have to point out that, even though it's in the East Bay, it's a nice address?

She dug in her purse and produced a ring of keys. "Let's take a ride in a brand-new Lexus."

"So," I hesitated, "there's money in dope. I'm impressed. I'm also tired. Can I go to bed now?"

"You're too broke to sleep."

She had me there. "So?" I said grudgingly.

"We have a plan, Ivy and I, and there's a paycheck in it for everybody. You, too. Eight or nine hundred bucks for a few hours' work. And it's completely legal," she added, "almost."

"Almost, she says."

"Come on, Curly," she cooed. "You need a break. Ivy needs a hand. Both of you need money."

"All too true," I said cautiously. "So where do you fit in?"

"I'm the enabler." She dangled the car keys off an index finger.

I folded my arms and set my jaw. "I refuse to steal organs."

"No keyboards involved," she laughed. "Just bring your guitar case."

"Why? I just got fired."

"Just the case. Leave your ax here. Do you have a piece of respectable-looking carry-on luggage?"

31

Four

Ten blocks later, Lavinia killed a Dalmatian.

We were crossing Dolores on 25th, she was speeding, and I barely saw the dog. It was accompanied by a woman dressed in jodhpurs and a quilted vest with a ruff collar, and it was attached to her by an inertia reel leash, the kind that extends from no length at all to fifteen or sixteen feet. The dog only needed about five of those feet to meet his undoing. His mistress was waiting for the light, but she was on the phone, too, turning one way and another and not paying attention. The dog followed its nose into the crosswalk. When the right front tire hit it square on the shoulder it sounded like a watermelon dropped off the roof of a five-story building. Orts of dog sprayed the undercarriage, the woman screamed, and we were gone.

Several blocks later, Lavinia asked me if we should have stopped.

"The dog's dead," I pointed out.

We were crossing Sanchez. "Did you hear what she screamed?"

"'Gates,' I think."

"Her dog's names was Gates?"

"Maybe she'll inherit its fortune."

Lavinia turned left on Noe and jogged right on Clipper. We crested Diamond Heights and a few minutes later descended Upper Market, half the nightlit city spread out beneath us. Nearly three miles away, next to the Lefty O'Doul drawbridge

32

at the edge of the bay, the Giants' baseball park was brightly illuminated. A thicket of fog the size of a small town drifted on the bay beyond it, glowing in the surplus illumination shed by bright towers looking down on the stadium. Beyond the fog bank twinkled the Oakland hills.

"When I was a kid in Nevada," I mused, "I was driving home one night from a date. In those days the eastern slope was far less populated than it is now, and a forty-mile stretch of starlit desert separated Reno and Nevada City. We lived on a ranch straight east of Mono Lake. The girl was a cellist I'd met at a summer music camp at Lake Tahoe, and she lived in Sparks. It wasn't uncommon to drive a hundred-mile round trip for a date. Forty or fifty miles to pick her up, back across the tracks to Reno or someplace where we could have some fun, see a movie or go to a party, then the other half of the round trip to drop her off and make it home again."

Lavinia lit a cigarette and held it out the driver's window between puffs, a thoughtful courtesy, considering it was her car.

"To accommodate the necessity of covering long distances efficiently, I'd dropped a late sixties four-barrel 327 into a 1950 Chevy pickup truck. I found a rare '59 transmission for it, a Chevy three speed with overdrive, and shoehorned it in there, which in turn required a Pontiac drive shaft and a Mercury rear end. I fitted it with wide tall tires in back and normal ones up front. That heap could cruise at ninety-five or a hundred miles an hour all night long. Had an eight-track tape deck, too."

Lavinia frowned quizzically at the nacelle of electronics in the Lexus dash, whose speedometer claimed a top speed of 145 mph and whence she could select any track in any order from five or six CDs.

"Have you ever seen an eight-track tape?" I asked.

She shook her head. "Never heard of them."

"All the truck's original electrics, like the headlamps, the taillights, the radio, were six volts. But the tape deck and everything on the V8, like the starter, were twelve volts. So I had an extra six-volt battery wired up in series with the truck's original six volt battery. The only place the second battery would fit was in the footwell in front of the passenger seat. There was a floor shift, of course, rather crudely cut in. Through the hole in the floorboards you could watch the asphalt streaming beneath the truck. My cellist had to be careful around that rig. She didn't want to get battery acid on her party dress."

Lavinia flicked her cigarette into the night. "It sounds to me," she observed, checking her mirror as she signaled and changed lanes, "as if this poor girl came a distant third to that truck and its tape deck."

"Well, that's interesting you should mention that, Lavinia, and I hasten to agree, if qualifiedly. Until I met that cellist, you might have been correct. But that cellist. . . ."

A Lincoln Navigator, at 6,000 pounds one of the largest SUVs on the market, abruptly passed us in the right lane. Its driver held down his horn and gesticulated rudely in our direction.

"Guy's panties are too tight," Lavinia suggested, braking as the Navigator cut us off and stopped, just in time, for the light at Clayton. Lavinia had to brake hard to avoid rear-ending it. "Does not this pig care that I am carrying a gun?"

I looked at her. "You are?" Lavinia said nothing. I turned back to the windshield. "Maybe the IRS is reviewing his offshore partnerships, so he needs to commit suicide."

We studied the vehicle—we had no choice. Just four inches shy of eight feet wide, burnished to an ebony luster, its bulk filled the entire windscreen. It's rear bumper was almost as high as the hood on the Lexus, which forced us to squint into the reflected glare of our own headlights. As for its sparkling windows, an American flag filled each of the two rear ones. A red, white and blue sticker on its left bumper read, *United We Stand*, and as Lavinia quoted it, she was quick to provide the phrase with a minor premise, *"On Top Of Everyone Else,"* and a conclusion, *"Or Else!"* She slapped my knee. "Pretty good, huh? Huh?"

"Yes," I agreed, "but it's unpatriotic." I pointed out the sticker on the beast's right bumper.

I'm Changing the Climate: Ask Me How!

"That's incredible," Lavinia marveled. "No way this jerk knows that motto is defiling his Global Warmer. Some prankster put it there."

"On the contrary. Maybe he's proud of it."

"Which makes for the bigger jerk?"

"That he knows, of course."

Lavinia nodded. "Then he knows."

When the light turned green, the Navigator emitted a strange roar and lunged forward. It sounded like a sand-blaster.

"He got a mile to that gallon," Lavinia said, as we watched the huge taillights diminish down Market Street.

A car behind us honked. Lavinia turned left.

"So," I continued, "one night, having delivered the cellist to her mother in Sparks a little earlier than we'd planned, on account we were making out in her driveway and accidentally leaned on the horn, which woke her mother up. . . ."

Lavinia laughed. "You've never played a note that wasn't smooth jazz, have you, Curly?"

"Hey. I'm telling you all this for a reason."

"You are?"

"Check it out. The way home was 43 miles through the desert. Not a stop sign, not a streetlight, not another car, no speed limit. There wasn't even a line painted in the middle of the road. It was way past midnight on a Sunday, and I was supposed to open up the Flying A station in Lee Vining at six A.M., where I worked

35

at the time, which left me about four hours' sleep. No problem. I was nineteen. I parked the tachometer at 3300 rpm in overdrive, which translated to about 92 miles per hour—no speedometer —and let her roll. It was late spring in the desert. The sage had begun to get hot enough in the daytime to release its scent into the cooler night air, but I was steering with a light touch, elbow out the window, and smelling the inside of my right wrist, on which I could detect the perfume of my cellist. I never knew what brand it was, but to this day I remember what it smelled like, and if I ever notice that smell in a club or a hotel lobby or on the street, it takes me straight back to that night. I can hear the exact pitch of the dual exhaust on that 300 horsepower V8, I can hear the chains rattle on the tailgate, I can hear the Grateful Dead's *Dark Star*, the longest cut ever released on eight-track tape, so far as I know. . . ."

"You're a fucking moron," Lavinia said.

"I entered one of those long desert curves that can take up a whole valley, and I saw the dog sleeping in the road, but that's all I had time to do before the right front wheel simply exploded it. It sounded like a wave hitting a seawall, a percussive splash that spewed large and small pieces of dog all up under the truck. It didn't affect the forward momentum at all. I was a mile down the road before I even thought to react."

Lavinia stopped for the light at 17th Street.

"Dogs, you know, way out in the country, they'll sleep on the road at night for the warmth the asphalt's soaked up during the day."

The light turned green and Lavinia turned left. "Did you stop?"

"What for? It was between me and that dog, and he was dead."

"Didn't you feel bad?"

"I just told you the story, didn't I?"

"So?"

36

"So it's thirty years later. Doesn't that tell you something?"

"Like what, Curly? That you're a sensitive moron? But that story just about made me puke. What if it had been a kid?"

"Kids don't sleep on asphalt in the middle of the night."

Lavinia was silent.

"Do they?" I asked uncertainly.

"You know what I've been thinking the whole time you were telling that story—since before your story, since we ran over the Dalmatian?"

"No. Since *you* ran over the Dalmatian, what have *you* been thinking about?"

"Telltail."

"Telltail? Is that a person?"

"That's the girl in my video. Tanya was her real name. Telltail was her nickname." She glanced my way, "That's T-A-I-L."

I nodded. "The girl who was killed in the liquor store hold-up."

"I'll never forget it. I dedicate every show to her."

"That's big of you. Do you send royalties to her mother?"

"No way. Telltail's mother was renting her out to her own boyfriends by the time Telltail was twelve."

"Oh, great, honey, let's grow a sociopath. So you keep the money."

"Hey. Curly?"

I turned to look at her.

"Did you keep that hotrod pickup truck?"

I raised an eyebrow. "Damn straight I did."

She turned right on Stanyan.

A half hour later Lavinia parked the Lexus in front of Lafayette Elementary on Anza between 36th and 37th Avenues, and pointed out a two-story bungalow across the street.

"What about it?"

37

"The address is 4514 Anza. Can you remember that?"

"Sure."

She pulled away from the curb. "Now we need a cab." She produced a cell phone and retrieved the number of Big Dog Taxi from information. When the dispatcher came on the line, she ordered a cab for a cafe called In Fog We Trust, on Cabrillo at 40th. She listened for a moment, then explained that the ride was six blocks, a wait, then another six blocks, but, not to worry, she'd guarantee a thirty-dollar fare. She listened for another moment, then patiently spelled the name of the cafe. She was parallel-parking one-handed on 39th, just above Balboa, by the time she hung up.

We retrieved the empty guitar case and carry-on bag from the trunk and walked two blocks to 40th and Cabrillo. There we found a lively little group of businesses, including a dry cleaner, a yoga school, a trophy shop, a bar, a Vietnamese restaurant, and a small grocery. In Fog We Trust was a natural-food cafe with a genuine, humming samovar looming over the back bar next to a pastry case. A couple of people played chess in the front window. A guy strummed a guitar on a bench out front. When he saw my instrument case, he quit playing.

The marine layer was gliding in to blanket the city for the night, and it was chilly. Lavinia and I walked past the cafe. As we neared the top of the block, the shy guitarist began to play again. From sixty yards down wind it sounded like Fernando Sor's "Tema con Variaciones."

"When you get to 4514 Anza, tell the driver to wait for you. Make sure he parks in front of the house, so whoever answers the door will see the cab. Your name is Stepnowski."

"What is that? Polish?"

"How should I know? You're looking for your brother. His name is Stefan and his wife's name is Angelica. Got that?"

"Stefan and Angelica," I repeated.

She looked at my head and frowned. "I wish we had a stupid

hat for you, but we don't. If whoever answers the door isn't too nervous to speak with you, they'll tell you that Stepnowski no longer lives at that address."

"Oh, dear."

"That's right. You've been on the road for a month and out of touch, but you came all the way from Philadelphia to gig with your brother's band until they find a new guitar player. The first job's tomorrow night, but you don't know where it is."

"You need Stepnowski's new address."

"That's correct."

"He owes you money?"

"He owes money to Kramer's World of Sound."

"Sal 'The King' Kramer? How much?"

"Seventy-five hundred dollars."

"Since when does Ivy Pruitt carry the weight for a job like this?"

"He gets pretty ugly when he's strung out. People are afraid of him."

"So where's that leave me?"

"You're big and you're bald and you got an octopus tattooed on your head."

"But these," I said, turning them palm up, "are an artist's hands. I don't use them to beat up people."

"So use your feet. If we pull this off," she persisted, "we have a bondsman who will go Ivy's bail for $1200. Once he's out, Ivy will need a little running-around money—"

"Is that what he calls it?"

"—say another six seventy-five. That makes eighteen seventy-five for Ivy. Whether these reprobates give up the gear or fork over cash, 'The King' gives Ivy half of whatever he manages to intimidate out of them. In this case, if we get the whole seventy-five hundred, you and I will split what's left after Sal and Ivy get theirs. That's nine hundred and thirty-seven dollars and fifty cents apiece. In other words, you fucking idiot, your cut will come to more than five month's pay at that crappy gig you just got fired from."

"As I was saying, these hands are capable of almost anything, A-minor-seven-flat-five, even."

"Good. Keep your wits about you and things will go peacefully. They almost always do. Here's your cab."

An orange taxi was pulling to the curb in front of the cafe as we returned. The cabbie popped open the trunk lid and got out to take my luggage. I told him I would keep it with me. He slammed the lid in disgust and got back under the wheel.

"Honey?" Lavinia said, as I loaded the guitar case through the back door. When I turned around she plunged her tongue into my mouth. I drew back, shocked. Lavinia smiled dreamily. "I never kissed sushi before."

"*Sushi* is generic," I said. "*Tako* is octopus."

"Whatever." She closed the door.

As we rolled away from the curb, the cabbie dropped the flag and glanced at the mirror. "Where to?"

"4514 Anza."

He stopped the cab. "That's six blocks from here. I drove all the way out here from the fuckin Tenderloin, man. You—"

"Hey, hey," I said, "take it easy. Didn't your dispatcher tell you there was thirty bucks in this ride?"

"He didn't tell me shit. He was trying to give the ride to some buttboy of his, but things were so dead in the 'Loin I beat him to it. But hey, man, six blocks. . . . The goddamn gate fee's up to a buck and a quarter and I—"

"That's stiff," I agreed. "But I got thirty toward your one twenty-five for a lousy twelve block round trip. Let's get it over with."

As we discussed the fare, I realized that Lavinia had neglected to negotiate expenses. Here we go, I thought: Ivy Pruitt has figured out how to get me to spend my money on him even while he's in jail.

40

"I used to play guitar," said the cabbie, as he turned up 39th.

"Yeah?" I said, without interest.

"Sure I did. All through the sixties. I knew all the tunes." He named five or six.

"You and the sixties," I said, "are making me carsick."

"Don't puke in the cab. You want me to pull over?"

"No."

"I never got laid so much in my life."

I interrupted. "Tell you what."

He looked at the mirror. "What?"

"Left on Anza. Do you still play?"

He shook his head. "Nah. I got married, had a couple kids, got a mortgage to pay, drink too much after work, *love* reality television. . . . You know how it is."

"I do," I lied.

"Yeah?"

"Yeah. Keep up the good work, don't talk about the sixties, and I'll make it forty bucks."

"Forty bucks? Thanks, buddy. Say, do you know the chords to—"

"There it is. Park here and wait. I'll be right back."

Forty-five fourteen Anza was the bottom half of a two-story duplex on the northwest corner at 36th Avenue. Two six-foot junipers sculpted into corkscrews flanked the windowless front door. There was a light over them. I pushed a button next to the mail slot and a doorbell chimed. A minute passed. I rang again. A window opened on the second floor, left of the door. "Who's there?"

I stepped back and looked up. An older gentleman in a smoking jacket was looking at the idling taxi behind me. The ceiling of the room behind him flickered with the blue light of a television. His hair was white and thin on the sides and nonexistent on top, but he had let the remaining tonsure grow very long and overcombed the strands, on the same theory, one supposed, that

41

farmers apply when heaping brush in a gully to inhibit erosion. The fog wind was trying to play with these strands, but they'd been moussed into stiff resistance. His cheeks were the white of clay, the color of meerschaum, not to say sallow, but shaved closely enough to promote asymmetric patches of razor burn on both. The eyes were, in fact, intelligent but distracted. Perhaps a televised movie had proved absorbing.

Having discerned that I was associated with the taxi in front of his house, the man crossed his wrists and dangled them off the window sill. One of them held a small metal tin.

"Good evening, sir," I called cheerfully. "Would this be 4514 Anza Street, San Francisco, California, USA, Planet Earth?" and chuckled like the chucklehead I like to tell myself I'm not.

The old man wasn't impressed. "Who wants to know?"

"David Stepnowski," I said. "My brother Stefan lives here."

"Stefan was your brother?"

"Was, sir?" My expression changed completely. "Was?"

"He no longer resides at this address."

"But he's okay?"

"I guess he's okay. How should I know if he's okay?"

"Well, sir, you just said, I mean, when you said 'was,' well, it's just that my mind. . . ."

"Nah, nah," the man said, waving the thought away. The tin rattled like a dried gourd full of seeds. "He just moved, that's all."

"Oh, well—but wait. We talking about the same guy?" I held up the guitar case. "He's a musician, right?"

"That's right. Does it run in the family?"

"Oh, we all sang in church. Stefan's a drummer."

"That he was—still is, probably."

"Well now, sir, this is strange. I've come all the way from Philadelphia to play with my brother's band, see—he still has his band?"

"How the hell would I know about his band?"

42

"Well, I mean, Stefan called me in Philadelphia a month ago. His guitar player quit or got pregnant or something. . . ."

"Busy guitar player."

"Yes, sir, most of us are, sir. . . ."

"Ever think about getting a real job, son?"

"Music is my life, sir." I put a headlock on the neck of the guitar case. "For better or worse."

"Yes," the man said thoughtfully. "I was young once. . . . So." He cleared his throat. "Care for a mint?" He rattled the tin.

"Thanks, but not on an empty stomach."

He opened the tin and took one for himself. After chewing thoughtfully for a moment, he said, "I take it you haven't spoken with your brother lately?"

"No, I haven't. We talked a month ago, right before I went on the road. He said that when I arrived, he'd have a job for me, and . . . and a place to stay." I set down the guitar case and pulled the police garage paperwork out of my hip pocket, squinted at it, and gestured toward the apartment door. "This is the address he gave me."

"It was his address until just a week ago. He moved quite suddenly."

"I've been all over America since then, sir. It's quite a place. Met all kinds of people. But I haven't thought to call my brother."

"I can understand that. What kind of songs you play?"

"Railroad songs, sir. I know every song Jimmy Rodgers ever recorded."

"Jimmy Rodgers!" the old man said. "The Singing Brakeman!"

"The very same, sir."

The old man grew pensive. "Your brother Stefan lived here almost two years. I heard a lot of music come through the wall, but I never heard a Jimmy Rodgers tune. Not one."

Well, I thought to myself, if there were actually a guitar in this case, I might play you one. To head off the possibility that

43

I might be asked to do so, I said, "I'm hoping to bring Stefan around to my way of singing, sir. But I don't know. He's a wild one."

"Mm," was all he said.

"Sir?"

"Yes, son?"

I shivered visibly. "Is it always this cold in San Francisco?"

The old man permitted himself a smile.

"I haven't eaten since yesterday," I hastened to add, "and this gig I mean job my brother was telling me about, it starts tomorrow night. We got a lot of music to learn between now and then, not to mention catching up on some sleep. Would you possibly know where he's moved to?"

The old man bit his lip. "I'm not supposed to tell."

"Not supposed to tell? Why forever not?"

"Must have to do with that other guitar player. Stefan said he was a bad element. Borrowed money from Stefan and drank it all up. Kept coming back for more. Skipped rehearsals. Showed up drunk for jobs. Stuff like that. Stefan's trying to get away from him."

"Oh, well, I can understand that," I said. "That's awful."

"I kept telling him that's the nature of the business he's in," the old man said pedantically. "The music business, I mean. Told him he ought to get off that path and turn to Jesus or stockbroking. But Stefan said if he was going to hell, he was going to take rock and roll with him, and there would be plenty of stockbrokers there waiting for him. Said the devil wouldn't have it any other way."

My neck ached from looking up at him, and it *was* cold out there. A horn honked behind me. "Hey," yelled the cabbie. "They're calling for a fare to the airport!"

Not liking an interruption while I'm performing, I glared over my shoulder. The cabbie held up both hands and said, "I'm cool, I'm cool," and settled back into his seat. I looked back at the landlord and smiled. "High finance."

44

He smiled thinly. "If you don't mind my asking, son, what's that on your head?"

"An octopus, sir."

After a moment he said, "Is that right."

I shrugged modestly. "Youthful indiscretion."

"Youth." Without looking into his tin he thoughtfully chose another mint. "And by the way," he said, as he placed it on his tongue, "stockbrokers belong in hell."

I grinned. "It sounds like you learned more from my brother than he did from you, sir."

The old man said slyly, "You brother's wife has lots of pretty girlfriends. She's a looker herself."

"Oh," I said, "that would be Angelica."

He beamed at the name. "They're a couple of rockin' robins, those two. Regular loveboids. Very close. Although I don't see what she—" He stopped, cleared his throat, and pointed the tin. "When you get to 112 De Haro Street, tell Stefan anything you damn well please. But when you see Angelica, tell her that old Ari Torvald misses her."

I brightened considerably. "112 De Haro," I said. "Yessir. I certainly will tell her, sir."

"That's Ari Torvald, now. From Anza Street."

"Ari Torvald," I repeated, retreating towards the taxi. "112 De Haro Street. Thank you so much, Sir! I'll send you an invite to our first gig!"

The old man shook his head. "Jimmy Rodgers and an octopus." He lowered the sash.

"Oh, boy." The cabbie rubbed his hands as I got into the back seat. "Potrero Hill, here we come." He slid a hand flatwise over the dashboard. "Alllll the way across the city."

I closed the door. "Forget it." The fare on the meter had reached thirteen dollars. "Drop me where you found me on Balboa."

"Sonofabitch. . . ."

"Do it."

He turned south on 36th Avenue and muttered imprecations the whole six blocks.

Five

De Haro Street extends north, from one of the worst housing projects in the city, up and over Potrero Hill and down to 17th Street, past the softball diamonds at Lazzeri Playground to the intersection of King and Division Streets, through what used to be a warehouse district. In the dotcom times—roughly the last ten years of the 20th century—you couldn't rent unimproved space in that neighborhood for less than $80 per square foot per annum, even if you could find it. After the dotcom crash, however, the vacancy rate climbed to 30% in less than a year, and suddenly you could take your pick from any number of nicely turned-out commercial spaces at about $20 per foot. Owners and landlords began to offer incentives. They even sank to renting rehearsal space to bands again. I'm sure some of them cried.

In the dotcom times a pedestrian could get run over crossing any street in these flatlands, day or night. Lucre-crazed SUV drivers ignored stop signs, pedestrians, other SUVs, even cops, certain that the gold rush would wait for no one. A worker flagging a lane of traffic while his crew backed a cement truck toward a pour was run over and killed by a man driving an SUV, steering wheel in one hand, a phone in the other. Whatever he was talking about proved to be more important than another man's life. Despite the presence of an entire construction crew, any number of other drivers, and the SUV's female passenger, all of whom bore witness, the hit-and-run driver was never caught. The dead flagman left a wife and three kids.

Not two years later the flatlands at the foot of Potrero Hill had become nearly as deserted by day as they were by night, as exposed as an intertidal reef by the recession of the tsunami of avarice. Gold rush over, the locals started to poke their heads out again in order to enjoy their restored tranquility—to wit, we saw a man in a pink tutu and tights and yellow dance slippers accompanied by a mincing, perfectly coiffed pink Pomeranian, the only citizens in sight, as Lavinia made a preliminary pass down the one hundred block of De Haro, and I counted down a series of roll-up doors along a waist-high loading dock: 116, 114, 112, 110. . . .

We circled the block for another look. The citizen and his dog had disappeared. A city is funny like that. You see something notable, turn a corner, never see it again. Across the street from the warehouse stood another, still with its loading dock; but its roll-up doors had been replaced by glassed-in office bays, its freight spur so hastily paved over that the street retained a phantom trace of rails. A vinyl sign dangled limply from the remodeled building's stucco parapet, advertising the availability of raw space from 450 up to 45,000 square feet.

"Man," I observed, "you might think that it looks like the seventies down here, it's so deserted, but I might think it could be more like the fifties."

"I've only seen pictures," Lavinia said.

"Me, too."

"Visions of the railroad earth," Lavinia said.

I turned to look at her. The shadows moved off the dashboard and over her hands on the rim of the steering wheel, sculpting her face. It looked like a flight of pelicans limning a swell. "My favorite Kerouac piece," I said.

47

She shook her head. "*Mexico City Blues* is better."

"I don't think so, but you're not alone; Michael McClure called it the great visionary poem of the twentieth century."

"Yeah, well," she shrugged, "he's probably never read *The Sorrow of War*, by Bao Ninh."

"I'd prefer to call that novel an elegiac triumph, and to hell with visionary."

"Curly," she purred, "you are the only person I've ever met who's read as many books as I have."

"More," I corrected her. "More than you have."

"After you starve to death," she cooed, "can I have your library?"

"I'll leave you mine if you leave me yours."

"Can't do that, I'm sorry to say. Ivy pawned the whole thing one box at a time." She softened her tone. "Don't I have anything else you want?"

I shook my head. "This doesn't look like a real address."

"What would you know about a real address? You mean it's not a toilet with a bed and a sink?"

"You slagging my crib?"

"No, I'm talking about your shitty apartment. When's the last time a woman was in there?"

I gave this a moment's thought. "About two hours ago," I replied. "At least, it used to be a woman."

"You know what I mean," she insisted.

"Not counting my guitar?"

"Don't be pathetic."

"None of your business," I replied pathetically.

"Don't you know any female octopi?"

"I wouldn't spend so much time with her, meaning my guitar, if she weren't the real thing."

"You wouldn't spend so much time with her, meaning your guitar, if you had a real thing."

"That," I conceded, "might be a brush with the truth."

48

"Anyhow, where people keep their stolen PA systems isn't necessarily where they sleep."

"And here I thought I was looking for my beloved brother."

"You might still be looking for your beloved brother. Nobody is saying our bird is still here—if he ever was here. Did that landlord look cagey to you?"

"Lavinia, think about it. When was the last time you saw somebody look cagey who actually was cagey?"

"Um. . . . The last time I saw a picture of Little Bush on the cover of *Time?*"

"That guy's not cagey."

"On the contrary, my mouse, I think he put one over on everybody, including himself."

"Speaking as a small rodent, I agree with you."

"If only there were a little Id to go along with it."

"Like when Clinton was President? But hey, now that we've established our San Francisco political credentials, we didn't come here to talk politics."

"No. We came here to talk money."

"What's the difference?"

Lavinia took a left around the north corner of the block, on Alameda, and parked on the wrong side of the street.

"Will it fit in your car?"

"What, seventy-five hundred bucks?"

"I was thinking we might get the merchandise instead. Seventy-five hundred dollars worth of PA system could take up a lot of space."

"That's just what he owes on it," she reminded me.

". . .Mixing console, the wire snake, speakers, microphones and stands, a rack full of amps and preamps, EQ, a patch bay. . . ."

"I forgot that you know something about this stuff."

"Almost as much as you know about documentary videos."

"Hey," she retorted sharply, "Every time I sleep deeply enough to dream, I pay for that experience."

"I hope you never have to go through another one like it. Sincerely."

"Telltail was my friend."

"I know that. Didn't you hear what I just said?"

"She was just a kid. We—"

"Yes, yes, of course. Kids stick up liquor stores several times an hour in America. If this were a Moslem country, we wouldn't have that problem."

Lavinia stared at me. "You don't feel my pain."

I stared at her. "No."

After a minute she said, "Let's get this over with." She pointed. "Hand me that piece in the glove compartment?"

"Piece?" I blinked. *"Visions of the Railroad Earth?"*

She gestured impatiently.

"No." I shook my head.

She unfastened her shoulder belt.

"Lavinia. . . ."

She leaned over the center console, opened the glove compartment, and removed a flat, black, automatic pistol. "Think you can open your door?"

I didn't move. It wasn't courage or even the lack of it, you understand—though I'm as pusillanimous as the next guy when it comes to guns. Everything is so obvious when it comes to guns. Everything's all figured out already. There's no leeway, no bargaining, no intellectual freedom. Guns kill people. That's what they're for. But it wasn't precisely the gun that was bothering me. What was bothering me was that, as with guns, I now knew everything I needed to know about Ivy Pruitt and his ex-girlfriend, Lavinia Hahn. And what I knew about them was, they kept guns around. They liked guns. I didn't want to get into it just then, at so inopportune a moment, into so sensitive a subject, but I was willing to postulate that what Lavinia regretted about the liquor store holdup was not that it had failed, or even that her girlfriend Telltail had gotten herself killed, but, on the contrary, that Telltail hadn't been toting something more lethal than a BB gun. Now wasn't the time to be getting into such quibbles, of course. Now was the time to be getting out of them.

Lavinia released the automatic's clip and inspected it. A row of snub bullets glowed dully under the streetlight. She jacked the slide and a slug hopped out onto the leather upholstery between her thighs. "Ivy usually handles the ordnance."

"Why am I not surprised to hear that?"

She jacked the slide again. The gun was empty.

"Haven't you had enough of shooting?"

"I've had enough of having no protection from it."

"Funny, I was just thinking that."

She fingered the ejected shell into the clip and the clip into the hand grip.

"Where does this leave me?" I asked.

She jacked the slide, which chambered a round. Then, aiming the gun at the floorboard between her knees, she let the hammer down with her thumb and set the safety. All very pro. But now she closed her eyes and lay the pistol flat against the side of her face, as if to cool her raging intellect. "Protected," she answered, "is where it leaves you." She tapped the length of her finger alongside the trigger guard.

"That's all this pistol is about?"

"That's all."

"Promise?"

"You sound like a little boy."

"I feel like one."

"A babe with a gun doesn't make you hard?"

"Are you nuts? I have to have, you know, *feelings* for a gun."

"Jesus Christ," Lavinia hissed. "No wonder that guy fired you."

"Hey," I retorted testily, "I got fired because a bunch of Oakland cops arrested me for buying heroin from two Mexican illegals and smoking it with Ivy Pruitt, who is a repeat offender.

51

I *never* go to Oakland. Put that fucking thing where I can't see it and let's get this sordid version of wage-earning over with. What caliber is it, anyway?"

"Don't feel so fine, ain't got my nine."

"Oh, the famous nine millimeter, storied of song and verse amongst punks and fuckups."

"It fulfills a great need between the .32 and the .38."

"And to think I traded my singleshot .22 rifle for my first guitar. The only gun I've ever owned. A rabbit gun."

"You never shot a rabbit, you ain't no friend of mine."

"Oh yeah?" I said. "How many rabbits you shot, Elvis?"

She didn't answer.

I nodded curtly. "Where's that leave us?"

"Fucking peacenik." Lavinia opened the driver's door. "Don't forget your guitar case."

"What for?"

"It worked once. Maybe it will work again."

"Maybe you should carry it," I grumbled, wresting it over the seat back. "As in, carry his ax, bear his children?"

"For a guy who can't get it up, that's thinking pretty far ahead." Walking in front of me, Lavinia raised the back of her blouse to park the barrel of the pistol under her belt, in the crack of her ass.

"Hmmm," I said.

"Don't mix your metaphors," she said.

We turned the corner and climbed a short set of creosoted wooden stairs. We weren't exactly innocuous; a mercury street-light laved our every move in a grayish blue. At the top of the loading dock a roof rat scurried along the splintered boards ahead of us and disappeared into a crack at the bottom of a roll-up door. "Eek," Lavinia said, without enthusiasm.

"Shoot it."

"I don't need the practice."

"You can hit a rat with a handgun?"

"Sure. But if it's carrying the plague, I want it to live."

"Lavinia. . . ."

"Yes, Curly?"

"Is a darkly pessimistic conception of mankind and the fate of the earth the other thing you have in common with Ivy Pruitt?"

"That and television. Until he pawned it."

"A veritable spiral into hell."

She nodded. "The intensity of it broke Ivy of two habits."

"You and television?"

"Yep."

"Which he replaced with the one big habit?"

"That would be correct."

The door of 112 De Haro was big enough to forklift a pallet of flywheels through, maybe twenty feet wide and sixteen high. In the lower left corner of its metal slats a mandoor bore a faded sign.

BAY AREA ICE, CO.
112 DE HARO ST ∎ SAN FRANCISCO
POTRERO 2595
"Icing the Fleet Since 1946"

"What fleet?" Lavinia whispered.

"There used to be actual maritime commerce in San Francisco," I whispered back. "We even had a fishing fleet." I touched the date. "I'd say some guy came back from the war and started himself a business."

"Which war?"

"World War II?" I suggested.

"Oh," she said vaguely.

"He's probably been gone a long time, too, along with this superannuated telephone prefix."

Having already lost interest, Lavinia got down to business. "If we should accidentally run into any normal people, you're still looking for your brother Stepnowski, okay? If we actually find

53

him, we're working for Sal Kramer, you're the muscle, and I'm the brains. Stay behind me and try to look like a tough guy with an octopus tattooed on his head."

"Beautiful," I lied.

She knocked on the door.

"But if it's so beautiful, why am I worried?"

She knocked again. "The only thing you've got to worry about is if Stepnowski really needs a guitarist."

"What kind of music does he play?"

"Metal." She knocked again, louder.

"Shit," I hissed.

"Hey! Step!" Lavinia shouted.

"Lavinia—"

"Look." She grabbed my arm.

We watched the door open about eight inches, as if by itself. We waited.

Silence.

Lavinia nudged the door with the toe of her boot.

It creaked on its hinges, of course, until it opened halfway and emitted a draft from beyond, a musty darkness rank with rats and transmission fluid, one of my favorite cocktails.

"Hello?" Lavinia called tentatively.

No response.

"Hey," I whispered, "nobody here. Let's go get married."

"That landlord guy might have called to warn him."

"If he didn't give us a bum steer altogether, you mean?"

She pushed the door wide open. Except for a slim parallelogram cast by the streetlight, illuminating a grimed and gouged concrete floor, we saw nothing. Lavinia pushed the door all the way open, until the slats in the roll-up door rattled slightly.

"Well," I said quietly, "there's nobody behind the door. Now what?"

Lavinia removed the pistol from her belt. "Let's see if they took the PA system with them." She slipped sideways over the threshold, out of sight.

"Man," I hissed, "you are tenacity in tight pants."

"Shut up and find the lights."

I stepped over the threshold and changed the guitar case to my right hand, so I could pat the sheetrock beyond the door frame with my left. There was a switch plate. As I opened my mouth to speak, Lavinia abruptly gasped, the two actions uncannily simultaneous, as if the gasp had come from my own mouth. I turned to my right. The neck of the guitar case hooked the door and nearly closed it. Now, for sure, nobody could see anything. Lavinia screamed. I threw the case to the right and myself forward, away from the door. Three muzzle flashes strobed the darkness.

Six

A long pause followed the gunfire. The only audio was the whine of my brand new tinnitus.

It was too late to get out of the building. The street light would make a target of anything in the doorway.

Crawling was an option. But to where?

I tried to recall what might still be in the guitar case. Strings and picks, for sure. A tuner? A stringwinder? Probably. The completely useless Pocket Chord Dictionary? Maybe. A Derringer? A boomerang? A ninja star? Certainly not. At least the Gibson hadn't been in it. If it had, I might have let myself be gunned down before I'd throw it across a room. On the other hand, while there are a lot of Gibsons in the world, the number of octopus-tattooed bill collectors is assuredly rare. I'd already done the arithmetic. As soon as I got myself out of this mess, there was going to be one less.

The smell of transmission lube slowly overwhelmed that of gunpowder. The sound of labored breathing slowly displaced the tinnitus.

"Curly."

Since it seemed to me that the business end of a firearm might easily search out the sound of my voice, I remained silent.

"I know that's the glow of your dome in the gloom, Curly. Look up."

I looked up. A shaft of yellowish street light angled down from a gap near the top of the metal door, right into my eyes. I squinted. "Has that little spot been specially on my head since the lights went out?"

"Ever since you hit the floor."

"So why all the shooting?"

"Somebody tripped me and there was a big crash," she said, somewhat defensively. "Over there."

"Somebody else is in here?"

"Was."

"You mean you shot somebody?"

"No. At least, I don't think so."

"What's that supposed to mean? Is he still here?"

She ignored this. "Did you find the lights?"

"I found some switches."

"Let's have a look."

"What about–?"

"I have a few rounds left."

"Oh, great."

"Whoever you are," Lavinia said loudly, "we're here on business. That's it. No other reason."

Silence.

"Okay?"

No response.

"Okay," she said grimly. "Let's get on with it."

I cautiously stood into a crouch and slid my hand up the sheetrock wall, sweeping the palm back and forth until it hit the switch plate. "There're four of them."

"What am I, an electrician?" Lavinia barked.

The first switch caused a rectangle of light to appear around the edges of the roll up door.

"That's the outside light," Lavinia said. "Turn it off."

The second switch instigated the creak of a belt getting traction on a pulley. A rooftop exhaust fan barely got started before I killed it. The third switch, once thrown, rebounded to its original position. The roll up door emitted a bang and rattled open an inch.

"Back! Down!" Lavinia hissed. "What are you doing?"

57

I bumped the switch in the opposite direction. The door banged shut.

The fourth switch illuminated the whole place with a ghastly energy-efficient ochre.

A sheetrock partition ran parallel to the garage door, about twenty-five feet inside the building. Lavinia was lying against it. The sheetrock was fire-taped—seams and screws had been hastily mudded, but any topping, smoothing or painting remained undone, which left a floor-to-ceiling and wall-to-wall hopscotch pattern of white dabs and stripes on a gray background, twenty feet high and maybe forty wide. At the far end of the room in a second fire-taped wall, at right angles to the first, stood a pair of steel doors, gray with no windows. Opposite, to my left, loomed an ancient cinderblock wall.

We were in a box.

Between us, on the floor of the box, a man lay face down.

Five feet beyond the body, Lavinia held her pistol in both hands, trained on it. Her pallor was more wan than usual, and her confidence was mostly gone.

The man wore a yellow pineapple shirt, black jeans, and white athletic socks. His hair was brush-cut and dyed yellow with a few magenta tufts drawn into spikes. A large pool of blood, perhaps a yard across, had spread away from him, toward me. Its surface had taken on a dull sheen, like the skin of a rotten apple. Its color was no longer red, precisely, but it was not yet brown.

"He lost all that blood before we got here," I guessed aloud.

"I tripped over him. After I fell I heard a crash. I shot three times." Lavinia moved her eyes to her left, then back. "Over there."

Further down the box, to my right, the guitar case lay on the floor, its lid sprung open and leaning against the outside wall beyond the far end of the garage door. It had a bullet hole in it.

"Nice shooting."

"He's dead. Isn't he dead?"

58

"Looks that way."

"I didn't shoot him. I shot over there."

"You shot my guitar case. Not this guy."

Her eyes darted to her left, then back to me. "What the hell."

"What was I supposed to do, get shot? The guitar case was a spontaneous distraction. Now that the lights are on, I see that somebody else bought the farm. Somebody I don't know. My friend, Lavinia, is perfectly okay. I'm delighted to see that my good friend Lavinia is okay. The same goes for myself. And I'm sorry that some guy I didn't know is dead. But the sum of the game is, not all that much has changed since five minutes ago."

She looked at me as if she might shoot me and cry, or vice versa.

"If you'll point that pistol somewhere else, I'll have a look at this guy."

She didn't move.

"Okay, I'll stay here. From this distance, anyhow, we can call a corpse a corpse. But this isn't some random corpse—right?"

Lavinia's lower lip quivered.

I considered the corpse. When I was an auto mechanic—in another life—there was always some engine reduced to a lump of iron, as inert and even less functional than a boat anchor. After a certain amount of tinkering, however, this configuration of parts might roar to life. No matter how much I learned about how it worked, this little miracle always amazed me.

Tonight, in this obscure warehouse, the opposite effect was at work, and it was no less curious. Not so long ago, this heap of laundry on the floor had been possessed of the free will necessary to dye its hair.

"Is it Stepnowski?"

"Can you see his left forearm?"

I could see it plainly. "There's a tattoo."

"What's it say?"

I turned my head to read it: "STAGE LEFT." I righted my head and looked at Lavinia. "You're kidding me."

"At least it's not an octopus."

"And on his right arm. . . ?"

She nodded impatiently. "What do you think?"

I shook my head slowly. "He was a drummer, all right."

"And his name was Stepnowski."

"Drummer or not, this is getting to be one expensive PA system."

Both hands still on the pistol, the pistol still trained on Stepnowski, Lavinia sat up against the wall. I saw no blood on her clothes. She must have tripped over Stepnowski's hands, which were flung before him, beyond the pool of blood, as if he were reaching for something. Or someone. Or, it occurred to me, quite as if he'd been dragged by his feet which Lavinia might have tripped over as well. But the pool of blood precluded dragging—didn't it? Or maybe he was knocked on the head, dragged here, and then he was shot. . . ? *Had* he been shot?

"Must have been unpleasant, to trip over that mess in the dark."

Lavinia's eyes enlarged. "It felt like he grabbed me."

So maybe it had been the hands.

Clearly, although she'd been screening a notorious splatter video in underground clubs up and down the west coast, nothing about the present experience constituted a matter of relish for Lavinia. It occurred to me that, night after night, Lavinia must have managed one way or another to avoid actually looking at Telltail's demise over and over again. Maybe it was too much. Maybe tonight was forcing Lavinia to re-imagine it. Maybe, on the other hand, I was giving her too much credit for introspection.

In any case, Lavinia seemed on the verge of shock.

"I'm going to approach Stepnowski."

Lavinia lowered the gun a little.

I stood slowly.

She raised the gun.

"Lavinia. . . ."

The gun drooped in her hands.

Stepnowski lay face down. I touched the nape of his neck. No warmth. I pressed a carotid. No pulse. The quick under his fingernails had lost its color. The arms were slightly stiff.

"I think this guy is dead."

"That's brilliant, Curly. Why don't you go through his pockets?"

So much for introspection. "I think he's been dead for a while, too."

"Your empiricism is underwhelming," Lavinia said. "Look in his pockets. Start with that back one." She pointed the gun.

A large bulge strained the fabric of one of the dead man's hip pockets. I hesitated. "Dead or alive," I said, "it's been a long time since I touched a guy's ass."

"What happened to those San Francisco credentials, Curly? Come on," Lavinia insisted. "Check it out."

I slipped my fingers under the denim seam, which was tight. The bulge proved not to be a wallet; it was a wad of cash, folded double. As I worked the bundle out of the pocket, the corpse farted.

"Woman," I winced, "Please note that I am earning my keep."

Lavinia didn't look so well herself, but she perked up when she saw the money. "If I were an actress," she muttered gamely, "I'd say that's a rôle worth considering."

There were eighty-seven one-hundred dollar bills, two twenties, one ten, and four ones. It took almost two minutes to count them.

Just like that, I was handling more cash than I'd ever handled in my life.

"He was good for it," Lavinia marveled.

"There's enough to pay off the sound system," I puzzled. "So what are we doing here?"

"Stepnowski was sixty days past his most recent payment,

which is a month beyond the pale. Sal couldn't get him on the phone, so he called Ivy."

"Between not being able to get away with it and not wanting to get your guitar-playing fingers broken, let alone get yourself killed," I gestured at the body, "this doesn't have to happen too often?"

Lavinia shook her head gravely. "Ivy doesn't happen too often. But this," she blinked toward Stepnowski, "this never happens."

"Now must be never."

She pursed her lips. "It's certainly more than I bargained for."

I held up the money. "What should we do?" Before she could answer, I added, "We should call the cops."

"If we call the cops," Lavinia suggested, "they'll try to prove that we did it. They won't look for anybody else."

"That would be a hasty conclusion. We only came here to collect a bad debt. It's unfortunate, I admit, that you had to bring along a gun—by the way, is it licensed?"

Lavinia rolled her eyes.

"So your pistol could be a little troublesome. Still, that's a long way from a murder rap. By the time they coordinate time of death with our whereabouts today, and get back the ballistics, and talk to Ivy and Kramer, we'll be in the clear. They'll keep your gun and that'll be it."

Lavinia cleared her throat and recited dully, "I'll be in the clear until they find the inventory of liquor store videos in my apartment. Then they'll start wondering all over again about who was driving the getaway car."

"What getaway car?" I was taken aback. "You mean for the robbery?" Of course that's what she meant. "Lavinia. . . ."

Lavinia looked morose. "Think of it as a youthful indiscretion."

I didn't like this development at all, even if, ultimately, it had nothing to do with me. What the hell is going on, I wondered. Is this the night I grow up? Reluctantly I said, "I guess you have a point."

62

"There's another one. The cops will impound that wad of money. It might show up in the evidence cage; it might not. It might even make it to the exhibit table at the hearing. Either way, we'll never get another chance at it. There will be no dough for Kramer, no cut for Lavinia, no bail for Ivy, and no rent for Curly."

"Damn it," I declared, "How come I never see things as clearly as you do?"

"Because I'm a businesswoman," Lavinia suggested. "And you are only a musician." She pointed her chin at the corpse. "Like him."

"That's a drummer," I said reflexively.

"Curly," she said, "I still have a couple of rounds in this piece, here. But I don't think I'm going to have to mention them just to help you out with your decision."

She crossed her arms, leaned against the wall, and watched me.

"You wouldn't. . . ." I blinked stupidly. "You would?"

She rubbed the pinky and ring finger of her left hand back and forth above her left eye, as if to ease a headache. "No, but, on the other hand. . . ." She dropped her hand and looked at me. "Have I got a choice?"

I scarcely credited that she would actually shoot me. But I said, "Tell you what. Let's count out seventy-five hundred dollars and put the remaining twelve hundred back in the guy's pocket."

"Whatever happened to in for a penny in for a pound?"

"Whoever killed him didn't do it for the money. If the cops think it was robbery and find us, we'll be in a fix. If they go on the theory that it wasn't robbery because they find a nice piece of change on the guy, who knows, maybe they'll get the real culprit before they get us, and Bob's your uncle."

Lavinia considered this. "Ivy will get Kramer's cut to him first thing in the morning. If the cops look into it, Kramer will tell them he got paid, the sound system belongs to Stepnowski, and he knows from nothing about the guy getting killed. Kramer won't drop the dime on Ivy unless the cops give him a good reason."

"Murder's not a good reason?"

"Sure it is. The best. Usually. But the fact is, we didn't kill the guy. Ivy can handle Kramer. They have a rapport. Kramer makes a natural dead end for that line of inquiry."

I turned it over in my mind, and gradually a metaphor took shape. A guy is about to jump out of an airplane. He's poised at the door. He grips the jambs with both hands. The slipstream tears at his hair and at the sleeves and the legs of his jumpsuit. He squints. The green light comes on and he jumps. As he plummets, he rights himself. It's time to open his parachute. He reaches for the ripcord. The ripcord is a rattlesnake.

"Sounds great," I lied. "Other than that. . . ."

"Other than what?"

"I don't like it.'

"I don't like it, either," Lavinia admitted. "But I don't know what else to do."

"For example," I said.

"Why belabor it?" she said testily.

"It's my style. For example: The cops will find Stepnowski's landlord. You know, the one we hornswoggled into giving us Stepnowski's address?"

"You," Lavinia pointed out.

"Pardon?"

"You hornswoggled him," she reminded me. "I drove to a gas station and gave some kid five bucks to hose the dog out from under my beautiful Lexus."

"You did? Really?"

"I did. Really. Don't you think that's the type of workaday moment that's liable to stick in almost any kid's mind?"

"They'll have to find him first."

"Yeah, they'll have to find him first. Meanwhile, a bald guy with an octopus tattooed on his head and carrying a guitar case was getting this address—" she gestured at our surroundings —"from Stepnowski's ex-landlord."

"Yeah," I said uncomfortably. "That was how it happened, wasn't it." After what seemed to be some very sluggish thought, I added, "But there were people in the cafe who saw us together. That guitarist out front, for example. The cabbie saw us, too."

"So? Why deny it?"

"I doubt we could deny it. But at some point, I would dearly like to dissociate myself from you." Then it occurred to me that, if the cops did make the connection, Stepnowski's landlord would in fact provide an alibi—for me, but not for Lavinia. If Stepnowski had been dead for an hour when we found him, as it certainly seemed he had been, I, at least, would be in the clear. The timeline of my alibi had several verifiable nodes in it. Lavinia and her gun would have to shift for themselves.

"Look, Curly," Lavinia said, "you've got a point. But first the cops have to decide they're looking for us instead of the guy or guys who really did this. Chances are excellent that Step, here, was into some bad business that we know nothing about. Fencing stolen musical gear, for example. After all, where'd he get eight grand? Maybe he's got a rap sheet a mile long. Certainly it's strange that somebody took the trouble to track him down and blow him away but didn't take the two seconds required to relieve a dead man of eight thousand dollars in cash."

"Like I said," I said, "I don't like it." But I said it half-heartedly.

She frowned at Stepnowski.

So did I.

"There was a wife, as I recall."

"Angelica," I remembered.

"Angelica," she confirmed. "Maybe it was a crime of passion."

"Maybe the bastard deserved it."

65

"Maybe, if we're lucky, we'll never find out."

"Let's get out of here." Lavinia stood up.

As she took her third step away from the wall, wary of Stepnowski, I pointed a finger: "Pick up your brass."

She stopped and rasied an eyebrow. "Good idea."

Though it was the last place I could imagine wanting to linger, I was reluctant to leave, or to act at all. In the face of a lot of lousy choices, I didn't want to undertake any of them. I thought of Raskolnikov, who kills on page 76 of *Crime and Punishment*, then spends the next 455 pages driving himself crazy about it. At least he, I reminded myself, was actually guilty of a murder. Nevertheless it seemed like it would be a lot less nerve-wracking to face the music up front.

Lavinia walked to the mandoor, making a wide circle around the corpse.

I peeled C-notes off the wad, sufficiently nervous to slightly tear one of them. When I'd counted twelve I folded the smaller denominations around them and returned the reduced bundle to Stepnowski's hip pocket. I tried not to think.

When I joined Lavinia at the door she opened her left hand and showed me three spent cartridges.

I turned out the lights.

There was no traffic on De Haro.

Halfway down the loading dock I said, "Wait!"

Lavinia, her nerves obviously frayed, spun on her heel and hissed, "Now what is it?"

"The guitar case."

"Oh, you stupid—" She glanced toward the door we'd just closed. "I'll get the car."

I grabbed her arm. "The hell you say."

She twisted away. "What's the matter, Curly?" she sneered. "I thought you were used to the bus."

"It's not that," I said evenly, watching her eyes. "It's just that the bus only takes exact change. All I have is hundreds." I patted my back pocket.

Her sneer went away. But before it did, I swear, I saw the thought glint through her eye: *I should waste this bastard and get it over with.*

"Go get the car," I suggested quietly. "Drive around the block; pick me up."

She hesitated.

"What's the matter, Lavinia? No gas money?"

She drew a breath. "Go get the guitar case. I'll get the car."

Back in the warehouse it was pretty quiet.

The light came on, like it was supposed to.

Stepnowski lay where we'd found him. Like he was supposed to. Like he wasn't going to walk away. Like he was going to lay where he was supposed to lay until somebody else found him.

The guitar case lay where sighted last, too.

Right where it was supposed to be.

I closed the lid.

I latched it shut.

I picked up the case.

Just like I was supposed to.

I turned off the light and watched the street through the cracked mandoor. The corpse lay on the floor in the dark behind me. The Lexus pulled up out front. Everything, animate and inanimate, did like it was supposed to do.

I closed the mandoor behind me and dropped the four feet off the loading dock to street level. I walked around the back of the Lexus, opened the passenger door, and dropped the guitar case onto the back seat. I dropped myself onto the passenger seat. I closed the door.

"Buckle up," Lavinia reminded me, and she drove us out of there.

67

Seven

Our next stop was a mere ten minutes away, up 7th Street and right on Bryant to Barrish Bail Bonds. Don't Perish in Jail, Call Barrish for Bail. Open 24 hours a day, 7 days a week, 365 days a year. Serving the People Since 1961. *Se Habla Español.*

After Lavinia spent about forty-five minutes doing paperwork, we backed the Lexus onto the sidewalk on Gilbert, an alley a few doors west of Barrish's and directly across Bryant Street from the many doors of the Hall of Justice, whence Ivy would be sprung in due course. A thick fog had rolled in, cold and damp. Lavinia produced a picnic blanket from the trunk ("Telltail just loved picnics.") and we cozied up under it with our money and a pint of brandy, the better to keep a warm eye on each other. I prevailed upon her to return the pistol to the glove compartment.

I stayed awake for about ten minutes, worried about spending the rest of my life in jail for crimes I may or may not have committed. Gradually, my eyes closed. At the threshold of dreamland, I heard Lavinia's voice. "Doesn't the leather back seat of a luxury vehicle make you feel horny?"

"No," I replied, pretending not to wake up. "It makes me feel homeless."

"Be that way," she groused petulantly. "Save it for Miss Right."

68

She reached between the front seatbacks and turned on the radio. It was 2:30 A.M. Harold Land and Clifford Brown were working out *Land's End* with Max Roach. We snuggled up.

"Don't you wish you could play like that," she declared.

"May it please the court," I kept my eyes closed, "counsel for the defense would like to stipulate for the record that, aside from the fact that there's no guitar on this band, the state isn't asking a question."

"I'll rephrase, your honor."

"Skip it. The answer is yes—yes, I say, yes—I've always wanted to play like that!"

"And you never will! Isn't that true? Isn't it?"

"Yes. Yes! Oh, god, oh god oh god. . . ."

"Bam! Guilty!"

"I know, I know, I know. . . ."

Roach's brooding tom elided into somebody tapping on the window. We woke up. Ivy Pruitt stood on the sidewalk, looking in. He was tapping the glass with his clasp knife.

Lavinia unlocked the driver's door and Ivy slid behind the wheel. "Man," he said, "all they talk about in that joint is ass-fucking and Jennifer Lopez."

"Who's Jennifer Lopez?" I asked sleepily.

Ivy started the engine, put the car into gear, and nosed onto Bryant Street. "Well, Curly," he said, looking to his left for oncoming traffic, "if you go from the latter to the former, it's a prime example of deductive reasoning."

"It's a prime example of wishful thinking," Lavinia snorted.

Across Bryant Street, the curb in front of the Hall of Justice was lined with black and white police cars, many of them double-parked. Hookers on bail descended the steps to the sidewalk and chatted with loitering cops. Ivy turned right, accelerated hard down Bryant Street, then braked to a dead stop for the light at Sixth, all within one hundred yards of the police station. Lavinia and I braced ourselves to avoid being thrown to

69

the floorboards. "Can it be said that a Lexus has floorboards?" I wondered aloud.

"Good question," Lavinia said, "but for sure it doesn't have an extra battery in the footwell."

"Fasten your seat belts," Ivy suggested mildly.

On the radio, John Coltrane started in on *I Want To Talk About You.* "The very idea of Oakland," Lavinia cooed, "fills me with a sense of adventure."

"Oakland?" I repeated ingenuously. "I'm not going to Oakland."

"Why not?" Lavinia asked frankly. "You don't even have a job to get cleaned up for."

Ivy's eyes snapped to the rear view mirror. "No job?"

"He got canned," Lavinia helpfully supplied.

The light turned green. "Oakland," Ivy announced, "here we come," and he floored it.

The brandy bottle tumbled to the floor and Lavinia and I were thrown against the back seat. "Wait a minute," I shouted from the tangle of arms and picnic blanket, as the Fifth Street on-ramp began to fill the windshield. Between Fifth Street and the bridge there are no more San Francisco exits. "I need to go home!"

There was a slight dip at the intersection of Fifth and Bryant, and Ivy had to swerve some thirty degrees to port to line up for the onramp beyond. The Lexus bottomed its springs, rebounded and angled left. Lavinia and I were thrown against the right side of the car in a heap. Before we untangled, we were on 80 East and heading for the maw of the lower deck of the Bay Bridge, not one hundred yards away.

"Goddammit, Ivy, I already spent a day and a night on your agenda. I've got my own trip to attend to."

The speedometer said we were doing eighty. Ivy's free hand was draped behind the passenger headrest. He turned up its palm in my face. "Gimme."

"I'll take you home when Ivy gives me my car back," Lavinia laughed consolingly.

70

Ivy laughed good-naturedly, then snapped the fingers of his free hand twice.

I got myself sitting up straight and counted six one-hundred dollar bills into Ivy's waiting hand. As I laid the seventh over the other six, I said, "You owe me twenty-five bucks."

Ivy folded the cash into the breast pocket of his shirt.

Lavinia tapped my shoulder.

I counted nine c-notes into her waiting palm. "You I'll owe thirty-seven fifty until I find change."

"Fine." She tucked the money into her blouse. "Buy me a leather teddy."

"Now, that brings up an interesting point," Ivy said, as I counted the remaining cash to make sure I hadn't shorted myself. "I owe Curly twenty-five bucks, Curly owes Lavinia thirty-seven fifty, and that comes to sixty-two fifty—no?"

Automatically I said, "Whatever you're thinking, count me out. Plus, you two owe me half of the forty bucks I spent on cab fare to the Stepnowski residence—"

"Forty?" Lavinia yelped. "I told his dispatcher thirty."

"I gave him forty."

"Unauthorized expenditure! That's one's on you, Curly."

"Hey, I got the job done, didn't I?"

She crossed her arms and looked out the window. "I told him thirty."

"Goddammit. . . ."

"Wait, wait." Ivy deigned to use both hands on the wheel long enough to swerve left one lane to pass a car and right one lane to pass another, the two vehicles doing a mere fifty-five or sixty, and then replaced his right hand on the back of the passenger seat, pinching the two stainless steel stanchions of the headrest between his thumb and forefinger as if they were some hapless robot's neck struts. "Hear me out," he said pleasantly to the rearview mirror.

"And you call this a business," I grumbled.

71

"You got a shot at amelioration, hoss," Ivy assured me. "It won't take but a little more grease to set us up with an eight-ball and a jock."

An eight-ball, for the information of those of you who live in Thomas Kinkaid communities, is one-eighth of an ounce or 3.54 grams. An eight-ball could be one-eighth of an ounce of anything, of course, of pea gravel or the pubic hairs of koala bears, but usually it's somewhere between three and four grams of cocaine.

But a jock? The jock was new to me.

"Not that I'm interested," I said, as the container cranes of the Port of Oakland streamed toward us, "but is a 'jock' when you get some buffed midget to ride your back for three hours while you snort dope out of a dog bowl?"

"Wow," Lavinia perked up, "whom do I call?"

"Nah," said Ivy, as uninterested in word play as he was single-minded about his career as a drug fiend. "Jock is short for jockey, which is argot for one gram of horse."

"Oh, *argot*, is it?" Lavinia said.

"Heroin again," I said tiredly to my window.

"But it's China white," Ivy explained helpfully. "Different from tarball. Different animal altogether. Purer, stronger, meaner."

"So the jock is a kind of moral equivalent to an eight-ball. How come I couldn't guess that?"

"Actually," Lavinia said, "it was the amount you didn't know, not the substance. Jock? Horse? Right?"

I threw up my hands.

"So," Lavinia said to the front seat, "what's the tab?"

"I can hook us up for a hundred and eighty on the eight-ball and maybe forty for the jockey. Two-twenty in all."

"Good price," Lavinia said. "By three that's. . . ."

Without hesitating Ivy said to the windscreen, "Seventy-three dollars and thirty-three cents. The penny's on me."

"It seems a privation, to go without," Lavinia suggested.

"At the very least," Ivy agreed. "So," he continued, "we can take advantage of this unit of fun to square up if I spring for $98.33, Curly rings in with $86.83, and Lavinia gets off, as it were, for a mere $35.83."

Ivy's agility with arithmetic seemed remarkably undiminished despite years of desuetude and drug abuse. It occurred to me to wonder whether the perseverance of this skill still coexisted with his no less remarkable and formerly effortless ability to count the most swinging and the most bizarre time signatures alike with an equally formidable dexterity. And, I continued to wonder, so what if he had? These and others of his talents have gone and will go entirely wasted until, one fine day, he dies.

"And then," I said aloud without enthusiasm, "I suppose we all go back to your place and get wall-eyed fucked up."

Ivy adjusted the rear-view mirror and said to my reflection, "You got a better place to go?"

"No," Lavinia declared with certainty, "he doesn't."

"Not to mention," I interpolated, watching the eyes of Ivy, "the place to score is conveniently located on the way to your place."

"Places," Ivy smiled. "But it's a true story." His eyes refocused on the freeway.

"Sometimes," I said to nobody in particular, "life is a perfectly bowled strike."

"Nothing more," Lavinia nodded, "nothing less."

I sat back, resigned to the joyride. What else did I have to do? The upper deck of the Bay Bridge, overhead since San Francisco, abruptly gave way to night sky. There was fog over only the bay here, its underside illuminated by the mercury lamps surrounding the gantries of West Oakland. The toll plaza whipped past and receded westward. Ivy centered the Lexus on the two lanes that became 580. We rose over The Maze, as are called the multiple lanes and freeways between Emeryville and the Bay Bridge approach, that merge and entwine and diverge there like heartworms in a commuter's dog, and we veered south.

73

Merely excepting Sonny Rollins' immortal cover of *Everything Happens to Me*, we rode the ten miles to the Fruitvale Avenue exit in silence.

Street level regained, Ivy turned west. A taco wagon rolling slowly east was followed by a large pit bull trailing three feet of logging chain. He trotted contentedly, oblivious of an Oakland squad car behind him with its rooftop lights on. Burger joints and liquor stores alternated with rib stands, a tortilleria, laundromats, bars and convenience stores on either side of the street, all of them shuttered for the night and many of them boarded up for good. Knots of men stood here and there on the corners anyway, each group attended by boys on bicycles or motorized scooters. Despite the obvious lack of commercial destinations, there seemed to be a lot of commerce.

Ivy turned into the apron of an open gas station, a rarity in this neighborhood where, if a door open to the street in broad daylight is an invitation to robbery, at three in the morning it's a guarantee.

But as soon as I saw the limousines and taxis lined up among the service islands, I realized that Ivy knew exactly where he was going and what he was doing. A crowd of men hung around the vending machines at one end of the service garage, some of them actually consuming soft drinks. Others paced and talked animatedly, while a few leaned over the black hood of an immaculately detailed Mercedes 600SL limousine. Two or three men wore the dark livery of the chauffeur—blazer or black suit, with tie—while a greater number affected the variegated non-uniforms of the taxi or jitney driver, each with a medallion on his breast or cap. Many of them smoked. Few seemed eager to sally back into the night. None of them would have cruised Fruitvale Avenue for a fare in any case.

Since it was handy and I had nothing else to do, I gassed the Lexus and cleaned the windshield while Ivy went into the office behind the pay window. Nobody else approached the window

74

while Ivy was doing his business. Striding back to the car counting his change, he was humming an old pop tune entitled *Downtown*, "downtown," among certain people, being yet another of the myriad slang terms for heroin.

He sat behind the wheel and closed the door. "Now."

Wrapped in the blanket, Lavinia said, without opening her eyes, "You score?"

"Halfway to paradise."

"This will have been the coke," she surmised, looking around.

"Marching powder."

Ivy nodded as he put the car in gear. "These folks like to stay awake while they work."

Next stop was a mile or two further west and two blocks south, where the neighborhood went from charmingly bedraggled to conspicuously worse. Here, most of the street-front commercial façades were boarded up and dark, but even the odd residential building brandished permanent plumes of black soot over plywood-shuttered windows. Rocks or bullets had taken out most of the streetlights and, before I realized what was going on, Ivy had made a turn and the pavement ended. A block later we pulled up behind a row of vehicles parked in front of a low wooden building that might have been on a back street in any cotton town in Mississippi. There were even crickets—a sound never heard in San Francisco, not fifteen miles across the bay. Twelve feet above the dirt lot was the bottom 2x6 of a wood-framed sign with dirty pearlescent plexiglass sides. Three or four fluorescent tubes inside the box, one of them burned out, backlit a corpus of dead insects, windrowed against a lower corner of the frame, and a single row of diminutive sans-serif black capital letters, which announced the place as Emil's Grotto.

The entrance to Emil's Grotto was an unpainted wood-railed screen door with an enameled Red Man Snuff sign for a push bar, rusted almost to illegibility. A nasty rumble from within proved to be Howlin' Wolf's *I Asked For Water (And She Gave Me Gasoline)*.

Ivy cranked the wheel, crooked his arm over his seat, and used the Lexus side mirrors to back it into a space between a brand-new burgundy Eldorado, waxed to luminescence, and a twenty-year-old Firebird with a broken rear spring, a spidered windshield, no hood, and two colors of primer.

"Curly?" Ivy put the Lexus in park and turned down the radio. "Whilst I negotiate these premises, would you mind perching up under this steering wheel with the engine running and the passenger door off the latch?"

"Here we go again," I divined.

"Just a minute." Lavinia threw off the blanket and sat up. "This is my goddamn car."

"Now now, little lady," Ivy drawled.

"Fuck you." Lavinia batted the back of the driver's seat with the heels of both hands. "Get out."

Ivy opened the driver's door and stepped out. Lavinia pushed the seat forward and joined him on the dirt. "Good luck, babe," she said, and kissed Ivy full on the mouth, just like she'd done to me just a few hours before, like a pint-sized Athena encouraging her man as he sallies into battle. Ivy pulled away from the kiss, slipping a fat bindle into her hip pocket as he did so. I slid over the seat to get out, too, but Lavinia pushed the seatback into my face. "Stay," she said, exactly as she'd have said it to a dog. She slid into the driver's seat herself and closed the door.

Ivy rounded the Eldorado and disappeared into the bar. The screen door patted the jamb softly behind him.

Lavinia leaned over the console, unlatched the passenger door, and retrieved her pistol from the glove compartment.

"Woman," I said, "haven't you had enough of that shit for one night?"

"Ivy's cool," she said, nosing the pistol between her seat cushion and the console, "but I'm not."

The Lexus engine was turning over, but I could barely hear it. Even at this hour, headlights and taillights were streaming up and down Fruitvale, a mere two blocks north. No vehicle, however, came down the dirt street to Emil's Grotto, despite its being wide open long after closing time, where Howlin' Wolf now made room for *Yola My Blues Away*.

"Skip James," I marveled.

Lavinia made no reply.

The spring on the screen door stretched tiredly. From the back seat, looking over the hood of the Eldorado, I could see the black fingers of a large hand with a pink palm easing the hinge stile through its radius, as delicately as if it were parting a lace curtain. A body launched through the door, remained airborne for nearly the entire length of the Cadillac, then folded like so much laundry into the gravel in front of it.

"Good night, Dawg," said a deep voice from the doorway. The door closed gently against the jamb, bouncing once.

"Ivy doesn't go by the name of Dawg around here, by any chance?"

"Not that I know of."

"Why the hell is he scoring junk in this godforsaken joint when he could be buying it from you?"

"Because I sell Mexican tarball. Here he gets China white."

It seemed like the difference between hydrozine and rocket fuel, but Lavinia put me straight. "It's the difference between fried rat and poached veal."

"Oh."

Emil's music segued to *Sittin' on the Dock of the Bay*. "Hey," I said, still speaking softly, "Otis wrote that in Sausalito."

"So?"

"It had to have been forty years ago. Maybe more."

Lavinia made no response.

"I was a bartender then. I—"

"Shh, quiet," she whispered.

77

The eighty-sixed customer was pulling himself up by the Cadillac's bumper. At length he stood, more or less erect, keeping one hand on the car's trunk lid to steady himself. He wore a rumpled brown suit, a tan shirt, and a yellow tie with a tie tack that twinkled when it caught the light. Despite the relative composure of his dress, it looked as if he hadn't changed clothes in weeks. With his free hand he brushed at his clothing ineffectively.

"A lifetime ago," I whispered.

"Yours, maybe," she answered, her voice nearly inaudible.

The man muttered curses steadily and incoherently, but also calmly and quite deliberately. He batted at the creases in his pant legs and tautened the lapels of his jacket. Dust motes circulated in the air beneath the fluorescent sign. As he turned in the light, not six feet away, we could see that the whites of his eyes were yellow and webbed by exploded capillaries. His face was ghastly, its high cheekbones accented by emaciation, its skin aged and lined and sufficiently dessicated and taut as to render its features skeletal. Abruptly he leaned against the Cadillac. He took a careful look around. His eyes passed over the windscreen of the Lexus without betraying any recognition of our presence. Then he stood nearly erect and ambulated past the hood of the Lexus. When he leaned forward, his feet sped to catch up, and when he leaned back, they slowed down. Though neither Lavinia nor I had any reason to fear this man, we both held our breath as he passed.

Three cars down the line he stopped at the trunk of a two-tone brown Oldsmobile and began fumbling in the side pocket of his jacket.

The spring on the screen door stretched and the door opened and closed again, patting its stops. Lavinia and I turned as one to watch Ivy walk briskly along the length of the Eldorado. He rounded its trunk but at the gap between the Lexus and the

Cadillac he froze in his tracks. As one, Lavinia and I followed his gaze.

The trunk lid of the Oldsmobile stood open, and the man in the brown suit was breaking down a double-barreled shotgun.

I leaned over the passenger seat and carefully gripped the passenger door armrest. Lavinia watched me curiously.

"We'd best be leaving," I hissed.

She pulled the transmission lever into gear, and our brake lights lit up the entire front wall of Emil's Grotto, in scarlet. As the car idled past Ivy I released the door and he tumbled into the passenger seat. "Go," he rasped hoarsely.

The man in the brown suit heard our tires on the gravel, closed the breach, and looked up. I slapped the back of the driver's seat. "Go, go!"

Lavinia stomped the accelerator. A mistake. The poor girl had probably never driven a car on an unpaved surface in her life. The front wheels of the Lexus began churning gravel up along its own undercarriage. As she cranked them to the right, as if hopefully, toward the lights of Fruitvale Avenue, the left rear of the Lexus banged the right front fender of the Firebird, parked to our left.

"Back off!" I shouted. "Back off!"

"Steer toward the skid!" Ivy shouted. But he grabbed the wheel.

"No more drivers!" I yelled, and chopped the side of my hand down between Ivy and Lavinia, breaking his grip. Ivy knew I was right. But this was Ivy Pruitt. A smile stole over his features and morphed into a grin. "It's on you, baby. . . ."

Lavinia straightened the car before it ran into a willow tree in the yard of an incongruously cute bungalow directly across the road from Emil's Grotto, but not before she scythed a rut through its lawn. The Lexus regained the street but its front end continued coasting toward Emil's Grotto while its tail wallowed the other way, the entire machine rotating slowly if loudly over

79

the gravel like a coracle adrift in white water. Lavinia recovered from this course, too, however, sawing gamely at the wheel without, unfortunately, backing off the throttle, so that gravel alternately sprayed the row of vehicles in front of Emil's and the rustic clapboards of the bungalow as she corrected her overcorrections, with agonizingly little forward progress. Finally she got the car aimed properly at Fruitvale Avenue, but with still no more than thirty yards separating us from the man with the shotgun, who by then had been granted all the time he needed to bring the stock up to his shoulder, to close one eye, and to sight along the gun's length. He pulled both triggers, and the back window of the Lexus abruptly disintegrated.

Lavinia screamed. The tires got a grip and screamed, too, as they suddenly found pavement under them, at which point Lavinia gamely floored it again. We accelerated as fast as that car would accelerate until we made the corner at Fruitvale, where Lavinia remembered to brake slightly before she ran the stop sign and took a right. We hadn't gone a block before Ivy calmly told her to slow down. She slowed down. Ivy took a look over the back of the passenger seat, then he looked down. There, he found me on the floor, jammed between the seats and flocked in safety glass, looking back up at him. I would have called him a choice motherfucker, but I didn't feel like swallowing glass to do it.

Ivy shifted his eyes toward the hole that used to be the back window and sucked a tooth. "I used to score my shit in a penthouse in Pacific Heights," he said. "But you know what, hoss?" He grinned at Fruitvale Avenue, unreeling behind us, and shook his head. "I just couldn't get along with those people."

Eight

I stretched out on the floor. Lavinia paced and smoked a cigarette. Ivy milled cocaine, the entire eightball, by means of a little red device designed to the purpose. Under its inch-and-a-half dome lay a screen through which, by twisting its top, coarse granules of cocaine were ground into a fine powder, which collected in a small cup that formed the mill's base.

Having processed the cocaine to his satisfaction, Ivy carefully deposited its refined dust onto the back of his all-purpose blue plate, rapping the screen lightly with the blade of his clasp knife.

He repeated the process with the heroin. He took his time, too. Like many dope fiends, Ivy Pruitt toyed with his monkey for as long as possible before allowing it to sink its teeth into him.

I slept like a poleaxed manatee for maybe twenty minutes, weightless in an amnion of exhaustion, then awoke with a gasp, only to find Lavinia watching me. "He's dreaming he's unemployed." Ivy suggested she leave me alone since, if I never woke up, there'd be that much more dope for the two of them.

I've mentioned that Ivy's apartment was pristine excepting certain moral issues, and this was true. It betrayed the almost neurotic attentions of a tenant who spent a lot of time wide awake with nothing to think about except dirt and nothing to do except relentlessly pursue it. I've also noted that the apartment was almost empty of possessions; but, looking straight across the floor, I spotted an overlooked cache of books stacked between the hot water heater and the sink cabinet. Since I knew Ivy for one of the waxing majority of global spawn who rarely read anything, let alone a book, I concluded that, having found this heap on the street or stolen them out of the back of a car, Ivy intended to sell them to second-hand bookstores in Berkeley. I let my eyes descend the spines of the dustjackets, and soon discerned a pattern. The books were *Steppenwolf* by Hermann Hesse, *Brave New World* and *The Doors of Perception* by Aldous Huxley, *The Female Eunuch* by Germaine Greer, *The Fire Next Time* by James Baldwin, *The Electric Kool-Aid Acid Test* by Tom Wolfe, *The Tibetan Book of the Dead* by Tibetans presumably, *Selected Poetry of Ho Chi Minh*, *The Second Sex* by Simone de Beauvoir, *Confessions of an English Opium Eater* by Thomas De Quincey, *Soul on Ice* by Eldridge Cleaver, *Howl* by Allen Ginsberg, *Naked Lunch* by William Burroughs, *The Strange Case of Charles Dexter Ward* by H.P. Lovecraft, *The Mind Parasites* and *The Outsider* by Colin Wilson, *Stranger in a Strange Land* by Robert Heinlein, *On the Road* by Jack Kerouac, *One Flew Over the Cuckoo's Nest* by Ken Kesey, *The Bell Jar* and *Selected Poems* by Sylvia Plath, *New American Poetry* edited by Donald Allen, *Tropic of Cancer* by Henry Miller, *Justine* by the Marquis de Sade, *The Joyous Cosmology* by Alan Watts, *Nine Chains to the Moon* by R. Buckminster Fuller, *Tarantula* by Bob Dylan, *The Three Stigmata of Palmer Eldritch* by Philip K. Dick, and *LSD My Problem Child* by A.B. Hoffman. At the base of the stack, like a sturdy pedestal to a column of questionable entasis, lay a thick *American Heritage Dictionary*, with dustjacket. I dismantled the pile and set aside all but the dictionary.

"These books are brand new," I observed, "with a common design, excepting the dictionary. What gives?"

"They sent the dictionary as a perk," Ivy said, not looking up from his task, "when I signed up with The Sixties Book Club."

"What's the big deal with the Sixties, anyway?" Lavinia asked, browsing through the stack.

"Nobody can remember," I said.

"I intend to collect them all," Ivy said.

"So you can sell them," I deduced.

"Of course." Ivy nodded contentedly. "They send a book every week. If you don't send it back within ten days, that means you've accepted it, and they send you a bill. Eight ninety-five each, including postage." He dipped a moistened fingertip into the powder on the back of the saucer and scrubbed the gums above and below his incisors with it. "Book dealers prefer their books unread, you know. It increases a book's value." He smacked his lips.

"And how much are these worth, on Telegraph Avenue?"

"Two bucks, two-fifty. Although that dictionary," he pointed the damp pinky, "should bring twenty-five or thirty."

"Beats a job," I said, leafing through it.

"I'll never sink that low again. Don't tear the jacket."

"'Cocaine'," I read aloud. "'A colorless or white crystalline alkaloid, $C_{17}H_{21}NO_4$, extracted from coca leaves, sometimes used in medicine as a local anesthetic especially for the eyes, nose, or throat and widely used as an illicit drug for its euphoric and stimulating effects.'"

"Only illicit since the Marijuana Tax Act of 1938," Ivy pedantically pointed out. He smiled. "But why quibble?"

"'Etymology'," I continued. "'French *cocaïne*, from coca; coca, from Spanish. See coca—' merely one entry up the column, as it happens. '1. Any of certain Andean evergreen shrubs or small trees of the genus Erythroxylum, especially E. coca, whose leaves contain cocaine and other alkaloids. 2. The dried leaves of such a plant, chewed by people of the Andes for a stimulating effect. Etymology: Spanish, from Quech•ua—'"

Lavinia interrupted her pacing. "What?"

I churned pages until I achieved the Qs. "'1. The Quechuan

83

language of the Inca empire, now widely spoken throughout the Andes highlands from southern Colombia to Chile. 2. a. A member of a South American Indian people originally constituting the ruling class of the Inca empire. . . . Etymology: Spanish, from Quechua'—get this—'*plunderer*.'"

Lavinia got it. "The Conquistadors called the Incas *plunderers?*"

"So it would appear."

"I'm changing the climate," she said. "Ask me how."

"There's nothing like a little etymology for fetching up the odd, telling epistemic relativism," I observed.

"Is that the same as irony?" Lavinia asked.

"Now for the 'aitches." I turned pages. "'Heroin. A white, odorless, bitter crystalline compound, $C_{17}H_{17}NO(C_2H_3O_2)_2$, that is derived from morphine and is a highly addictive narcotic. Also called diacetylmorphine. Etymology: German, originally a trademark.'"

Even Ivy took note of that one.

"I *did* change the climate," Lavinia marveled. "Ask me to do it again."

"There's nothing like a little etymology for fetching up the odd, telling *je ne sais quois*," I reminded them.

"Those fucking Nazis might win yet," Ivy observed darkly.

"It's always a possibility," I agreed. "One more?"

"This is almost as interesting as the drugs themselves," Lavinia suggested.

"Speak for yourself," Ivy suggested back.

With the blade of his clasp knife Ivy carefully began to mix the heroin and cocaine, drawing inscrutably calculated amounts of each from their respective heaps, thoroughly dicing them together, then organizing the result into long, thin lines. The table in front of him began to take on the qualities of an aerial photograph of a turkey farm.

Lavinia requested another definition.

84

"Sure. How about. . . . 'Alkaloids: Nicotine, quinine, cocaine, and morphine are known for their poisonous or medicinal attributes. . . .'"

"Mostly poisonous, you bet," Lavinia commented.

"But oh so medicinal," Ivy reassured us.

"Last etymology," I promised. "'Alkalai. From Middle English, from Medieval Latin, from Arabic al-qalIy, the ashes of saltwort, which comes from al, the + qalIy, ashes, which in turn is from qalAY, which means . . . to fry.'"

"Perfect!" Lavinia squealed.

"Ah to fry," Ivy agreed appreciatively, "lonely as a bird."

"Lonely as a crowd," Lavinia corrected, "and," she reflected, "Arabic."

"Sons of bitches might win yet," Ivy speculated.

"On the other hand," I closed the dictionary, "heroin is Old World, while both nicotine and cocaine are New World. So the score's two to one. Who knows?" I rapped my knuckles on the floor. "The Last Superpower Standing might win yet."

"Globalism!" said Lavinia. "Cigarettes and cocaine all round!"

"It's no wonder we are the last superpower," put in Ivy.

"I like the emphasis on 'we,'" I told him. "It conveys solidarity."

"Always glad to be of service. Although," Ivy added thoughtfully, "when that superpower is nothing but one big we, when there's nobody left out, when it's truly global, then we'll see what's what." He produced a candy-striped drinking straw and set about knifing it into three equal lengths. "Marx predicted, a century and a half ago, that when capitalism goes global, it will destroy itself."

I frowned. Hadn't this idea come up already? "It sounds like Marx had more faith in capitalism than I do," I remarked suspiciously.

85

Lavinia narrowed her eyes. "How the fuck did Marx know that?"

"Better you should ask," I suggested, "how does Ivy Pruitt know it?"

"I'm going to be more specific than that," Lavinia said, as we gravitated toward the table. "How can we sit here doing drugs knowing, as we now know, that dedicated, talented, intelligent and well-funded people are determined to destroy us and our way of life?"

"Same way we sat here doing drugs before we knew it," Ivy pointed out. He handed a two-inch section of straw to each of us. "Keep your straw to yourself because, you know, Hepatitis C is extremely communicable." He snapped a finger.

Transgressing the boundary between cosmetics and flesh, Lavinia inserted an end of a straw into one of her petite nostrils and bent over the array of lines.

"What did you say?" I asked.

"A mere fleck of contaminated blood in a dollop of mucus," Ivy replied, watching Lavinia, "is all it takes to transmit the virus that causes Hepatitis C."

"Ivy," I said. "Are you–?"

"If a straw has your number on it," Ivy interrupted, leaning into his own pair of lines, "then it has your number on it." He snorted twice, smoothly and deliberately, then sat back in his chair with a satisfied air. "Son of a bitch, at fucking last, I am one with my numinosity. Curly, you're on deck."

I felt like I was on a deck. If that stack of books from the sixties had tampered with my equilibrium, the idea that Ivy Pruitt might have an incurable and fatal disease seriously moiled it.

As I leaned over the table to do my pair of lines, however, I gave everybody else a reason to be nauseous, for a steady stream of glass particles cascaded out of the cuff of my shirt, littered the surface of the table, and polluted every single line and heap of dope upon it.

86

I jerked away my arm, but that reaction only sewed additional fragments over the table, more or less as if I were seeding it for a crop of martini glasses. I couldn't have contaminated the scene more thoroughly if I'd done it deliberately.

The room fell silent.

Earlier, in the street in front of Ivy's place, Lavinia had kindly brushed the glass off my clothes with a folded road map. I had removed my jacket to shake it out, but not my shirt. While there was no hair on my head to capture glass fragments, quite a few had fallen out of the ear that had been uppermost when the window shattered.

If twisting the tip of a finger in that ear would not have been a good idea, snorting a speedball cut with the odd particle of glass seemed a worse one.

I straightened up, carefully laid my straw on the table, and stood away.

I cleared my throat.

"Oops?"

"That," Ivy said, staring dully at the table, "does not count as positive feedback."

Lavinia sniffed. "We are experiencing technical difficulties." She looked hopefully at Ivy. "Should we stayed tuned?"

"I might be able to think again in about sixty seconds," said Ivy. "Stand by."

"We could cook it up and geeze it," Lavinia said hopefully.

"That's bright," I said. "Even supposing that you enjoy needlework, a single particle of ground glass is bound to give you a rush, as it courses through your bloodstream."

"Hell," Lavinia sniffled defiantly, "if impurities in drugs killed junkies, there wouldn't be any junkies."

"I didn't mean to suggest it would kill you," I said patronizingly. "I meant to infer that it would be an unusual experience. Sensational, possibly."

"So what are we waiting for?"

"Don't mind me. Help yourself." The room fell silent again. I looked toward the front door. "Was that a rooster?"

"Every day," Ivy responded dully.

Lavinia brightened. "That's what we'll call it. The Oakland Rooster. A speedball cut with ground glass. We'll be famous."

"The sun is coming up," I said. "Coining argot is inappropriate."

"Safeway," Ivy said.

"Why would you call it a Safeway?" Lavinia said. "Oakland Safeway?"

"Open 24 hours."

"Does that include now?" I asked.

"That's a good question," Lavinia said. "Answer it, Ivy."

Ivy spoke in a monotone, as if he were in a trance. "Go to Safeway." He extended his hand. "Buy an egg poacher." He twisted his hand and retracted it until it touched his chest. "Bring it to me."

"Egg poacher?" I asked.

Lavinia blinked. "How much of that shit did you do?"

"Ten or twelve blocks." Still staring straight ahead, Ivy extended his arm toward the east. "Straight past the columbarium."

"An egg poacher," I repeated.

"You'll pay for it," Ivy suggested tonelessly. "Get on your hoss.

"But if it works," he added, addressing me directly, "we'll split it three ways."

Nine

Nyctalopia is the term for night blindness. A person who is nightblind might be a *nyctalope*. So, what is a person with day blindness? Or a person who won't work? *Jobalope?*"

"That would be Ivy."

"We're both squinting. How about *diurnalope?*"

"If it weren't for these shades," Lavinia said, "I'd have driven straight into that cemetery wall."

It was one of those mornings we Californians like to think happen only in California, which may be one thing we're right about. No humidity, of course: none. Which means cool in the shade, warm in the sun. Predawn, it's cool with the certain prospect of future warmth. A few wisps of coastal fog remain in the east, as if deliberately, a small committee to welcome the tangelo hues of the ascending dwarf star. The blues of the sky run a gamut from cornflower, backlighting the wisps, to blueberry, straight up, and violet as you move west, all the way to the contusive horizon, where sky and sea can't be determined as agreeing on a boundary. The latter color is a disturbing one, as of an integument having sustained a mighty pummeling in the night, implying that now, as of yore, we have no idea of the terrible machinery that animates it.

Still, with the exception of maybe a half-hour's shuteye grabbed in the back seat of the Lexus while we waited for Ivy Pruitt to get

89

himself processed out of jail, and my twenty minutes on the floor of Ivy's kitchen, Lavinia and I had been up all night. Despite a couple of pairs of shades retrieved from the glove compartment, which I gingerly teased past the black nine-millimeter that lived in there like a hibernating puff adder, the daylight hurt our eyes. And though she was driving quite reasonably along the back streets of Oakland, the slipstream, tugging at the hole where the back window used to be, tugged also at our few remaining calories. We hadn't gone a block before Lavinia had the heater on. That Lexus was some kind of luxury car. Everything in it ran quietly. Though the fan was on full blast KCSM didn't have to work very loudly to serenade us with Cannonball Adderly's exquisite cover of *Autumn Leaves.*

"Are people who wince at daylight universally called musicians?" Lavinia asked, apparently just to make conversation.

My answer was, "That guy didn't have shoes on."

"What guy?"

"Stepnowski. In the warehouse."

Lavinia frowned. "He didn't?"

"The socks on his feet were white but not very dirty and seemed randomly dispersed."

"Randomly dispersed. . . ."

"Like a pair of shotgunned puppets."

She thought about this.

"Sorry," I said. "I have shotguns on the brain this morning."

"He was on a loading dock. . . ."

I nodded automatically, though in fact I was mulling something else entirely, namely the fact that, having counted out our money, we hadn't spared the time to take a look around the rest of that De Haro Street warehouse. But I said, "That's a very interesting point."

". . .Because the next conclusion would be that Stepnowski was killed someplace else."

"And dumped on the loading dock."

90

Stopped at a red light and facing directly into the sun, we thought about it. Lavinia dialed down the heater fan. "He was a little guy. Could one person, alone, have deposited him where we found him?"

"A hundred pounds is still a hundred pounds."

"He weighed more than a hundred pounds."

"Very likely."

"So, two guys with a watchamacallit left him there."

"A dolly? A handtruck? A forklift?"

"But what about the pool of blood?"

"What about it?"

"How much blood in an adult human?"

"Ten pints."

She looked at me, puzzled. "How do you know that?"

I shrugged. "You can only practice so much. Since I don't drink seriously, never watch television, and can't afford a social life, I read."

Livinia kept on watching me for a bit, then turned to face the windshield. "Huh."

"The real question is, can you be an adult human, and a drummer, too?"

The light turned green and the tune was over. I turned off the radio. Driving, Lavinia said, "If only we'd had a look around."

"I was just thinking that thought."

"We might have found his shoes."

"Or no shoes."

"How much is ten pints, anyway?"

"Fifty bucks, if it's Guiness. . . ."

She wheeled us into a Safeway parking lot. A neon sign atop two concrete pillars high above the store remained illuminated: OPEN 24 HOURS; poppy red letters against the robin's-egg blue of the sky.

"Why didn't we have a look around, again?" she asked, as she guided the car into a parking space.

"We got what we came for, and there was a dead guy on the floor."

"Right." The parking lot was nearly deserted. Delivery vehicles of every size and description, from bakery vans to Safeway's own tractor-trailers, surrounded the store. "Nothing about us being chickenshit."

"Not a cheep."

"Yeah. We got what we came for and we left."

"That's my take on it."

The supermarket's doors opened automatically. The lighting was very bright. Lavinia took a shopping basket from a stack inside the door and handed it to me.

"We're just here to get the egg thing," I pointed out.

"What the hell," she said. "When's the last time you had something to eat?"

I considered this. "I can't remember."

"So what comes immediately to mind?"

"Orange juice, coffee, hash browns, toast, butter, jam, and . . . eggs." I looked at her and she looked at me and we both said, "Poached eggs."

"Sounds good to me, and I don't even eat breakfast."

"A lot depends on what Ivy wants an egg poacher for."

"We can always fry them."

"I bet he doesn't own a frying pan. You'll have to get salt, pepper, sugar, paper plates, cups, forks and spoons, too. He has a couple of knives."

"How about a coffee percolator?"

"How about running water?"

Lavinia made a U turn and came back with two liters of bottled water, which she placed into the basket.

"Gas," I said. "I know he has gas."

"I'll bet a gas stove was his single requirement for signing the lease."

"The back-porch view of the Inevitable was just a bonus."

"He didn't think twice about it."

I followed Lavinia as she selected a pound of bacon, a dozen eggs, a quart of milk, a variety of picnicking products. As she added paper towels to the basket, I said, "Maybe we should just go out for breakfast."

"Don't fuck with me; I'm waxing domestic."

We rounded an end cap of tortillas stacked five feet high. "Corn or flour?"

"Corn."

"How about ground pork sausage instead of bacon?"

I shrugged. What the hell did I care? Despite the three-way split, I was still holding more cash than I'd held in a very long time. In years, maybe. Why not go for steak?

Lavinia gathered enthusiasm as she accumulated groceries. She crossed over the back aisle to a wall of meat products and retrieved a pound of ground sausage. "You are in for huevos rancheros like you never had before. For which we need salsa."

"Right here. I guess those Mexican kids leave a little culture behind them every time they get deported."

"And all we offer in return is NAFTA. Excuse me, sir."

A man wearing an apron with a feather duster in one back pocket and a price-sticker gun in a hip holster didn't turn around from a pyramid he was constructing with half-pint cans of peas. "Yes, ma'am?"

"Do you have such an animal as an egg poacher?"

He was a big man with dill pickle fingers that dwarfed the cans he was stacking. "Aisle Six." He jerked a thumb over his shoulder as he turned to look at us. His bloodshot eyes and ragged voice betrayed the fatigue unique to the middle ground between the end of a night shift and the beginning of a second job. It was obvious that the man was exhausted. We should have been helping him, instead of the other way around. Lavinia noticed it, too. "Thank you, sir," she said tenderly.

I glanced at a sign overhead. "This is aisle Four."

93

The man acknowledged Lavinia's civility with a tired smile and turned back to his pyramid. "Enter Six from the front of the store," he advised us. "Get your egg poacher and exit the way you came. That way, you'll avoid a direct encounter with the man who's taking a shit in School Supplies."

For once Lavinia was nonplussed. "School Supplies?"

"It's at the other end of Six."

"Ahm," I hesitated, "is this a regular customer?"

"He's *real* regular," the clerk said.

"Where are your security people?" Lavinia asked.

"Security don't want nothing to do with him."

"What about the cops?"

"Cops got real crime to attend to."

"Where's the manager?"

"Crying in his office."

We walked to the row of cash registers at the front of the store, crossed over to aisle Six, and peered cautiously around its end cap, which consisted entirely of pineapples.

"He wasn't kidding," Lavinia said.

"I never thought so. There's the kitchen stuff. Only twenty feet in."

A speaker overhead reproduced *Hello Goodbye,* by the Beatles.

"Let's go."

We had to scan the display. Salt shakers. Knife sets. Chafing dishes. Can openers. Sauce pans. Fondue forks. Wooden-handled barbecue spatulas. Refrigerator magnets. "Get a pot-holder," I suggested.

"God almighty," Lavinia said, angrily throwing a pair into our basket. "What the hell has that guy been eating?"

"Cheap wine, I'd guess."

"What do you know about it?"

"What's to know? You are what you eat?"

"Look. There's a goddamn egg poacher."

She pointed out a plasticized package containing a saucepan

94

with lid, five shallow semi-spherical metal cups, and a flat, round flange with five holes stamped out of it.

"It looks like a hubcap."

"It cooks eggs by steaming them in these cups." She stood on tiptoe to pull down the package. "The cups fit into the hubcap, which covers the saucepan, half-filled with water, which you put on the stove. . . ."

"I got it I got it—get it."

"I can't reach it. . . ."

From thirty feet away came sounds not unlike those to be obtained by spitting on a hot griddle, with moaning in between.

"God almighty. . . ."

As the woman at the cash register ran the egg poacher over the bar code scanner, she said, "First thing we sold off Six in a while."

I nodded. "No wonder the manager's crying in his office."

"He said he'd turn this store around." She scanned the sausage. "But the store's turning him around."

"Curly, look."

Lavinia pointed to a San Francisco *Examiner* in a rack of tabloids and fashion magazines at the entrance to the check stand. Its headline read, "FAMED DRUMMER MURDERED."

"Famed?" I said. "That guy was no more famous than road tar in the average fender well. He—"

Lavinia elbowed me sharply in the ribs. "I heard it was converting to a tabloid format." She pulled a copy. "And sure enough. Yuck. Last I heard," she added, holding it so I could look at it too, "they no longer publish on Saturday or Sunday."

"They never had a Saturday edition," the checker said. "And as soon as that Hearst tit dries up they'll suspend Monday through Friday, too. Mark my words."

95

Lavinia folded the paper. "But the guy who redesigned the *Examiner* redesigned *The Wall Street Journal*, too."

"What are you trying to tell me," the checker retorted with unexpected venom, "that shit stinks no matter how it's packaged?" Lavinia laughed out loud, but the checker wasn't amused. "I will never forgive how that ass-wipe *Wall Street Journal* crucified Bill Clinton. Every day for eight years."

"They don't publish on the weekends, either," Livinia pointed out.

The checker vehemently totaled the register. "My uncrowned king!"

In the parking lot, Lavinia spread the *Examiner* over the trunk lid of the Lexus.

Acting on an anonymous tip, police discovered the body of Tenesmus drummer Stefan Stepnowksi in a Potrero District warehouse early this morning.

Few details were available by press time. Citing the confidentiality of an ongoing investigation, a police spokeswoman disclosed only that a Caucasian male had been shot at least once at close range and that he probably died instantly. The body was discovered in a pool of blood behind the unlocked door of a warehouse on De Haro Street at 12:41 A.M.

Although the police spokeswoman refused to confirm the victim's identity, pending notification of next of kin, the Examiner *night desk was able to determine through informed sources that the murdered man has been positively identified as Stefan Stepnowski, famed drummer of the short-lived thrash-metal band Tenesmus. Though releasing only one CD before disintegrating over disagreements about the band's creative direction, the influence of Tenesmus extended far beyond the scant ten months of its existence. Music acts as diverse as Pocono Harris, Star Chamber, Robohammer, and Unclaimed*

96

Deceased often cite the band's pioneering sound. A fan who works the night copy desk at the Examiner *reports that despite their initial success none of the members of Tenesmus was able to capitalize on the notoriety of the band's first and only recording,* Scarred By Chains. *That album has been out of print for at least ten years due to contractual disputes, the fan said, and Stepnowski was widely presumed to have been the sole surviving member of the band.*

"What a depressing mess," Lavinia said, as she started the car. "And what about the man's poor wife?"

I settled the groceries in the footwell of the passenger seat. "I never heard of Unclaimed Deceased."

"Three guys dress like morgue attendants right down to the necrotic cosmetics and perform songs about getting high on formaldehyde and necrophilia and the smell of dead Easter lilies, which act they manage quite handily to turn into a metaphor for greed in corporate America, and you never heard of them? Where the fuck have you been?"

"Re-reading *The Octopus* by Frank Norris," I said.

Livinia rasied her head with a start. "Is that where—?"

"I guess they expressed something about the human condition that needed expressing," I interrupted.

"They've sold *millions* of records, Curly."

"Sometimes the shit works and sometimes it doesn't," I observed glumly.

She drove us out of the parking lot.

"Christ," I said after a while. "The *Examiner* used to be a great newspaper."

"That was then. This is now. Don't litter."

The sun was up but it was still early. We stopped at a red light. On a power line above us a pair of rosy finches perched, facing opposite directions, and twittered merrily.

"I can't believe they decided to call that guy famous," I groused as we pulled through the intersection. "He was nobody."

"A nobody in a pool of blood," Lavinia said.

"Are you going to start up with that again?"

"If he was shot some place else, then dumped on the loading dock, why was there so much blood?"

I rolled up the *Examiner* and stuffed it in the grocery bag. "I asked myself that while I was still looking at him."

"If he was shot at close range, accurately enough to kill him, it seems logical he would have bled out on the spot."

"So he was lounging around the warehouse with his shoes off. Somebody found him and killed him. So what?"

"I wish we'd looked for his shoes."

"Why? What are you saying? That Stepnowski was killed somewhere else, the killer collected his blood, moved the body and redistributed the blood around it, all to confuse the police? It seems like a lot of trouble. What the hell for?"

"Exactly." Lavinia tapped a fingernail on the steering wheel. "The killer didn't want anybody to know where the killing happened. He or she didn't want anybody even to suspect that it happened someplace else. So he or she went to a lot of trouble."

"But not so much trouble as your little brain is going to. How do you collect blood from a gunshot wound? You pick the guy up and hold him over an empty bucket?"

"Sure. Why not?"

"Because dead people weigh too much. You ever heard the term dead weight?"

"Man, Curly, you take things too literally. I wasn't even interested in this idea until you decided the setup was wrong. Now you're so pissed off you think it was my idea. Don't be such a cheap date."

I looked out the window. I never minded staying up all night for the right reason. But staying up all night for the wrong reasons—which far outnumber the right ones—is nothing if not exasperating.

Another block passed. "Besides," Lavinia said, "Stepnowski was a little guy. Real little."

Ten minutes later, as we were walking around the side of the garage to Ivy's back steps, she said, "It's interesting to think about."

"Personally, I'm trying to forget that guy, face down in his own blood."

"Maybe it wasn't his blood."

"Maybe those weren't his socks."

"Maybe it wasn't his money, either."

"It wasn't his money. It was our money. Wait." She stopped. "You mean somebody moved the body *and* planted the money on it? Because—wait, don't tell me—because they knew we were looking for him and when we found him we would take the money and go away and not tell anybody about it, thereby implicating ourselves in the murder and ultimately muddying the identity of the true murderer into the bargain?"

"Exactly."

Lavinia paused with one foot on the first step, turned halfway back toward me, paused again, turned forward again, and paused again. Then, abruptly, she resumed climbing the staircase.

"Maybe he wasn't even dead." She took a step. "Maybe he wasn't even really there." She took another step. "Maybe he was a hologram."

"Now you've got a theory. . . ."

99

Ten

Ivy was sitting right where we'd left him, staring into space and tapping the vinyl table top with opposite ends of his soda straw, reversing its length within his fingers between taps.

"Hi, Ivy," Lavinia said pleasantly.

"The fuck you been?"

"Shopping." She pulled the egg poacher from the bag I was carrying and showed it to him. "Remember?"

He took it. "I could have been jonesing, you been gone so long."

"Hey, Grumpy, think of the alternative." Lavinia shucked groceries out of the sack onto the kitchen counter. "Everybody could have stayed here and bled to death from having shards of glass lodged in their maxillary sinuses."

Ivy eyed the groceries with a mixture of suspicion and disgust.

I unrolled the *Examiner*. "Check it out."

He pushed it away. "I don't read the papers." As he stood, he retrieved his clasp knife from its belt holster and slit the plastic perimeter of the egg poacher package, spilling its contents into the kitchen sink.

Lavinia distributed her supplies over the limited counter space. "Now, then. How about a nice, hearty breakfast?"

100

Ivy half-filled the saucepan with water and set it on the front burner of the stove. "Get that shit out of my way."

"Come on, Ivy. Curly and I are hungry. When's the last time you ate?"

"I don't eat. Make room."

Lavinia made a face. In that moment I thought we were in for a recapitulation of a domestic argument typical of the two years Lavinia and Ivy had lived together. The setup was perfect. Neither of them liked being told what to do, and both liked to tell others what to do. But Lavinia knew it wasn't worth it, and Ivy didn't care. She shoved the groceries to the back of the counter and stepped aside.

Contrary to appearances, Ivy had busied himself during the first fifteen or twenty minutes of our absence. First, he'd carefully scraped all of our speedball hors d'oeuvre off the edge of the table top and onto the surface of the blue saucer. Next, he'd set about two cups of water to boiling. Then, he'd cut an eight-inch patch out of a clean tee-shirt, which he'd stretched over the mouth of a empty wide-mouthed jar and, after dimpling the cloth with his thumb, he'd secured it there with a rubber band. Then he waited.

Now Ivy half-filled the poacher's saucepan, placed it over a lit burner, and placed egg cups into four of the five holes in the cover flange. The fifth cup he half-filled with tap water.

"Hey," said Lavinia, noting the setup. "You going for your own cooking show?"

"That sounds like work," Ivy said. "Don't get your hopes up."

"Yeah," Lavinia said thoughtfully. "Work. . . ."

Ivy used the edge of his knife to tip an inch or two of speedball into the fifth egg cup, which he began to pass back and forth through the flame of a second burner while stirring the solution with the tip of the knife. "Turn it down a little."

All three of us stood around the stove, watching the egg cup heat. Ivy held it by the flat metal tab that extended off its perimeter. "That's too hot." He cursed and set the egg cup on the stove top, waved his fingers in the air, blew on them, and finally held them under the faucet, thoughtfully watching as cold water trickled over them.

Abruptly Ivy walked out of the kitchen door and down the back steps. Lavinia and I looked at each other. Two minutes passed, then three. Lavinia turned off the cold water. The saucepan began to rattle, and Lavinia lowered the flame.

Ivy came back through the door with a straight pine twig six or seven inches long and about an inch in diameter. He quickly shaved its bark into the sink with his clasp knife, then sliced a diameter about a half inch into one end of it.

With the tip of the knife he worked one of the empty egg cups out of the five-hole flange, flipped it into the sink, and ran water over it. When the cup had cooled to the touch, he pressed its metal tab into the slot at the end of the stick, so that stick and cup became a ladle. He held it up for everybody to admire.

Lavinia nodded approvingly. "Didn't you attend survival school in the Navy?"

"101st Airborne," I reminded her.

"As if he'd ever let us forget it," she retorted.

Ivy transferred the dope and water mixture from its original egg cup into the ladle, replaced the empty cup into the flange, and started over again.

He passed the wood-handled cup back and forth over the second flame and stirred it with the tip of the knife. Little bubbles began to form at the bottom of the cup. Soon enough, the mixture of powdered heroin and cocaine began to dissolve.

Lavinia and I were fascinated.

"But Ivy. . . ." Lavinia said.

Ivy grunted.

"Are you getting set to geeze this stuff?"

"I don't geeze," Ivy said.

102

"Neither do I," I stipulated, just in case anybody was listening.

Ivy shook his head disdainfully. "You probably weren't even inoculated."

I pointed at my head. "What do you call this?"

"You got a point."

Lavinia giggled. "I know you never geeze," she told Ivy impatiently. "That's why I'm asking."

To geeze is to inject directly into a vein using a needle. What Lavinia was getting at, however, is that usually a street drug which comes as a powder (though people shoot tarball too; people will shoot anything), as ours had, needs to be converted into something shootable. As a rule it's mixed with a little water in a spoon which is heated over a flame until the powder goes into solution. Then a little piece of cotton wadding, such as is to be found cinched behind the placket by the button threads on your better brands of shirts and blouses, or, more commonly, twisted around the ends of an ear swab, is placed in the spoon. The liquefied drug is drawn through this cotton filter by a needle into the barrel of a syringe and, *voilà*, one more or less purified fix.

Next time you see ear swabs strewn around the sidewalk in front of one or another of your cozy local neighborhood stoops, you'll know what you're looking at.

By the way, while it is commonly held that the bit of cotton will filter impurities from the drug solution, it is not necessarily so. Moreover, a tiny filament of the cotton itself is likely to slip up the bore of the needle, as the piston is drawn back, and slip right back down it when the solution is injected into the bloodstream of the user. The subsequent reaction is called "cotton fever;" the symptoms are not pleasant, and their intensity is capable of exceeding any pleasure to be derived from the drug. Such is the junkies' communal humor that, witnessing a fellow user suffering the painful jactitations of cotton fever, they almost certainly will

103

laugh at him. Whosoever experiences its effects, however, laughs not; he may even die. Although, as junkies never tire of reminding anybody who will listen, especially each other, if impurities or embolisms killed junkies, there wouldn't be any junkies.

"So what are you cooking it up for, then?" Lavinia persisted.

"Quiet. Let's see if it works."

With a final swirl of the knife blade, the contents of the egg cup went into solution. "Okay." Ivy removed the cup from the flame and set it on the rim of the sink. "What do we have here?"

"A big spoon, is what we have here," I observed.

"True story, looks like." We watched as the eddies in the solution, still quite transparent, slowed and nearly stopped. "There." Ivy pointed his knife. "See those little dots?"

Tiny specks, like grains of sand, bounded along in the mild turbulence.

"And look," said Ivy. "There."

Lavinia leaned closer. "Where?"

"It comes and goes—there—see?"

What seemed to amount to little more than twinkles of light followed along in the wake of other, parti-colored grains.

"Glass," Lavinia said. "The others look like sand."

"Sand and glass are related, aren't they?" I speculated. "I wonder which would do the most damage?" Lavinia winced. "Hey," I pointed out, "I didn't even mention microscopic impurities, let alone soluble ones."

Ivy straightened up. "Those grits could be anything—including grits. But we got to work with what the good Lord has given us to work with."

"I hate it when he brings God into the picture," said Lavinia.

Now Ivy tipped the improvised ladle over the piece of cloth covering the mouth of the jar. The solution pooled there for a moment, then slowly began to seep away. In the end, a clear solution covered the bottom of the salsa jar, and a tiny, dirty collection of grits and bits of glass lay heaped in the bottom of the cloth dimple.

"*Voilà,*" Ivy said.

"Well I'll be damned," Lavinia said.

"So far, so good," I agreed. "Now you'll do the whole batch?"

"True story, Curly."

Within fifteen minutes Ivy had brought two cups of water to a gentle boil and carefully stirred the entire saucer of speedball into solution, which he then ladled onto his cloth filter. When he was finished, larger pieces of glass lay along the bottom of the saucepan. Atop the cloth filter, there remained trash sufficient to half-fill a teaspoon. It significantly slowed seepage through the filter.

Now Ivy removed the cloth from the mouth of the jar and transferred some of its solution to a single egg cup. Then he put the cup with the speedball solution into its hole in the egg poacher and covered the flange with the saucepan lid. He turned up the heat and stared at the saucepan. "I knew a guy, once," he said thoughtfully, "who started having headaches. When they got worse he called them migraines. Later, in the dark, he'd see flashes of light. They were very real to him, like heat lightning outside his window. But the flashes were generated inside his head." The saucepan began to mutter. Ivy waited. When steam began to leak out of the seam between the rim of the lid and the rim of the pan, he reduced the heat until the water merely simmered.

"Well," Ivy continued, "of course my friend was a junky, but he was also very well off, and along with his money he had health insurance. He also had a very sympathetic doctor, one of those guys who looks the other way when it comes to your real health problems and just does what you tell him to do. That doctor led to another and another and another, until my friend found a neurosurgeon willing to operate on my friend's head." Ivy touched his forehead at the hairline, above his right eye. "Here."

"And?" Lavinia wanted to know.

"Impurities," I guessed.

Ivy held up a finger. "A grain of something was lodged in a capillary in his brain. Tiny, but plenty big enough to dry up that part of the cortex, which left the poor motherfucker with headaches, flashes of light, and pain."

"Really?" Lavinia said. "There's a part of the brain that—"

Ivy waved this off. "Who knows how the brain works? They sewed up his head, sent him home, and—presto."

"Change-o?"

"He was cured?"

Ivy nodded. "No more headaches, no more lightning flashes, no more fainting spells. But. . . ."

"But?" Lavinia and I asked together.

"But he had epileptic-type seizures for the rest of his life. Right away he wasn't allowed to drive. Later, he couldn't be left alone. They got worse and worse until he died, about two years down the road."

"The seizures killed him."

"No," Ivy sucked a tooth. "He died of an overdose."

"You took the word right out of my mouth," I said with disgust.

"Gross!" exclaimed Lavinia.

"The operation disturbed more than it cured," I surmised. "But it didn't disturb the idiot's habit."

"What is that, Curly?" Ivy cracked the lid on the egg poacher, and peered under it. "Some kind of moral?"

"Moral?" I replied. "What instruction do you take away from that story?"

"That's easy: The brain is a delicate thing. If you're going to fuck with your brain, it pays to eliminate the unknowns."

I ruefully shook my head. "Unknowns like sand and glass in your bloodstream?" We all tried to see under the lid. "Was the overdose deliberate?"

106

"It could have been. He was pretty fucked up." Ivy shrugged. "If it wasn't, it should have been."

Lavinia and I shared a look.

"Well," Ivy smiled and turned off the flame. "We're all gonna die, anyway."

"Just have a look out the back door," I said quietly.

Ivy removed the lid from the poacher.

All the egg cups were empty, except one.

"See that white stuff?" Ivy said.

"Pure speedball," I realized.

"One hundred percent," Ivy agreed.

"My god," Lavinia breathed, and she looked at the saucer of contaminated heroin and cocaine. "So much for the dry run."

Twenty minutes later, all five egg cups were half full of cloth-filtered speedball solution, the lid was on the poacher's flange, the saucepan was on the boil, and my cell phone rang.

"Jesus Christ, I've been shot," I jumped, fumbling at my belt. "I haven't had a call since the French Revolution."

"It's probably for me," Ivy said mildly, turning down the heat under the egg poacher.

Annoyed, I said to the phone, "Hello?"

The phone growled back. "For a lousy seventy-five hundred bucks you had to whack the fuck?"

"Tell him I'm busy." Ivy eyed the flame. "Tell him to call later."

"I beg your pardon?" I said to the phone.

"Did you at least get the goddamn money?" the phone replied.

"Who is this?"

"Well I guess this ain't Ivy Pruitt," the phone said, adding with a shout heard round the room, "because that prick knows who I am!"

"Mr. Pruitt is in a meeting," I replied primly. "May I take a message?"

107

"Since when is a fuck in the shitter and he can't talk on the goddamn telephone?"

Ivy peeked under the saucepan lid.

"What," the phone screamed, "he needs both hands to wipe?"

"I'm sure I can't answer that, sir."

Ivy replaced the lid.

"Put on Pruitt," the phone demanded. "This is important!"

"A call from Mr. Important." I held out the phone. "He insists on exchanging insults with you personally."

Ivy took the cellphone. "Yo, Sal—" he began. "—What?" He listened. "Wait a minute, why should we kill the guy? He paid off. We went away." Ivy said, to us, "Did you guys shoot that Stepnowski guy?" I shook my head. Lavinia rolled her eyes. "No," he said to the phone, "they didn't shoot him. Obviously, that shit happened later." He listened some more. Then he said, "How many repos have I—? No, no, no, Sal, I beg your pardon, it's more than twenty. Yeah. Has anybody gotten killed—who? That wasn't my gig, dickhead, that was Tony's gig. Yes, *your* nephew. Who, in turn, as I recall, got himself killed just last Christmas. So much for nepotism— Of course it was cash. Cops? How did—? A receipt. . . ?" Ivy frowned. Then he said, to nobody in particular, "The cops found a World of Sound receipt in Stepnowski's hip pocket." I looked at Lavinia, who bit her lip. "Shit!" Ivy said, and angrily turned off the flame under the saucepan. "No, Sal, not you, I'm trying to cook some breakfast here. Sure I eat. He told you what? So what's a cop know about it? Oh. Ouch. What? All hundreds. Sure. . . . I'll send it over with Curly. Watkins. Yes, yes, *the* Curly Watkins." Ivy winked at me. "Sure you know him. He's probably another guy who owes you money." Ivy shrugged and rolled his eyes. "Okay, Sal, today you don't know him. What the fuck difference— Illegal? Since when? Oh. Yeah. Well, yeah, sure, of course murder's against the law." Ivy waved an impatient hand at the saucepan.

108

I plucked the lid off the egg poacher with one of the new potholders and set it down on the stove top. In the die-cut platter, each egg cup was frosted white, like so many UFO windshields of a crisp winter's morning, say, but in fact they were more like the sclerae of a five-eyed dragon.

A real delicacy.

"Sal, you don't give a shit about Stepnowski, so get off it. The bread's here, you'll get it this afternoon. When? What's the big deal? Curly's not there, he's here. Sure. Here is Oakland, but— Okay, Okay! Fuck you, too. And very much."

Ivy held the phone at arm's length, made a face, and pitched it to me. I caught it with the potholder and turned it off.

"A fucking receipt," Ivy muttered disgustedly. "I thought you guys went through his pockets."

"Curly went through his pockets," Lavinia corrected him, somewhat defensively. "I only touch live men."

"Pocket," I corrected them both. "The dough was in the first pocket I checked, so that was that."

Ivy wasn't even listening. "Whatever happened to the handshake deal?" he groused. "Isn't a man's word good for anything anymore? Fucking paper trails. . . ."

His attention fell upon the egg poacher, and his mood shifted. After a close inspection of the cooling saucepan, he happily scrubbed his hands together.

"I'll take the vapor trail," he said. "Every time."

Eleven

Sal 'The King' Kramer's World of Sound is on Folsom at Sixth, right across the street from a place called the Brainwash, where you can watch your clothes tumble dry beyond a soundproof glass wall while you sit in a comfortable chair eating a cheeseburger with a beer and pretend to listen to live poetry while in fact browsing the sex ads in the back of the *Bay Guardian*.

The poet Jim Carroll once observed that, while he enjoyed fronting a rock and roll band, when the gig was over, he wanted silence. The guys in his band, however, would go home and listen to music. He couldn't figure it out.

What I can't figure out is drummers who go down to Kramer's World of Sound and pretend to test-drive the most expensive kit in the inventory, by way of practicing their paradiddles, at ten o'clock in the morning. Another thing I wonder about is how Sal Kramer can stand to smoke a nickel cigar at that hour—or any other, for that matter. Traffic was inexplicably light, so, as we sank down the Fifth Street ramp, westbound off the Bay Bridge, I expressed these concerns to Lavinia.

"That's easy," she said. "They're connected—the practicing drummers and Sal's cigars, I mean. Plumbers smoke cigars to mask the smell of shit, right?"

"You know," I admitted, "I never thought of it that way."

She tapped her right temple. "Vassar."

110

"I got another question."

"Shoot."

"What about that back window?"

As she made a right at Seventh, broken safety glass rattled over the rear window shelf. It sounded like the percussion instrument known as a rainstick.

"Insurance. Ask me a hard one."

"Okay, how much dope will be left by the time we get back to Oakland?"

"Any amount of dope divided into a zero like Ivy equals zero dope left over."

"Vassar," I concluded.

She nodded.

"Do you think Sal was making it up, insisting that we had to bring his thirty-seven fifty to him immediately?"

"Otherwise Sal would have no choice but to admit to the cops about siccing Ivy onto Stepnowski?"

"Which would force the cops to admit to themselves, disappointing as that might be, that Ivy was under lock and key in their own basement the whole time Stepnowski was getting himself killed?"

"But wasn't his payment to the bail bondsman in cash?"

"Hundred dollar bills, in fact."

"Of which Stepnowski had some twelve examples in his jeans when they found him." Lavinia looked at me. "Right?"

I shrugged. "The paper didn't say anything about it."

"How much do cops make?"

"About that much a week, I'd think. But don't get your hopes up."

"I guess we're about to find out," Lavinia said, grasping the steering wheel with both hands. "Here we are."

Actually, we'd been in the World of Sound's parking lot long enough for Lavinia already to have parked and turned the engine off. Immediately to our left, a purple two-story cinderblock wall

111

with yellow flowers and green leaves painted on it emitted deep thuds.

"It was generous of Ivy to allow us a couple of fat bumps apiece before he threw us out," Lavinia said. "I was really tired."

"Me, too," I admitted. "Not that I care about the stuff."

"But it made you feel better, didn't it."

"Sure did."

"Real better."

"Yeah. It's too bad we didn't take the time to make breakfast, too."

Lavinia shrugged. "What can you do in the kitchen of a man who says food makes him paranoid?"

"Eat his breakfast for him."

"Isn't that some kind of business homily?"

"You're asking me about business?"

The thudding stopped. One minute elapsed peacefully. Beyond the hood of the car, orange nasturtiums bloomed along the base of a chain link fence.

"Hey, Curly, remember what Saint Augustine said?"

"Fuck no."

"If you can understand it, it is not God."

Another minute of silence passed.

"That speedball sure is nice."

"Yeah."

"Tell you what."

"Tell me anything you want."

"If we manage to navigate through today without getting arrested, let's celebrate with a little speedball."

"Good idea."

"Just a little."

"Yeah."

"Couple hits each."

"Sure."

"Get us through the night."

112

"Yeah."
"We could even have sex."
"What did you say?" I asked mildly.
"Let's get this over with."

Sal 'The King' was sitting at a desk within a glass-walled cubicle in the back of the store, the atmosphere inside of which reeked of an electrical fire doused by soy sauce. It looked that way, too. Invoices, pieces of cardboard, cymbals and drumheads in and out of their cartons, drumsticks and curly cords, packs of guitar strings and styrofoam coffee cups littered every available surface. The fax machine was overflowing faxes into an overflowing wastebasket. A gold record hung among framed and autographed concert posters and band photographs on the wall behind the desk. Everything was askew and covered with dust.

"Fuckin' junk faxes," Kramer said to nobody in particular, reading a page as the machine excreted it. *"Repair Grandfather Clocks At Home In Your Spare Time for Big $$$!"* He threw the sheet to the floor. "That's my fuckin' paper they're wasting, my toner, my phone line—I should pay for this shit and read it, too? I pay some recycler he should cart them faxes away, I pay some kid he should go to the Office Depot to buy me more fucking cases of toner and paper. . . . I'd like to fax the Federal Tax Code up this clock guy's ass. This grandfather clock guy's costing me money! Look at this!" He snatched up another sheet from the floor. *"$99 Disney Vacation!* Fuck! See that 800 number? Tiny print, right? Tough shit. Buy yourself some glasses. Says, If you feel that you've received this fax in error, please call 1-800-HIY-ASAP and request that your name be removed from our database. Right!" He threw the sheet to the floor. "Look at this!" He pointed his cigar at the wastebasket. "How many faxes you think are in there? A thousand? A million? It's a fire hazard! I got time to call all these jerkoffs? No! *They* should call *me.* And beg me—*beg* me—not to kill them when I

113

catch the cocksuckers. I pick up this phone—" He jabbed his cigar at a telephone hidden beneath a coil of audio cable on his desk. "And right now," he snapped his fingers, "the guy is dead." He snapped his fingers again. "Grandfather clock guy is a dead grandfather clock guy." He abruptly collected himself. "What am I saying? Here I am, raving on and on about junk faxes, for chrissakes—junk faxes! I should kill somebody? For a junk fax? And right here in my office are a couple of musicians, a couple of envoys from the most sensitive tribe on the planet." He waggled the cigar. "My children, disregard the petty concerns of the workaday world, and take a deep breath. Center yourselves. Now." He exhaled a gout of fetid smoke toward Lavinia's breasts. "Tell me what kind of gear you need, and what kind of credit problems you have. And. . . ." He tapped his chest with the forefinger of his cigar hand, "Sal Kramer will show you how you can afford it. They don't call Sal 'The King' for nothin'. Hell, I knew Joe Ellis when he couldn't even blow out the candles on his birthday cake, let alone hold down first desk in the pit on *Andrew Lloyd Webber's Greatest Hits!*—that show's been camped at the Orpheum for, what, twelve years? Joe still had hair when he started that gig." He pointed the cigar at Lavinia. "You hearda Joe Ellis?" Lavinia shook her head. Sal took one of Lavinia's hands between his, the cigar protruding from his fat fingers like a zeppelin leaking fumes. "Joe Ellis didn't have a watch to keep time with when I sold him that horn. On credit, too. One hundred percent financing! But 'The King' believed in Joe. 'The King', for no money down—"

I suddenly said, "Joe Ellis didn't buy that trumpet from you."

"He— What?" Kramer squinted through the cigar smoke at Lavinia. "Who let him in here?"

"Lambert Deutschen sold his trumpet to Joe Ellis in the basement of the Great American Music Hall in 1988 for enough cash to buy an ounce of blow, a thousand bucks, about one sixth what that horn is worth. It was a dark hour in the history of jazz.

114

But if he hadn't sold it to Joe, he would have sold it to somebody who didn't know what it was. But you know what, Kramer?"

Kramer hadn't taken his eyes off Lavinia's breasts. "Tell him to go away, sweetheart."

Lavinia got her hand back and said, "What, Curly?"

"If Lambert ever asked Joe to return his trumpet, Joe would give it to him."

Lavinia frowned. "Didn't Lambert Deutschen die of a heart attack while snorting cocaine off the dashboard of a car behind a club in Detroit about ten years ago?"

"That's not the point." I stabbed my forefinger at my chest and said, "I saw the look in Joe's eyes when that deal went down. I—"

"What the fuck were you doing there," Kramer interrupted, "cleaning the toilets?" He smiled lasciviously at Lavinia. "Not for nothing do they call Sal Kramer 'The King', baby." Confused and alarmed, Lavinia looked back and forth between us. Sal 'The King' Kramer called me a motherfucker and stood up. I advised Sal that on the contrary he was the motherfucker, and stepped up to meet him.

We embraced.

"Curly."

"Sal."

"Long time."

"I've missed you."

"No you haven't."

"Okay, I haven't. How you been keeping? Let me look at you." Sal held me at arms' length.

"Ah, I don't look as good as you, Sal."

Sal's smile faded. "That's true. You don't look so good." His face assumed a pained expression. "Where's my money?"

"It's all bullshit." Lavinia shook her head. "Why should musicians be allowed to talk? Why can't they just play music

115

and go afterwards to a shelf in a closet away from the rest of us, some place where they can't make normal people crazy?"

I produced the wad of hundreds.

Kramer plugged the cigar into his mouth, took the money, sat into his office chair and counted the bills into the styrofoam lid of a take-out carton. "Thirty-seven." He looked up. I handed him fifty in small bills. He counted those, too, then stacked the lot. "Okay."

Kramer cleared a windrow of cut-sheets and invoices away from a computer monitor on his desk and began to mouse around. "Receivables. . . . Stepnowski. . . . Balance due. . . . Wait a minute." He peered at the screen. "There was a synthesizer." Sal swiveled his chair. "You see a keyboard lying around Stepnowski's place? Specifically," he turned back to the computer screen, "a Kurtzweil FX-11? Fifty-five keys? Black?"

"Nope," I said.

"Nope," Lavinia affirmed.

"He bought it a month later." Sal swiveled to squint at the computer again. "Sonofabitch. The guy's dead, and the account's still open."

"Somebody should tell him," I suggested.

Sal swept the clutch of audio cables off the phone and touched a preset. A woman came on the speaker almost immediately. "Beat me, Bwana, order me about."

"Invoice number 2381-16," Sal said. "It's a synth. I'm moving it up in the cue."

"I'm on it like brown on rice." The woman rang off and Sal went back to mousing. "She's a vegetarian so she gets to talk like that," he told the computer screen. "The Peavey 1430 Sound Reinforcement System is now . . . paid in full and . . . right here we write off . . . the recovery fee. Save. Okay. Now print, you bastard."

Tractor-fed invoices began to inch up out of a box on the floor into a printer, which stippled noisily.

116

"Curly," Kramer spun his chair, "How the fuck did you get mixed up with Ivy Pruitt?"

"I've known Ivy for years, Sal. Same as you."

"But you're a working musician."

"So? If I only hung out with working musicians I'd be as lonely as Nixon after Watergate."

Sal shook his head. "Ivy Pruitt's nothing but trouble, Curly. Not only that, you should stick to what you know how to do, which is playing the same ten songs three sets a night five nights a week, and leave Ivy Pruitt to do what he knows how to do, which ain't playing no music."

"I'm up to eleven tunes, Sal," I pointed out, but I could feel my cheeks coloring at the slant the conversation had taken. I didn't understand it, but neither did I think Sal Kramer had any right to give me this kind of advice. On the third hand, I had no doubt that I was in over my head with Lavinia, let alone Ivy Pruitt, but I had no intention of giving up that information to Kramer. Worse, Sal was right. It was a bad idea to be associating with Ivy Pruitt. Everybody in the business knew he was a junky, and if word got around that I was hanging out with him, club owners might suddenly discover that there is an amazing number of people out there willing not only to play ten or even eleven songs over and over again but to sing them too, all night long, for no money at all.

But I wasn't about to give Kramer the satisfaction of knowing that I agreed with him about the last twenty-four hours, most of which I'd spent spending money I'd taken off a dead man, getting shot at on a back street in Oakland, not to mention buying, transporting and consuming heroin and cocaine, not to mention playing no music whatsoever; all because of Ivy Pruitt.

"Hey," I protested lamely, "we all got our troubles. Ivy Pruitt, for example, is a disabled veteran."

Sal 'The King' Kramer closed his eyes and shook his head.

117

"The taxes I pay," he muttered, "and that fucking guy gets a check every month?"

"Plus," I added, "he's a friend of mine."

"And mine," Lavinia put in.

"You a musician?" Kramer asked her.

"No," Lavinia said. "But I love music and the people who make it."

"Jesus fucking Christ," muttered Kramer.

"Hey," I said, "She's catching on."

The phone rang. Instead of taking it on the speaker, Kramer picked up the receiver. "Yeah?" He listened, looked at each of us, then said, "No. They just left."

Lavinia and I exchanged glances.

"How the fuck should I know?" Sal barked. "No, I don't know the answer to that, either." He sighed loudly. "Look, Garcia, Folsom Street is the only way out of my parking lot and it's one way going east. You want I should catch them for you, too? Get a move on. They can't be far. I was going to call you," he said, exasperated. "They just went out the door, for chrissakes. You're welcome." He slammed down the phone. "Fuckin' cops."

"Cops?"

"You two kill that guy?" Sal said to the wall in front of him. "Stepnowski?"

I said, "Sure we did. Blew him away for a bad debt. Iced him. Anything for you, Sal. He had it coming."

Sal spun the chair to face us. "Anything for the money, you mean. Did Ivy at least split the commission with you, I hope?"

Lavinia said, "He didn't have much choice."

Sal was looking at me. "What's she talking about?"

"Ivy was locked up at the Hall of Justice all day yesterday," I told him. "We tracked down Stepnowski and got the money back on his behalf. Ivy handed off the job for half the take specifically so he could get himself bailed out."

118

"Ivy was in jail again?" Sal assumed a pained look. "How in the hell. . . ? This ain't your racket, Curly."

"You're telling me."

Sal looked at Lavinia's breasts again, but addressed me: "This is what's in it for you?"

Lavinia shrugged ostentatiously. "It was the only way to come up with enough dough to spring Ivy."

"What was he in for?"

"Paraphernalia," I said.

"Chickenshit," Sal snorted.

"That was the Oakland beef," I specified. "The DA didn't want to pursue it. That sprung me and it should have sprung Ivy, but they trucked him over to San Francisco for some prior he'd run out on. Driving on an expired license, something simple like that."

"Expired license," Sal repeated acidly. "You a special friend of Ivy's?"

Lavinia stood straight and smoothed the front of her jacket over her breasts. "You might say that."

"So why didn't you just bail him out? Loan him the money?"

"Why didn't you?" Lavinia countered.

Sal shrugged. "I'm a businessperson."

"Same here," Lavinia said.

"You'd never see it again," I suggested.

"He knew better than to call me," Sal said. He looked curiously at Lavinia. "So he called you."

"Not for a loan, though." She nodded. "He made me a proposition. It looked like easy money. I went straight to the address you gave Ivy, but Stepnowski had moved. I tried to get the landlord to tell me where Stepnowski was. No soap. The landlord all but told me that if I'd come inside and fuck him, he'd tell me where Stepnowski was. Right. And I was hatched out of an egg last week."

"Really?" I said. "He didn't try to get me to do that."

"Maybe the guy's got standards," said Sal.

"Maybe a girl does, too," Lavinia countered sharply. "Anyway, Ivy's next idea was to get Curly to run the brother-from-out-of-town routine. We had to redistribute the action but, hey, without Curly there was no action. Ivy knew Curly looked weird enough to pass for a musician and an enforcer, too, if he kept his mouth shut. And he knew Curly could use the money."

"Pass?" I said.

"What an operator," Sal said, "a fuckin' polymath." He waggled a flattened hand. "Tentacles in two worlds."

"Any fool can see the sensitive soul beneath this tattoo," I suggested.

"A youthful disfigurement," Sal declared acidly. "Like a war wound."

"You're speaking from experience?"

"Fuck no." He jerked the thumb of his cigar hand to indicate his own chest for a change. "I dodged the draft for my country. It was the sixties. You shoulda been there. But," he cleared his throat and spit into the trash can, "you weren't."

"Please note, Sal," Lavinia interrupted, "that Curly got the job done? He conned Stepnowski's new address out of the landlord; we drove over there; we found Stepnowski dead." Before I could stop her, she went on, "The money practically fell out of the guy's pocket, but Curly took care of that, too. Personally, I wouldn't have touched it."

This elicited a long look from me: I didn't believe her.

"Give credit where credit's due," she persisted, "You ever go through a dead man's pockets?"

"Not lately," Sal said.

Him, I believed.

"Stepnowski had plenty of money on him. We took our bite — your bite, too—left the rest, and got out of there. End of story."

"Left the rest?" Kramer appraised her with a look.

"There was another twelve hundred on the guy," I said.

Sal looked back and forth between us. "Really?" he beamed. "That's true?"

"That's it," I said. "That's the truth."

"What about it, Sister?"

"It's the truth."

"That's it, then," Sal said loudly. "Let's get this over with."

I looked around. "Who you talking to?"

With an air of distraction Sal picked up a pencil, inserted the eraser into one ear, and stared at nothing. I looked at Lavinia. She looked at me. We both looked at Sal. Stirring the pencil, Sal looked at Lavinia's breasts. The office door opened behind us. With a little fresh air came the sound of someone belaboring a ride cymbal.

"Who was that on the phone?" I asked as I turned around. A guy in a trench coat was closing the door. He wore a tie, knotted but loose. He had wavy, jet black hair and smooth, closely shaven cheeks. He was in his late thirties or early forties, almost as tall as I am and half again as heavy. He had tired eyes that didn't look like they were falling by the World of Sound to score a pair of xylophone mallets.

"Lieutenant Garcia," the man said by way of answering my question. "Homicide."

121

Twelve

The King," I faced Sal, "my ass."

"Guy sticks up the store," Sal grumbled half-heartedly, "it takes them all fuckin day to get here."

"Murder isn't a cash register, Kramer," Garcia replied. He jerked a thumb at the door behind him. "Beat it."

Sal looked a little startled. This was his office, after all. But Garcia stepped aside and Sal lost no time in getting out. A uniformed cop posted in the hall closed the door. Garcia turned around and held up a pistol, its barrel impaled on a pencil.

"Yikes," said Lavinia, "so you're the guy who smashed my back window and stole my roscoe out of the glove compartment?"

I cringed.

Garcia said quietly, "This isn't high school, Miss Hahn."

"That's true," Lavinia nodded. "Do you have a warrant?"

"Lavinia. . . ."

Garcia forestalled me with a smile. "I do have a warrant," he addressed her, "if you'd like to play that way." He patted his breast pocket. "But if you so choose, you're going to lose. Perhaps you'll hear me out first?"

"Perhaps she will," I insisted.

Lavinia had so much trouble with authority that she was perfectly capable of flying in the face of Garcia's winning hand, even if she went to jail for it. Jails, in fact, are full of such people. Much as a scientist would watch a frog's leg to which he's attached an

122

electrode, Garcia watched Lavinia. I watched her, too. My fate was a little too wired into her decision for comfort.

But some stroke of reasonableness stayed her contrariety. "So," she finally said, "talk."

Garcia talked. "Through a miracle of technology we've established that a second pistol fired three rounds at the scene of the Stepnowski murder." Garcia let the pistol turn around the shaft of the pencil like a slow noisemaker, whose ominous appearance made up entirely for its silence. "But that gun didn't fire the shot that killed him." When the handle came around, we could see that the clip had been removed. Garcia looked past it at Lavinia. "Same caliber, different gun."

"On cop shows on my television before I pawned it," I interrupted, "ballistics tests took weeks."

"It's probably been several years since you pawned it," Garcia said, with only mild condescension.

I nodded. "Ten, fifteen, twenty."

"Other than the march of progress," he said, with no condescension whatsoever, "you haven't missed a thing."

"What's so hot about this murder case?" Lavinia asked. Despite her reasonable decision of just a moment before, her voice had reclaimed its accustomed note of antagonism. "Don't you have important dead people to investigate?"

"Oh yes," Garcia replied mildly. "But there are reasons to fast track this particular case."

"What reasons?"

The gun began to turn again. "By the additional miracles of computerized record-keeping and gun control legislation, we have also established that the registered owner of a Lexus parked in the lot next to this very building has no gun permit. In fact, even if this handgun is registered, its serial numbers have been filed."

Lavinia pursed her lips.

"So the pistol will remain in our custody until such time as it meets its ultimate fate as one of the many guests of honor at the annual Police Athletic League fundraiser, barbecue, and ordnance meltdown."

It seemed to me that, while Garcia was letting Lavinia slide on at least two gun charges, he almost had to be aware of how she earned her living. "I sense a drift, here."

"It took almost two hours to follow up on the tip that sent us to the De Haro warehouse," Garcia said. "But a homeless guy who regularly sleeps on the roof of a building across the street from 112 De Haro gave us a first-rate description of you two, along with the license plate number of a Lexus registered to one Lavinia Hahn." He shifted his eyes to me. "He mentioned a guitar case, too. We found one in the trunk of your Lexus." He shot a cuff and checked his watch. "By now it's at the lab. Which reminds me." He opened the door. "Lavoix."

Officer Lavoix turned around. Even with most of her raven hair tucked up under her service cap, she proved to be one of the prettiest cops I'd ever seen. "Lieutenant?" she said.

"You got a Number 3?"

Officer Lavoix produced a briefcase out of which she retrieved a large padded envelope, into which Garcia dropped the pistol, followed by its clip. From a spiral pocket notebook he recited a case number, which Officer Lavoix copied onto the flap. "Run this down to Pickering," Garcia told her. "Suggest that he check it against the De Haro rounds. Come back and get me."

"Yessir." The door closed again.

"If it hadn't been for that homeless guy, whose name is Jake Carter, you two would be in a world of trouble."

Lavinia had a little more to hide than a mere unregistered gun; but I, for one, intended to play this frolic straight up the middle, because I had nothing to hide. I needed a murder rap or an accessory rap or any rap at all, let alone more face-time with cops and junkies, like Beethoven needed earplugs.

"I appreciate the consideration, Lieutenant," I said politely.

"So, given this homeless guy, what's your understanding of the shooting on De Haro Street?"

Garcia didn't exactly beam at this ass-kissing, but Lavinia, for once, kept her mouth shut. "Carter had just settled in to read a little Shakespeare by headlamp when he heard three shots. He didn't check it out right away and, in any case, Jake wouldn't want to stick his head up before he'd turned off his headlamp. Besides which he's street-wary. Other people's troubles are not necessarily his, and gunshots in the city aren't exactly uncommon."

"Sad to relate," Lavinia commented pointedly.

"Yeah, well." Garcia thinned his lips a little. "Jake took the trouble to put down his book, turn out his headlamp, get out of his sleeping bag, and take a careful peek over the parapet wall."

"And he saw—?"

"The street was deserted. The Lexus was there already, but it didn't attract his attention at first. He was just about to give up when the outside light at 112 blinked on and off."

Lavinia could not restrain herself from commenting: "Son of a bitch."

Garcia smiled without amusement.

I hurried it along. "So Jake settled in to wait."

Garcia nodded. "Jake was just about to give up again when a woman came out of the metal door at 112 followed by a tall, bald, skinny guy." Garcia paused before he added, "Jake described the woman as 'skanky'."

Lavinia gasped, then burst out with, "This insolent fuck, this dregs of society thinks just because he's looking up from the gutter he's got perspective?"

"What's the matter, Lavinia? You've been dressing skanky for years. It finally worked."

"Fuck you, you shitbird guitarist."

Garcia said tiredly, "They argued. . . ."

Lavinia rounded on him. "About what?"

125

Garcia shrugged. "At that distance, Jake couldn't make it out. But after a little consultation the guy re-entered the building. The woman scuttled—"

"Scuttled?" Lavinia shrieked.

"We have it on tape," Garcia pointed out mildly.

Lavinia hissed like a cat.

"—Scuttled along the loading dock and down the stairs at the corner, where she got into a recent-model Lexus parked westbound on Alameda Street, and took off. No more than a couple of minutes later, just as Jake was thinking it was time to go back to *Richard III*, the Lexus reappeared eastbound on 15th, made the corner onto De Haro, and stopped in front of the warehouse—northbound on the wrong side of the street— long enough for the bald guy to join her. Now the bald guy is carrying a guitar case. Interestingly, Carter observed that this case seemed too light to have an instrument in it. The bald guy hefted it wrong. He was careless with it. Carter's words."

"Your Shakespeare scholar is pretty sharp," I remarked.

"Nosy bastard," Lavinia grumbled.

"We left the guitar behind," I explained politely, "in case things got rough."

"How rough is murder?"

Nobody answered that one.

"Jake is sharp," Garcia agreed. "He doesn't seem to be a lush or a hophead or crazy, either. He's just homeless."

"Probably used to be a CEO," Lavinia suggested.

"He likes the freedom. Lucky for you. From his perch Jake could see the clock on the old Folger's tower at Brannan and Spear. It was twenty-five minutes to ten P.M.," he added politely.

"Damn," I said.

"More luck," Garcia smiled. "Jake will make a good witness. Any defense lawyer would play him like a violin."

"Oh shit, oh dear," Lavinia said, "defense lawyers are expensive."

"I couldn't agree more," I said.

Garcia shrugged. "The ballistics test on Miss Hahn's pistol will about tear it for me," he said, "if it comes up the way I think it will. We haven't nailed it yet, but Stepnowski's forensics should peg his death as approximately coincident with Curly's visit to the Oakland jail, yesterday afternoon, six to eight hours before we can place either of you on De Haro Street. So I guess," he clasped his hands in front of him, "you two can go ahead and get married."

That got a laugh from me.

"Don't make me puke," Lavinia barked. "What kind of self-respecting girl lets herself get married to a guy with an octopus tattooed on his head?"

"Youthful indiscretion covers both categories." I rubbed the flat of my hand over my pate. "Darling."

"And a musician!" she noted spitefully. "Where's the white picket fence?"

"On the album cover."

"Marriages have started on shakier feet," Garcia said sententiously.

"But not on eight slimy ones," Lavinia said.

"Arms," I said. "They're arms."

"With suction cups!"

"And a beak."

"Disgusting."

"The better to have and to hold."

"Eew!"

Garcia said, "I'd like to disregard the various felonies and misdemeanors littering the landscape, in order to get to the nut of this case."

"Some people have a hard time keeping their eye on the ball," I said appreciatively.

"Some people," Lavinia archly observed, "have a ball to keep an eye on."

I nearly retorted that calling heroin retail a ball to keep an eye on was going a bit far, but I confined my reaction to a scowl. If Lavinia was determined to sass her way into a hat full of felonies by way of distracting the world from her complicity in a shoot-out in a liquor store, she was welcome to them.

"Ever heard of Narcotics Anonymous?" Garcia asked suddenly.

With the effrontery that comes only from someone convinced she's pulled the wool over the eyes of the entire world, but especially over her own, Lavinia drew herself up to her full height and declared, "Narcotics Anonymous is for people with drug problems."

"Is it not," Garcia said.

"Next question." Lavinia set herself to brushing an invisible particle of lint off her sleeve.

Garcia, who in any case was obviously interested in something else altogether, shrugged. "Okay. I was about to say that I'm fairly satisfied with your version of the story, so far as it goes."

"Are you the guy who needs to be satisfied?" I asked.

"There will be the DA, when the time comes. The disposition of witnesses and evidence will be his call. But he takes suggestions from me. Plus," Garcia inclined his head toward Lavinia, "he's soft on victimless crime."

Lavinia declined to rise to this bait. "And that time will come when?" I asked.

Garcia shook his head. "When we nail a suspect."

"Do you have one?"

Garcia said nothing.

"Nobody?" Lavinia abruptly asked. "Stepnowski was a has-been musician trying to rip off a music store. How low can you go? He couldn't have had many friends left."

Garcia looked blandly at her. "Being friendless and ripping off King Kramer are not killing offenses—wouldn't you agree?"

"Uh, right," Lavinia admitted. "Not at all."

"Did you talk with his wife?" I asked. "Did he have a band together?"

"We found his address book at the warehouse. It was full of musicians and club owners, producers, sound engineers and not a few drug dealers, but a lot of the numbers are out of date. So far only one person, a bass player, admits to associating with Stepnowski, but it's been two years since they played together. Nobody seems to think Stepnowski had a band organized at all."

"That's really sad," Lavinia said, almost to herself.

I said, "The De Haro warehouse seemed ideal rehearsal space. Why else would he have it? Was there a bunch of gear there? How about the PA system he bought from Kramer?"

"Nothing. In the room behind the one in which you found Stepnowski, we found an odd selection of parts—a small guitar amp, some cables, a couple of mike stands—but no mikes—a ruined double-neck guitar, a broken reel-to-reel tape machine, a ukulele, two or three folding chairs. . . . Nothing like what you'd expect in a working studio. No grand piano, no amp stack, no gobos, no mixing console, no patch bays or electronics racks— nothing like that."

Lavinia frowned. "What are gobos?"

"Portable sound baffles," Garcia patiently explained. "There are many kinds, but you position them around a player and his gear to isolate or shape his sound. Especially a drummer."

"You know what gobos are?" I asked. "How come?"

"Well," Garcia said, a little color rising to his cheeks, "I used to play a little bit. We had a band at the Police Academy. We called ourselves The Rookies. On *La Bamba*, we rocked."

"On *La Bamba*," Lavinia repeated, "they rocked."

"You don't play anymore?" I asked kindly, ignoring her.

"Not since I graduated, got married, had a couple of kids, made Lieutenant."

"Not since you got a life, in other words." Evidently, Lavinia felt compelled to make this point.

"Was there a kit?" I wondered.

"Not a drum to be seen."

"How about clothes—or shoes?" Lavinia threw me a glance. "Shoes and clothes and stuff."

"No clothes," Garcia said, looking curiously at her. "His shoes were missing when we found him."

"Same here," Lavinia confirmed.

"Curious," I mused. "His landlord told me he had moved there."

"Ah, the landlord," Garcia said.

Lavinia and I said together, "What about—" We exchanged a glance. "Him," I finished. "Yeah," Lavinia added.

"We think Stepnowski was set to blow town. The bass player told us that Stepnowski had called him out of the blue, quite recently, not to set up a gig or rehearsal but to flog a bunch of gear to him. The bass player claims he wasn't interested. A drum kit was mentioned. So were a synthesizer and a Peavey sound system—board, speakers, amps, EQ, cables, and enough microphones to cover a four-piece band, with multiple mikes for drums, a four-track cassette recorder. . . . A truckload of stuff. Which reminds me. Stepnowski owned a cab-over Econoline van. It's painted flat black. We haven't found it yet. Have you seen it?"

Lavinia and I both shook our heads.

"That must be the system Sal sold to him," I guessed.

"Very likely."

"So what's the hustle?"

"It's a standard one," Lavinia put in. "Ivy tells me it's Sal's biggest headache, to which shoplifting's a distant second."

Garcia pricked up his ears. "The inimitable Ivy Pruitt."

"Let's leave him out of this," I suggested.

Garcia looked tentative. "That might be possible."

Lavinia explained. "Guy starts buying stuff from Sal, little stuff at first. Drumsticks, mike stands, a set of speakers, all his trivial supplies. He gets a line of credit going. He buys more stuff—a drum machine, maybe a whole kit. One day he turns up with a bunch of stuff to trade and a little cash for sweetener. He's got a story, too, like his band has landed an extended club gig or a recording contract or a short tour. At any rate, he's got to make some moves equipment-wise. He trades in everything Sal will take off his hands, throws in some cash, gets the rest on credit, and walks out of the store with a top-of-the-line synthesizer, a computerized lighting board, a 24-track mixing console—whatever."

"And until he manages to resell the gear for cash," I realized, "he makes his payments right on time."

"If he's really desperate—strung out, a wanted man, whatever—he'll drive to Reno and pawn the gear immediately to one of the big pawnshops there. That's extreme, however, because a pawnshop won't give top dollar. A private sale is much harder to trace and the money's always better. But either way it's *pffft*," she pushed air with her tongue between her front teeth, "the guy and the gear are gone, and Sal is stuck for the balance."

"Which is when Kramer calls in Ivy Pruitt," Garcia said.

"Yeah, but first Kramer has to figure it out," Lavinia nodded. "If the artist times it right, Ivy won't happen until long after the account comes past due—at least thirty days after a missed payment. Hell, a guy could sell the stuff and keep making the payments until he's safely in Patagonia."

"Stepnowski had a lot of money on him when he died," Garcia said. "He must have moved a lot of stuff. By the way," he smiled, "it goes down very well with me that you two took only what was owed you and left the rest. Very well indeed." When even Lavinia had nothing to say to that, Garcia added, "It speaks volumes about your sincerity."

I said carefully, "Stepnowski was into Sal for seventy-five

131

hundred. The PA system was worth thousands more. If he sold it for half what it was worth in order to move it quickly, he—"

I stopped.

Garcia said, "You were saying?"

"Shut up," Lavinia said simply.

Garcia fingered an audio cassette out of the side pocket of his trench coat and held it up for us to see. "Not to worry. We have the context. We're still adding to it."

I looked at the minicassette, then at Kramer's desk. Amid the clutter at least two microphones weren't even hidden. I looked at Garcia, who smiled. "Fast track. With Kramer's cooperation, of course." He returned the cassette to his pocket. "Assuming Stepnowski sold the missing synthesizer and his own drums too, eight grand sounds like a plausible minimum."

"Eight thousand seven hundred and fifty-four dollars. I counted it myself. There should have been twelve hundred dollar bills, two twenties, one ten, and four singles in Stepnowski's right hip pocket when you found him. Folded once. With all the presidents looking the same direction."

"We subtracted only what was owed to Sal," Lavinia hastened to be redundant. "No more."

"It speaks volumes toward your integrity and your motive," Garcia reiterated, a little bored.

Now that she knew she was speaking for the record, however, Lavinia felt compelled to ham it up. "For our good conscience, too."

"Yes," Garcia said, his tone darkening. "Your good conscience."

I ventured to suggest that he had it all figured out.

"That's possible, Watkins," Garcia said mildly. "You don't see any other angles?"

"What about the anonymous phone call?" I thought a moment. "What about the guy on Anza Street?"

"That creep," Lavinia said.

132

"He told me his name," I said. "Torvald."

Garcia didn't consult his notebook. "His first name is Eritrion. Calls himself Ari. We talked to him."

"And?"

Garcia shrugged.

I said, "After he spilled the new address, he made a special request of me."

"Which was?"

"He wanted me to be sure to say hello to Stepnowski's wife. He said she and her girlfriends were very pretty, and he missed them."

"Ugh," Lavinia said.

Garcia smiled. "He didn't mention that to me. Then again, I had Officer Lavoix running interference."

Lavinia frowned. "What's that supposed to mean?"

Garcia appeared to patronize her. "Perhaps you noticed," he said, "that Officer Lavoix is . . . attractive?"

"So what'd the guy do," Lavinia snapped testily, "drool his way through the interview?"

"Well," Garcia said, "we might have stayed all night. Asked him anything. Fine by him."

Lavinia looked at me. "Are you just going to sit there and listen to this sexist bullshit?"

"Hey," said Garcia, "it's just a fact."

"What are you talking about?" I said, although I knew exactly what she was talking about, and what she was about to start yelling about, but when I looked from Lavinia back to Garcia again, Garcia compounded her anger by offering a man-to-man shrug, with no attempt to hide it from Lavinia. "Bitches," he might just as well have said aloud. "You can't live with them, you can't live without them."

"Angelica," I said quickly, to forestall Lavinia blowing her top. "Wasn't that her name?"

133

Again, Garcia didn't bother to consult his notebook. "Angelica is her name."

Lavinia abruptly frowned and turned her attention away from Garcia, back to me. Because she had been hosing dog off her undercarriage while I taxied to the Anza address, she hadn't overheard my interview with Torvald, and now she had to admit that, while she had no idea what went on during my visit to Anza Street, Mrs. Stepnowski had never come up.

"So?" I asked. "Where is Angelica Stepnowski?"

Garcia nodded grimly. "That may well turn out to be your basic nine-millimeter question."

Thirteen

On the sidewalk in front of Kramer's World of Sound, a gentleman was reading the *New York Times*. He was perched on the edge of a redwood planter built around a jacaranda tree, his feet propped on the front axle of a shopping cart that carried a TV face down in a stratum of empty bottles, with the newspaper spread over its back. He wore several layers of athletic clothing, a mismatched pair of fingerless bicycling gloves, high-ankled combat boots without laces, and cobalt blue wraparound sunglasses.

"Hey, Mister."

"Yes?"

"Let me ask you something?"

"Sure."

He folded his newspaper. "There's a great deal of discussion in here about pedophilia." He gravely tapped the paper with his forefinger. "A great deal of discussion."

"Is that so?"

He raised his sunglasses until they revealed his eyes, which is how Californians demonstrate their sincerity to one another. "Do you think that's what people mean when they refer to America as a youth-oriented nation?"

Further up the sidewalk, Lavinia had backed the Lexus out of the parking lot onto Folsom Street. She touched the horn.

135

"That's the first laugh I've had in two days." I gripped the man's hand and pumped it. "Thank you so much."

The dark glasses fell back into place.

"That guy spare-changing you?" Lavinia asked as I got into the car.

"No. He wanted to share a joke."

"Really? What's a homeless guy find that's funny?"

"Us."

"You and me?"

"All of us."

"No wonder he's on the street. To get by in this life, you have to take it seriously."

"Like you do?"

"Damn straight."

We caught a red light at the Moscone Center. Lavinia said, "Well?"

"Well what?"

"Think Ivy's got any dope left for us?"

"I don't care."

"That makes three of us, but it begs the question."

"You want to drive all the way back to Oakland on the extremely remote chance that Ivy Pruitt saved us some drugs?"

"Aside from the fact that I live there, and, not that I'm strung out, but, yes, I'd like to see if Ivy's got any messages for my monkey. Furthermore, you got a better idea?"

"Yeah," I responded belligerently. "I'm going to find myself a job so I can eat next week and maybe restore my self-respect a week or two later."

I'd never heard Lavinia laugh so hard.

"Curly, what are you talking about? You've got nine hundred dollars in your pocket."

"Son of a bitch." I felt the left hip pocket of my jeans. The wad was still there. "I completely forgot about it." I really had forgotten about it; more cash than I'd had in hand in years, and

136

I'd forgotten about it. "I need a business manager." I whistled and sat back against the seat. "This changes everything." I pointed. "Look at that Moscone Center. It's a conventioneer's dream. Ain't it beautiful?"

"Not so beautiful as the Sony Metreon, up there on the corner."

"Talk about your product placement. As the sun sets on western culture, that piece of shit throws a shadow over the conscience of an entire city."

"You've got a nickel in your jeans," Lavinia said, "so what do you care?" The light turned green. "How about it?"

"If you're going to Oakland, drop me at Third and I'll take a bus. I really do need a job. Not to mention a shower and a shave and about twelve hours' sleep." I touched my hip pocket. "I can use this bread to get the Honda going. The transmission problem, an insurance payment, new brakes—and smog, I've got to smog it this year. Rent and the Honda will take every cent. The nine hundred is a windfall, I'm grateful, I hope it's a long time before I see another dead body, and goodbye."

"Gee," Lavinia drummed a fingernail on the rim of the steering wheel, "why don't you finish college while you're at it?"

"If I don't take advantage of the opportunity, I'll just pay the rent and piss away the rest and wind up riding the bus to gigs again anyway. Public transportation is a pain in the ass at night. Most people don't mess with a six-three bald guy dressed in black leather with an octopus tattooed on his head, but once in a while at a dark and lonely bus stop, I'll glimpse a couple of punks sizing me up, measuring whether they can take me down for the guitar and my wallet. One night I'll have one too many beers in me, and they'll pull it off. It won't be the first time, either, I might add. Then where'll I be? If I live through it, I mean, with all my fingers intact so I can still play, and my brain suffciently underconcussed so I can remember the music."

"Still waiting for the bus, is where it leaves you."

137

"Exactly. And since they'll steal my cell phone, too, I'll have to wait until I get home before I can call my one sympathetic friend and tell her what a loser I am."

"She'll always be there for you, Curly."

I looked at Lavinia. In her profile I could see years of heroin —or could I? She didn't look all that bad. Her features were a little puffy, and there would be another chin one of these days. But her violet eyes were almost delicately, if falsely, lashed, and the hennaed bangs that arched over her prominent forehead cut the midday glare behind her like a cold beer cuts a hangover— no, like a saint's corona. Madonna of the poppy. Nice. Plus, the small padlock key that depended from her earlobe had a strange effect on me. I couldn't figure it out.

Lavinia's key earrings reminded me that I'd once read that Ford's new model that particular year was called the Probe, and that the Probe had been designed for and marketed to single working women. This furrowed my brow and led to all kinds of speculation involving small teams of highly paid FoMoCo psychologists in a secret unmarked building on the outskirts of Detroit. In fact it's probably true. But I came to the conclusion that maybe women as a social group feel that, all their lives, one way or another, literally or figuratively and like it or not, they were constantly being probed by men and a masculine culture and that, in driving something called a Probe, maybe a woman could convince herself that she was in charge for a change, instead of a victim as per usual.

The Probe was the success story of the year.

Go figure.

Lavinia's key earrings provoked similar speculation. A key could be considered the male prerogative, the male arrogation, the symbolic object of the male search or persistence to fit it- self to that symbol of female mystery, the lock. So, in wearing her keys in plain sight, Lavinia was symbolically pre-solving half the battle, arrogating the arrogator, as it were, and teasing him

138

too. The mystery of the lock remained. And the key, after all, remained merely a key, merely a symbol.

"Curly. . . ."

Altogether, she looked well. Pretty, even. Heroin is unpredictable. Given an even temperament, enough money, a clean connection and privacy, a junky can maintain an even keel for decades. A best friend, a lover, her own mother might never figure it out.

"Curly. . . ."

Nobody but a fool would knowingly fall for a junky.

"Yes?"

"You were saying?"

By now we were all the way down to the east end of Folsom Street. We'd already passed the next-to-last on-ramp to the Bay Bridge.

"I was saying, it'll be late. Two, three in the morning, maybe."

"I'll be up."

"Really?" I looked at her.

She smiled. "Really. . . ." There's a stop sign on Folsom at Beale, and Lavinia observed it. At that time it was an odd part of town. A mere three blocks from us, straight east, a broad sliver of the bay showed between two buildings at the foot of Folsom, where it dead ends into the Embarcadero. The Bay Bridge arced across the gap, toward Treasure Island and the East Bay beyond. Though we were more or less in the heart of San Francisco, however, only parking lots and half-built buildings surrounded us. And so there was little traffic in this neighborhood, excepting commute hours. Lavinia pulled through the intersection and parked at the curb, directly in front of the oldest remaining wooden building in that part of town, which, once upon a time, had housed a blacksmith. She left the engine running.

"Okay, Curly, what's it going to be?" She put the transmission in park and looked at me. "Oakland in the Lexus? Or Hayes Valley on the bus?"

139

I looked at her. It was midday. It had been at least thirty-six hours since either of us had slept. The two fat lines of speedball we had nasaled apiece, not four hours earlier, had worn off. I was tired, and Lavinia had to be tired, too. Our most recent attempt at nourishment, forty dollars worth of groceries, languished on Ivy Pruitt's kitchen counter, a thirty minute drive from where we currently found ourselves. Once we got there the priority of rest and food over drugs and derangement would be reversed.

I decided to roll the dice.

I leaned toward Lavinia and put my hand on her shoulder. She let me pull her closer. We kissed.

Her response was tentative. That is to say she didn't exactly kiss me back, but she didn't pull away, either. That is to say, she let me kiss her. The radio was playing *Autumn in New York*. Which meant nothing, you understand. It's just that I remember it.

After a minute we let our lips separate, so we could breathe. Sinus congestion, you should infer. I said, "Let's go to your place." I smoothed her hair. Mousse had made it coarse. Her violet irises floated in jaundiced cream. "To hell with Ivy," I added huskily.

Her eyes were watching her fingertips tarry over my scalp. I might have taken this attention as significant, but experience told me that she was tracing the length of one or another tentacle. If I told you that some girls can't resist this indulgence, would you believe me?

"I'm grateful at least that you didn't suggest we go to your own foetid little pad," she said tenderly.

"I'm trying to show respect. Plus, the nature of relationship is compromise."

"On the other hand, how do you know my place is any less squalid than yours?"

"I'm an optimist."

We toyed with one another. Physically, I mean. Mentally too, I suppose, we toyed with one another. Entoyment. Was that a word? It is now. There was an element of suspense, although the

140

outcome was never really in doubt. It was the element of hope that was suspenseful. A tiny element of hope that made for a tiny element of uncertainty. But there was never all that much doubt. After a minute Lavinia couldn't think up another way to go about it and, in fact, she didn't care. So what if she thought up a cagey or devious or delusional way to go about it? I wouldn't be fooled. So she simply said, "Can't we go to Ivy's first?"

Our toying ran down of its own accord, like a top drained of spin. Another minute passed. Our hands were hardly moving at all. Her eyes slid eastward.

"The bridge is right here," she said.

"Yeah." My eyes watched hers. "It is."

"Easy on," she shrugged, "easy off."

I massaged her shoulder. "My idea precisely."

She laughed without amusement. "We can do that later."

I tapped one of her ear keys. It swung back and forth.

"If you still want to, I mean," she said.

Every time the key swung back toward my finger, I touched it again, just perceptibly adding to its momentum, like pushing a monkey on a swing.

After a full minute of silence I said to the earring, "Do you really think that Angelica Stepnowski murdered her husband?"

Lavinia didn't move. The little key swung back and I tapped it once, twice, three times. Then the musculature beneath the fine down that covered Lavinia's cheek rippled and I heard, "Musicians are hard to live with."

"Tell me about it."

"Drummers are the worst. All those paradiddles, whatever you called them. What a drummer calls etudes everybody else calls noise."

"But they love it."

She nodded. "It's still noise. But a musician has to practice. You'd think a woman who would marry a drummer would realize what she was letting herself in for."

141

Her eyes met mine and we shared our inner depths, two aquariums that wanted cleaning. I looked away. "That's what you would think." What the hell was I expecting?

Lavinia said, "A musician wants to fuck; then he wants to play music. That's his life."

"Oy," I agreed. "It seems so simple."

"But a man is a man," Lavinia continued. "Some men are good, some bad. So a guy's a drummer. So what?"

"That Garcia guy thinks it was a crime of passion," I noted. "That's why the money wasn't taken. The only person in this picture to feel passionate about Stepnowski, theoretically, would be his wife."

"He's entitled to his opinion. And it lets us off the hook."

"'Like loveboids'," I said.

"Who?"

"Stepnowski and his wife."

"Angelica."

"Loveboids."

"How do you know?"

I shook my head. "I don't."

"Then why do you say so?"

"That's what the landlord told me."

"That guy? Yuck."

"I know what you think of him, but that's not the point. Listen to what he said. They were like that." I entwined two fingers and held them up. "A couple of loveboids."

"I wouldn't believe that guy if he told me George W. Bush was a puppet of the oil industry."

"Why not?"

"Because he's a creep, that's why."

"Bush?"

"No. Yes. But I meant the landlord."

"He was right about the De Haro Street address, wasn't he?"

"Yeah, so? Look what we found there."

142

"That is what I'm looking at. Why did he send us there?"

"Because you tricked it out of him."

"What if I wasn't so smart as we think I was?"

"What do you mean?"

"What if that guy knew Stepnowski was already dead?"

"How would he know that?"

"Because he killed him?"

"Oh, yeah, right. For what? Back rent?"

"For the sound system."

Now she was amused. "Stepnowski was a nowhere drummer that had over eight thousand bucks on him when he died. The only way he could have gotten that much dough was to sell that sound system. The King said so, Ivy said so, and I say so. If somebody set him up to rip him off for it, they would have cleaned out his pockets, and they sure as hell wouldn't have missed eight grand in hundred-dollar bills. Am I right? Then Garcia's right, too. It was a crime of passion. Stepnowski's wife killed him cause he had a girlfriend. Or his girlfriend killed him because he had a wife. Or they both hired him killed because they were sick of paradiddles. Now please can we go get high?" She touched my cheek and smiled tenderly. "You can fuck me later, if you want."

My phone rang.

Fourteen

Curly, where are you?"
"You want to know something about musicians? When somebody they know calls them on the phone, they never have to ask who it is. Sound, to a musician, is identity. "I'm languishing in a purgatory of my own design, Ivy. Where are you?"

"In sunny Oakland, Curly, and I'm higher than Dizzy's double D."

"That's peachy."

"You sound like you're still with Lavinia."

"How perceptive."

"Don't you know better than to try to make it with your old buddy Ivy's ex-girlfriends? A chick just can't go from the percussion section to the strings, Curly. Not one with ambition, anyway. And don't go trolling among the reeds for cast-offs either, while you're at it. It's like Bird going from Dizzy to Miles. A real comedown."

"That opinion has been around for a long time, Ivy. Step out your back door and you'll get an argument from a dead man on that one."

Ivy said, "Miles was buying the Bird's dope for him."

This rationale of that opinion has been around for as long as the opinion. But what difference did it make to me? Musically, I couldn't hang with any of those guys. The mere fact that such irrelevant op-ed material had even come up represented an

144

anomaly in Ivy's single-minded pursuit of the poppy. Which only meant, of course, that he was momentarily out of the business of pursuing it.

"Call the tune. I gotta go beg a man for meaningless, underpaid employment."

"Forget that guy. I'm here to make your day meaningful and overpaid. How'd you like to make five hundred bucks in two hours?"

"Oh, no, Ivy," I laughed. "I have frolicked in lucre's golden shower enough for one week. It was just yesterday in fact. Twice in two days might kill me."

"Okay," Ivy said. "Seven-fifty."

I glanced at Lavinia. Since it was Ivy calling, her radar was on. Avarice had dwindled her pupils to pinpricks.

"Two hours of work," said Ivy. "Max."

"Here," was my answer, "talk to Lavinia."

Before the phone was even on her ear, she said sweetly, "Hey, needle-dick. What's up?"

As she listened she frowned. Then her face began to darken. Then she shook her head, no, but her mouth said, "Yeah, but. . . ."

I looked out the window. Commuters had begun to inch along Beale Street, a block south of us. A double line of their cars had begun to back up from the Harrison Street on-ramp, where it merged eastbound onto the Bay Bridge. It must have become three-thirty, somehow. Time flies until your drugs wear off.

I sighed at the windshield. A seagull overflew the roof of the Lexus, over the automobiles creeping across Beale, and drifted down the last two blocks of Folsom to the waterfront; mulling its options, no doubt, whether to further enguano the statue of Harry Bridges or, if it was built yet, the monument to Herb Caen. Then maybe the gull would glide on down the Embarcadero and around the corner to Fisherman's wharf, there to get in on the remains of one of those rounds of sourdough bread, about the

145

size of a five-eighths frustum of a bowling ball and filled with crab chowder, that the tourists buy and eat a third or half of and discard into the gutters along Jefferson Street. From there, well, who knows, maybe there will be one more good year in which to follow the fleet to the herring before both the fish and its fishermen become extinct.

Altogether, despite the vicissitudes of progress, San Francisco is still a great place to be a seagull.

"Hold on." Without bothering to put her hand over the microphone, which is hard to figure out how to do on a cellphone anyway, Lavinia said to me, "Ivy checked in with Sal."

"If they don't talk to each other, nobody else will," I replied.

"Sal got a call from Angelica Stepnowski."

If I had any more dog in me than I already do, my ears would have pointed at her. "And?"

"Remember that synthesizer Sal was wondering about?"

"Yeah. . . ?"

"She's got it. Wherever Stepnowski got all that dough, he didn't get it from selling the synthesizer."

"Good," I said. "As her public defender bobs and weaves through the many shadows along her path to death row, maybe Angelica will learn one or two Brandenburg Concertos."

"That's not the proposition."

I closed my eyes. "Of course it's not. Ivy wouldn't be calling if that were it. Ivy hates Bach. There's no money in Bach for drummers."

The cellphone emitted incoherent squawking.

I said, "Let me guess. If you, because you have the car, drive to wherever Mrs. Stepnowski is and pick up this synthesizer, and maybe pick up Mrs. Stepnowksi too, and bring it all down to the World of Sound, Sal 'The King' Kramer will make it well worth your while." I pointed at the cell phone. "And Ivy's, too. Is that it?"

Lavinia clasped the phone to her breast. "You are so smart."

146

"No," I said.

"What?"

"Letter N, letter O. Go do it yourself."

She shook her head. "No way."

"Why not? It's more bread for you and Ivy."

The phone emitted incoherent squawks. "What?" Lavinia put it to her ear. "Okay, okay. . . . Yeah. . . . No." She began to shake her head. "No," she said sharply. "The guy's a fucking creep, that's why." She raised her voice. "I'm not going out there without Curly!" She handed me the phone.

"If you can get the car off that bitch," Ivy said, "the split will be seven-fifty apiece."

"How about I just do the whole thing myself and leave both of you out of it?" I suggested. "What then?"

"Curly," Ivy said patronizingly, "Sal isn't going to hand this contract over to you, because Sal knows that guitar players got no balls. They're too worried about their hands."

"Listen, Ivy—"

"Let's get one thing straight: This is my gig. You work it for me or you don't work it at all—get it?"

"Fine," I said. "Adios."

Ivy's tone changed without missing a beat. "Come on, blood. It's easy money. The chick's waiting for you to come get the thing. It's practically in your lap. Borrow the car."

I knew what Lavinia would say but I asked anyway.

She mouthed the words: "No fucking way."

I said into the phone, "No fucking way."

Ivy said, "Shit. Come get me, then."

"Go get him, then," I said to her.

Lavinia looked thoughtful. "Is there any dope left?"

I repeated the question into the phone.

"What dope?" came the response.

Lavinia threw a hand toward Beale Street. "The bridge is already backed up."

147

"It'll be an hour before she gets there, plus at least an hour back."

"Forget it," Lavinia said loudly.

After a pause Ivy said, "Okay. We're back to fifteen hundred split three ways."

One month's rent and change for two hours of riding around. I looked at Lavinia. "Five hundred bucks, and I go with you." She frowned. I waited. She nodded. "Deal," I told the phone.

"Good." Ivy cleared his throat. "There's a catch."

"Oh," I said to nobody in particular, "there's a catch."

"What catch?" Lavinia said.

"You gotta front five hundred bucks to the Stepnowski broad."

"*What?*"

"It's half the down payment. She gets the cash to blow town, Sal gets his synth back. That's the deal."

"Naturally, I get reimbursed."

"Naturally."

"With interest?" I sneered.

I could almost hear Ivy shrug. "Fifty bucks."

This took me by surprise. "Really?"

"Really."

"Sal thought this up?"

"I suggested the fifty. The rest is Mrs. Stepnowski's idea. But Sal's game. That keyboard is worth a lot of dough and the guy only made two or three payments on it."

"This is way too complicated."

"No it isn't," Ivy insisted. "Drive over there, give her the five hundred, get the keyboard. As soon as you're out of there, call Sal."

"What for? He'll be closed by then."

"He'll be there. He'll be waiting for the call."

"I smell a rat. What's the big deal?"

Silence.

148

"Spill it, Ivy. I want to know what I'm getting into."

After a long pause he said, "As soon as you call Sal, he'll dime her to the cops."

After a pause I said, "Breathtaking. Simply breathtaking."

"They want her for killing her old man," Ivy explained helpfully. "And for reasons too deep and murky for us to plumb, like maybe Sal rents a sound system to the Policeman's Ball every year with no competitive bids, maybe some cop has Sal's nuts in a vice."

"But Sal wants his action first."

"That's affirmative. If he doesn't get it now, he'll never get it."

"That sounds affirmatively shitty to me, Ivy."

"It's business," Ivy said. "What's this chick to you? You fuck her or something?"

"Not like you and Sal are going to fuck her."

"Well, what'd I tell you about drummers? Not to mention guys who run music stores?"

"Nothing I don't already know."

"Come off it, Curly. I'm being straight with you. That's what's going down. Get a move on."

"What's the catch?" Lavinia said.

"In for a penny, in for a pound," I replied.

"So what else is new?" Lavinia said.

"What's to stop her from blowing me away like she did her old man?"

"Without you the synth is worth nothing to her," Ivy explained sensibly. "It's a straight up trade, and Sal knows where you are. So do I, for that matter. She'll play nice."

"I couldn't feel more secure if I were wearing adult diapers."

"This is getting more like a job every day," Ivy groused.

"Until you break a sweat," I said, "you will know from nothing about jobs."

"Thanks for reminding me. You remember the address?"

149

"4514 Anza Street."

"That's correct. Either she's there or at 4516, right next door. It's the landlord's house."

"What's he got to do with this?"

"Beats me. Maybe it's the only place she could go. Maybe he's soft on her."

"That's true. He is."

Ivy cared about sex like he cared about designer furniture.

"Yeah, well, it's a Kurtzweil FX-11."

"We'll find it."

"At last. I'm beat. It's time for me to go home."

"You're beat," I said wearily. "Where are you?"

"I'm on the pay phone at the Columbarium."

A chilly bank of fog roiled the cypresses in the western reaches of Golden Gate Park, their limbs furled and bucked slowly in the gusts as if they were under water. By the time we got off John F. Kennedy at 36th Avenue, the sky was low and gray enough to have dimmed the Outer Richmond to a preternatural darkness. As we crossed Fulton at the northern boundary of the park, a wind blustering straight off the Pacific T-boned the Lexus hard enough to shake it on its springs. The shattered safety glass on the back shelf spun in the eddies of cold air like so much dust.

Nothing had changed at Anza and 36th, though it seemed like two weeks since we'd been there instead of 24 hours. By what was left of the daylight, 4514 was still the boxy, two-story, non-descript cottage it had been the night before, a single unit with neither garage nor ocean view, typical of the cheaper homes built on the edge of the continent after World War II, painted white then, and gray once since, in 1960 or so. Its foundation plates would prove to be dry-rotted, along with the first foot or two of wood above the ground. The boards of a small laundry porch out back will have rotted through as well. The double-

150

hung windows on the weather side of the building would be painted or nailed shut on the first floor, except for the window in the bathroom, which would be propped open by a long-gone tenant's paperback copy of Philip K. Dick's *Martian Time-Slip*. A fifties-style TV antenna rotted nearly to transparency by the salt air tilted and oscillated in the wind that slipstreamed over the flat roof, its vanes and feelers trained eastward like the limbs and even the trunks of coastal cypresses and Monterey pines, sculpted by two lifetimes of relentless afternoon westerlies. The roof itself would prove to have been layered with rolled asphalt time and again, one- or two- or at most three-year protection against the near-horizontal rains fed by the tropical moisture locals call the Pineapple Express, which travels 5,000 miles, all the way from Hawaii, several times per winter, to test every seam, joint, and crack in California construction mores.

Lavinia parked across the street and reached for the glove compartment. I stayed her hand. "Haven't we had enough gunplay for a first date?"

She looked me frankly in the eye. "A girl likes to play with a full hand."

"I'll keep it full," I said, moving her hand to my lap, "later. For now, let's just get Sal's keyboard and get out of here."

Lavinia gave me a tentative squeeze. "I almost forgot what it's like."

"That's too bad," I said. "As a rule, it's worth remembering."

She nodded; whether thoughtfully or skeptically, I couldn't tell. "Let's go."

Both stories of 4514 were dark, but Lavinia touched the bell button anyway, twice. No answer. We walked next door.

There had probably once been a lawn, but someone had paved it with pink cement. This in turn had faded to a mauvish flavor of gray discoverable in the plumage of road-killed pigeons. A brick path between these two forlorn patches divided around a blasted bird bath of pebbled concrete, streaked with guano, in

151

whose bowl lingered unwanted beach detritus—shards of sand dollars and of mussel and abalone shells, pebbles and bits of coral, the arm of a starfish, collected no doubt by children long since become park bench pensioners—and out of whose center spiraled the corroded remains of two strands of reinforcing wire, about which once perhaps twined a comely cement naiad, her smooth integument reduced by willful teenage baseball bats long since to armature and crumbs.

Hardly had Lavinia fingered the bell button on this building than the door flung wide open to reveal a perspiring Eritrion Torvald. His hair was tousled, his sallow complexion flushed; he wore a pinstriped dress shirt, tail out and like himself much worn, like himself unwashed. His bridge, consisting of four upper front teeth, was askew, and there was fervor in his eyes. His shoelaces were loose, his fly half open, and he had a keyboard synthesizer under one arm.

"Mr. Torvald?" Lavinia said, a tad disconcerted, "I'm Lavinia Hahn, from Kramer's World of Sound? We . . . met once before." A strange look darted through Torvald's eyes, which I interpreted as a gleam of triumph. It faded when Lavinia added, "This is Curly Watkins, my associate."

Torvald peered up at me nearsightedly. "Well if it isn't the brother from Philadelphia." This perspicacity came my way unexpectedly, and he knew it. I bade him a good evening. Torvald didn't acknowledge the greeting. He adjusted his bridge, which decreased his overbite, and let his lower lip dip into a smile. Abruptly the muscles around it went slack and the smile concentrically dissolved, as if sinking into the quicksand of his face.

Lavinia said, "Your tenant, Angelica Stepnowski, is expecting us. Is she here with you, by any chance?"

Torvald took a step back into the room, away from the door, but did not usher us in, saying. "She's been spending a lot of time with me, poor thing. Such a shock. You heard about her husband?"

152

"We heard," Lavinia said. "On behalf of all of us at the World of Sound, I'd like to express our sympathies."

"The poor thing. Such a nice boy, too. I've always liked musicians. Rented to a lot of them over the years. Surfers, too. They always have nice girlfriends. Some of them can cook. You know, like, Hey Daddy, what's cooking!" He showed a completely mechanical smile of mostly false teeth. He hadn't shaved, and the stubble was the dirty white of over-the-hill tile grout.

"Yeah," Lavinia said without enthusiasm. "Cooking."

"I've just come from the apartment." He showed us the keyboard. It was a Kurtzweil, a fancy item with lots of buttons, a built-in hard drive, and fifty-five keys that, I happened to know, have a grand piano feel to them. A power cord and a couple of MIDI cables encircled it. "Angelica asked me to retrieve it for her." He looked at Lavinia uncertainly. "She said you would bring it back to the dealer?"

Lavinia nodded. My rôle as The Muscle was to remain in the background, silent and ominous, but I nodded, too.

"You can trust the King," Lavinia assured him.

Especially, I thought sourly, if you're Angelica Stepnowski.

Torvald bowed in a courtly manner entirely out of keeping with his physical appearance. By a bum out of Beckett, the gesture might have been funny. By Torvald it was almost unnerving. When he straightened up, he cradled the synthesizer like a toothy papoose. "Angelica said Mr. Kramer would refund the down payment so she'll have enough money to cremate poor Stefan. Is that so?"

Lavinia was at a loss to respond to this. How were we to know what kind of story Angelica had cooked up for the old man? "Five hundred dollars," I said, "regardless of the amount of the down payment."

Torvald blinked as if he'd forgotten I was there, and fixed his stare on my boots. From there he let his eyes crawl up me like a

153

pair of snakes re-entwining a caduceus. When they met mine, he said, ". . .Cremate. . ."

Lavinia spoke. "I guess you have all experienced quite a . . . an unpleasant shock, Mr. Torvald."

As if eagerly, he smiled in her direction. "Yes," he said, a little saliva moistening his fricatives. "A shock."

"We have the refund," Lavinia said, "in cash. But I need to hand it over to Mrs. Stepnowski in person, and she needs to sign a receipt."

Torvald was stealing glances at Lavinia, trying not to show too much interest, but in fact appraising her much in the way a needy teenager might, who had a compulsive imagination fueled by unlimited access to Internet pornography. I was beginning to see what Lavinia saw in him.

"I'm sure. . . ." He stopped and cocked his head, as if listening. He looked behind him. He shifted the synthesizer under one arm. He fumbled in the breast pocket of his shirt and came up with a rectangular metal tin. He thumbed open the hinged top and extended it, still looking over his shoulder. "Care for a mint?"

Lavinia, again, seemed at a loss for words. I said, "No thanks." Lavinia nodded faintly, but she said, "No, thank you," too.

Torvald pinched out a mint for himself, capped the tin, and replaced it in his breast pocket. He set the mint on his tongue, already whitened by earlier mints, and closed his mouth. His cheeks hollowed as he began to suck, looking thoughtfully, now, at Lavinia.

"Uh," Lavinia said, "you say that Mrs. Stepnowski is here? With you?"

A fierce draft of chill wind blustered down the street behind us. It ruffled the pair of tapered junipers flanking the front door and peppered the backs of our legs with particles of sand.

"Damn," Lavinia shivered, "I'm dressed for Oakland."

Torvald squeezed his eyes nearly shut and relinquished one

hand from the synthesizer to grasp the stile of the front door, to keep it from crashing against the hinge jamb. For a moment it seemed as if he were about to close the door behind him and leave us shivering on the sidewalk. Whatever he was thinking, he suddenly recollected himself. "Angelica's lying down in the guest bedroom." He stepped aside, gesturing with the keyboard. "Please. Come in."

Despite the cold Lavinia hesitated, clutching the lapels of her blouse to her throat.

Torvald bowed slightly, looked up at her, and smiled politely. "Please. We're all a little out of sorts this evening."

Lavinia wavered, then stepped over the threshold.

I followed.

Torvald closed the door behind us.

I heard the click of the dead bolt. An urban reflex on Torvald's part? But across the room on a low cabinet stood a very large television monitor, perhaps four feet on the diagonal. It was on and it depicted a bare room with beige walls, badly lit. The camera angle shot up from the floor, not ten feet from a woman with cornrowed blonde hair, who was strapped to an unpainted wooden throne in the center of the shot. She wore only shreds of undergarments. Though her head had sunk to her chest, bobbing slightly with her breathing, it was plain to see that a gag encircled her head. Her skin glistened with sweat.

Lavinia saw this too. It was impossible not to see it. In the stunned silence strange sounds came from a pair of big speakers flanking the television. The bound woman was mewing, like a kitten.

I spun to face Torvald, but he was ahead of me. I had time to see his move but no time to react. Already the synthesizer had been in full swing, impelled by all the strength he could lend it at arms' length, arcing like a baseball bat, and it cracked the side of my head with enough force to fell me like a lamppost struck by lightning.

155

"Congratulations!" Torvald spat out the mint and his incisors with the word, upended the keyboard, and tamped my head against the floor, with prejudice. As my senses swam like so much spilled beer through the fibers of the carpet pile, he thanked me for delivering to him the "final woman," and hit me again.

The last thing I heard was Lavinia's scream.

Fifteen

Eritrion "Ari" Torvald was a nice man until his wife, Malita, died.

Then he became nicer.

Until you got to know him.

Weekly, Torvald hosed down the two patches of pink cement that flanked the path from the sidewalk on Anza Street to his own front door. Then he hosed down the brick walkway to the two story bungalow next door. "Income property," he called his bungalow. "Aprons," he called his pink patches. "Washing my aprons," he would say, "rinsing my assets," and he would touch an eyebrow, as he surveyed his property, preening before his real estate as if it were a reflective window. Inquiries about the ruined birdbath met with a sad, "Malita loved it so."

The rental unit, social security, and an out-of-court disability settlement reached nearly four years after a ballpoint pen fell twelve stories onto his head as he was walking past a building full of non-profit art organizations on New Montgomery Street —these covered all his needs, as well as those of his lawyers, and then some. Torvald was one of those people who makes both money and trouble by apparently doing nothing. Nothing, that is, if you don't count Torvald detailing his Mercedes with a toothbrush every Sunday morning. Nothing, that is, if you don't count Torvald busing downtown to the Department of Parking and Traffic with a fold-up aluminum walker every business day for two months until the harried bureaucrat he had zeroed in on, a woman—whose husband disappeared after refinancing their house, cleaning out the bank account, and cashing in their life insurance policy, sticking her with their Down's Syndrome two-year-old and a mortgage payment equal to thirteen-sixteenths of her annual salary—who, desperate to rid herself of Torvald, issued him a blue disabled parking placard to dangle off the stalk of the rear-view mirror of his Mercedes, enabling Torvald to violate municipal parking statutes throughout the state of California with impunity.

Nothing, unless you count his secretly, by night, renovating the basement under his house. Minor excavation was required. San Francisco is a sand dune. Torvald transported some of the excavated sand to the parking lot below the Palace of the Legion of Honor and dumped it off the cliff there, scooping out four five-gallon buckets, the most he could get into the trunk of the Mercedes, a single one-pound coffee can's worth at a time, like a man feeding pigeons. He also dumped sand at Chrissy Field while it was being restored, and at the Giants' new baseball park while it was under construction. But it was the mammoth Catellus Project, nearly four hundred acres in the heart of the city, that received the majority of the sand. Nobody noticed the difference. Everybody thought Torvald was busy doing nothing.

Nothing, that is, unless you count the meticulous, incremental, glacial in pace, glacial in ineluctability, conversion of his basement taxidermy lab into two sound-proof rooms, which, as he almost let slip to the one neighbor who asked what was going on, just before that neighbor moved without leaving a forwarding address, Torvald intended to be a recording studio. Hence all the sound-proofing: fiberglass acoustic bats between staggered studs behind triple-sandwich walls—one layer each of plywood, fiberboard, and sheetrock glued and held in place with screws until the glue dried; then the screws were backed out and their holes caulked and sanded smooth; the entire wall covered with a special acoustic fabric—with a one-inch air gap between the sandwich walls and the surrounding eight-inch concrete retaining walls; 'floating' concrete floor; a ceiling built much like the walls, except it was suspended from the ground floor by special isolators, each carefully calibrated as to the amount of load it would be expected to carry.

Quite a project to have been carried out almost entirely in secret, entirely at night or on weekends, by a man who, to all outward appearances, did absolutely nothing the whole time.

Absolutely nothing, that is, unless you count the compulsive repetition of viewing and reviewing a meticulously curated collection of videos, some two thousand and forty hours of them, the temporal equivalent of one year's attendance at a regular job, cataloging them by date, length and number of cassettes constituting each volume, and alphabetically, too. Each volume had a name associated with it, although two of them had the same name, purely a coincidence of course, for the name, Sheila, was common enough, which Torvald had resolved by the simple expedient of labeling the respective productions "Sheila I" and "Sheila II". Torvald also indexed the collection as to male or female, race and age, stages and degrees, types and frequency of practices, as well as to his estimation of overall artistic value, both intrinsic and relative; as indicated by three to five stars.

Inferior material, of zero to two stars, he deleted.

Doing nothing, that is, unless you consider Torvald's ultimate ambition: editing the highlights of his collection into the greatest snuff movie the world would ever see, the raw material to be discovered in a pseudonymous safe deposit box long after his demise, coevally long after a Trojan Horse, which he'd downloaded off a hacker site, had propagated his feature-length triumph world-wide in its entirety, all hundred and twenty-one compressed minutes of it, by capitalizing on a virtually unknown but chronic weakness specific to Microsoft Corporation's monomaniacal conflation of their own Internet browser with their own operating system.

These feats Eritrion "Ari" Torvald had nearly accomplished, and he had done so entirely in the guise of a man who never accomplished anything at all, of a man who wasted days wandering the aisles of hardware stores and plumbing supply warehouses and lumber yards and electrical wholesalers, of a man who had nothing to do.

If Torvald had delusions of grandeur relative to the success of his film, he had next to none when it came to its production. Lately he had transferred hundreds of hours of his early career from beta and VHS to digital media and, in this regard, part of the secret ultimately revealed to his disappeared neighbor was true. There *was* a recording studio under his house, whose sole double-paned window looked onto a soundproof room with a wooden chair against one wall and two video cameras on tripods with a third stedi-cam, and a floor that subtly but surely and very accurately sloped concentrically down to a four-inch drain in its center.

The drain, being far below grade, had necessitated a sump pump, which, activated by a switch on a float in a sunken barrel, rapidly evacuated whatever flowed down the drain whenever the contents of the barrel reached a certain level. Sometimes this barrel took a long time to fill up. Other times, like when Torvald hosed out the studio, or when he heavily employed the mess-hall-grade garbage disposal to which removal of the plate covering the floor drain gave access—at such times the barrel filled again and again, and the pump kicked in and out with great frequency.

Torvald had a lot of trouble with this pump. After much research he'd purchased a model that could handle anything—the volume of a hundred-year storm or a glutinous bolus of machine-masticated gristle—but after the pump was buried deep below one of the two pink patches in front of his house (both of

160

which he'd torn up and repoured to ensure an accurate color match), when it lifted effluent up to the level of the sewer line under Anza Street, a construction project Torvald could hardly have conducted in secret, but managed to accomplish on four consecutive weekends while Mr. Tweedy, the nosy neighbor, was fly-fishing with his grandchildren in New Zealand, and while the Department of Building Inspection was locked up like it is on any weekend, fifty-two weekends a year, Torvald discovered that, despite its flawless performance, the pump made too much noise. Specifically, the float-activated relay that triggered the pump voltage emitted a click, inexplicably audible from anywhere along the sidewalk in front of Torvald's house.

Having allowed a decent interval for grief—after Torvald began telling the two or three people who asked why they hadn't seen his wife lately that Malita had vanished while on a trip to Mexico; presumably, if unobserved, having fallen off the stern of the night car-ferry between Mazatlán and La Paz while Torvald was in the foredeck bar trading shots of mescal with a one-armed bullfighter—Mr. Tweedy began to nag him about the strange clicking and humming noises coming from beneath the patch of pink concrete abutting their common property line.

Torvald explained to Tweedy about how PG&E appeared and dug up the street in front of their houses while Tweedy was on that fly-fishing trip to new Zealand two years ago with his grandchildren, though he had no idea what for and hadn't given it much thought at the time. But he, Torvald, had also noticed the funny noises and having assumed that it had something to do with the uninterrupted flow of electricity and/or gas to and/or from the Outer Richmond, found himself having gotten so used to the noise he didn't even notice it anymore, which, as Torvald wound up his yarn watching Mr. Tweedy with a certain look in his eye, a look he'd formerly been accustomed to focusing on his wife the last few months of her life, would be, he broadly hinted, Mr. Tweedy's first best course.

In fact it was true that Anza Street had been repaved while Tweedy was gone, so Torvald thought his exegesis had a good chance of skirting Tweedy's radar. But Tweedy was another of these guys you see around the Outer Richmond who apparently have nothing to do all day but detail their car with a toothbrush and groom the hedges framing the perimeter of their parcel with cuticle scissors and wash the street-facing windows weekly. It took Tweedy almost three months to do it, but one day Torvald hearing muted conversation parted the curtain of his parlor window to find a little blue PG&E truck parked in front of Tweedy's house and Tweedy standing on the property line with a PG&E engineer who held an unfolded blueprint, both men staring down at the patch of pink. Torvald let the curtain fall back into place and stood there, as if in repose, until he heard the engineer's pickup truck drive away.

Torvald knew that PG&E had no jurisdiction over whatever it was that might be under his front yard. But the very fact that Tweedy had managed to pester the vast PG&E bureaucracy until it relented to the extent of actually disembarking a human representative to appraise a situation that, in any case, must have seemed vague to them in the first place and beyond their purview in the last, demonstrated at a stroke to Torvald that Tweedy was possessed of a tenacity which occluded even that which had fomented the coup of Torvald's handicap parking placard. It was at that exact moment, not one second before and certainly not one after, that Tweedy transmogrified into a walking dead man.

The slow-motion denouement of that transmogrification is, and remains, recorded as Torvald's third video, a volume entitled "Calvin." "Calvin" was pretty good, too; although, as went Torvald's career, no production ever eclipsed the savagery of "Malita."

Not quite three volumes later, when Tweedy's grown grandson and the young man's wife made the sad trip all the way from New Zealand to see Tweedy declared legally dead and his estate probated, Torvald expressed sympathy without being too nosy, and made them a fair offer on the house, which, if they accepted, would save them the trouble of cleaning it up and selecting a real estate agent, putting it on the market and sorting through the offers, accepting one and waiting through escrow, closing, and so forth. They refused. Torvald began to look at them in a funny way. But after a moment's consideration he relented. One thing about Torvald, he was not a stupid man. Far from it. It was probably too obvious a setup, he reflected, for him to buy the house and rent it out to young girls, one at a time, who would then disappear, one at a time, and whom, after due diligence, he would then replace one at a time. Cool idea, bad execution. What Torvald wanted was good execution. Torvald reasonably presumed that eventually some cop or relative would come along and figure things out. As a force of nature, that was the job of inevitability. Even though Ted Kaczynski, the Unabomber, had disproved the theory that inevitability doesn't need any help, by the same token Torvald was in no hurry for the inevitable to happen to himself. But it was precisely this fundamental awareness, that it was inevitable that he get caught, that ena- bled Torvald to engage his ambition with such virtuosity as he brought to bear. Because he knew that in the fullness of things he would be caught; for, in fact, if he was successful, his work would come into the light of the world by design. He would have to be caught. This rationalization of the fear of inevitability, itself a triumph of logic the test of which his nerves would welcome, a fear which moreover he came to consider a mere titillation, enabled Torvald to focus the full amperage of his intelligence on his aesthetic achievement. As a side effect, his quiver acquired the dichotomous pincers of bold finesse, efficient recklessness, patience that could spring into celerity, and brazen stealth. It was like having a tool box full of complicitous scorpions—efficient, servile, and alacritous.

A week later the grandson and the wife came back with a real estate agent and accepted his offer. He walked through the two-story cottage with them. It was the first time he'd ever been in Tweedy's home, and everything remained as Tweedy had left it. Torvald was amused to find a photo of Tweedy's long deceased wife in a cheap frame on the mantel in the living room. Torvald had a similar photo of his own deceased wife, on his own mantel, to keep up appearances. But Tweedy's mantelpiece also displayed pictures of the grandson and the boy's father, who had married Tweedy's daughter thirty years before. There was a photo from that wedding, and another of the grandson at his own wedding, with Tweedy in both. Torvald heard that day, for the first time, of the deaths, years before, of Tweedy's daughter and her husband in a plane crash, which occurred in the course of the pursuit of their Christian mission in Burma.

Two years before, the cops investigating Tweedy's disappearance had turned off the TV. They'd found the bed made up, as it still was, with an old crocheted coverlet folded over the footboard. The place had been neat and clean, then, but now it smelled very much of disuse, of abandon, of mice and mildew, of dust. A saucepan on the back of the stove contained what looked like a petrified chicken soup. It had been there for so long it had no odor at all.

Traces of fingerprint dust were still to be found here and there, on the mantel, on a corner of the kitchen table, on the casing of the front door, on the corner of a window that faced the street, on the toilet handle, on the handrail of the staircase. Torvald was very interested in these details, too, though he didn't say as much.

The deal closed without a hitch. The grandson and his wife took all the photos and Tweedy's fishing gear and the crocheted coverlet and returned to New Zealand forever.

After escrow closed and he took possession of the keys, Torvald hired a young and enthusiastic illegal immigrant to clean the place. He hired him off the corner of Cesar Chavez and Valencia and, fresh from Michoacán, the kid was proud to be seen by his street-corner acquaintances in the front seat of a well-kept Mercedes—from the rear-view mirror of which Torvald had taken the precaution of temporarily removing the blue handicap placard. Slim and handsome, soft-spoken and hard-working, quick to laugh, enthusiastic and gentle, the boy finished the job in one long day, right down to washing the windows.

As the sun set beyond the bank of fog which almost always lurks off the northern coast of California, Torvald invited the kid to stay for beer and quesadillas.

By sundown two days later, "Xavier" had became Volume V.

Sixteen

Torvald took his time in renting his new unit. It took him a while to figure out how to do it efficiently. Being a landlord wasn't really in his line. He'd noticed it seemed to be in many other people's lines, however. But, whereas most of these people did it so they wouldn't have to work, Torvald had a separate agenda.

And it wasn't that Torvald minded working. He just didn't want anybody to know he was working. Not until later. Not until it was time for them to know.

During the late nineties, the dotcom years—which turned San Francisco upside down as thoroughly as beatniks did merely to North Beach in the fifties, or as hippies did merely to the Haight Ashbury in the sixties, or as gay liberation did to merely the Castro, Polk Gulch and Folsom Street in the seventies, or as cocaine did to merely the entire city in the eighties—Torvald did as most other landlords did. He held a single open house for one hour at noon on a Saturday, then sifted through the resulting sixty-odd tenant applications for someone fitting his specifications. In the glory days of the landlord's market, it was that simple. The first specification? The prospective tenant's ability to pay two or three times what the apartment was worth. As for other specifications. . . .

166

Soon enough, Torvald had a comely twenty-something in the unit. Oddly, he thought at first, she was never home. Tranquility reigned, albeit somewhat lonesomely on Torvald's part, but soon he figured it out. Since her rent was equivalent to two-thirds of her salary, his young tenant had to work all the time to come up with it. But that was only half the story. Unceasing work was in the nature of her 'employment sector'—the dotcom world. Unstinting labor was part of its 'culture.' That is to say, if working seventy hours a week for two years on the outside but not entirely remote chance that it could make you a millionaire can be called 'culture,' then that's what it was.

This default privacy was such a gold mine for Torvald that he forestalled fishing off the company pier, as it were, and did his fishing elsewhere, steering his operation entirely into off-shore, as it were, opportunism.

Finally, however, he succumbed to the temptation. It began when Kerry gave him a month's notice, as specified in the lease. She had located another apartment for the same price in the Western Addition. The new apartment was smaller than Torvald's unit, but to Kerry it represented a quick bike ride to work. Parking near her job had become out of the question, and the ride from Anza and 36th to Folsom and Eighth, whether by bus or bike, was just too long. Another nice thing about it was that Kerry could continue to live alone while seeking her fortune. Privacy is worth a lot, as she remarked to Torvald. Torvald couldn't have agreed more.

The end of the month was a Wednesday, but Torvald cut her the requested slack and let her wait until the following Sunday to move out so she wouldn't have to interrupt her six-day work week. He smiled and told her not to worry, he would pro-rate the four days according to the thirty-one in that particular month and subtract the amount from her cleaning deposit. See, he said with a smile, how easy I am to get along with? She thanked him, her tone a touch sarcastic.

167

It takes years of experience and a focused mind to achieve control of one's tone, Torvald said to himself as he looked at Kerry thoughtfully; but youth has other advantages.

Kerry didn't own much. Torvald watched her move all her possessions with her brand-new Jetta in five trips by herself.

When the car was loaded for the last time, she came to his door to return the keys. He suggested she give him her new address so he could mail her the cleaning deposit, less the prorated rent, as well as forward any first-class mail that slipped through the post office's notoriously porous forwarding mechanism.

She'd already had cards printed. She handed him one, said goodbye, and turned to walk away.

Before Torvald quite realized what he was saying, he verbalized an impulse. If she wanted to come in for a moment, he would write her a check. He remembered how it was, he added, to be young and moving house by yourself; it was expensive and it was hard work. Neither the computation of the simple interest —which by law he owed her on the deposit, which pleasantly surprised her—nor the subtraction of the four pro-rated days, was higher mathematics. He was sure the balance, almost a month's rent, would help.

She was sure it would help, too.

She stepped inside.

Thus initiated production on Volume IX.

"Kerry."

When two police officers came by a week later to inquire after the missing girl, he showed them a check made out to her and a stamped envelope with her new address written on it. He'd been about to lick the envelope and walk it to the corner mailbox when the doorbell rang. When he first moved from Indiana to San Francisco to be a hippy in the sixties, as he told the two officers, you could leave mail at your door for the postman. No longer. You had to make sure it was in a mailbox. Sir, one of the officers told him, the bad guys got keys to all those drop boxes.

168

Torvald begged the officer's pardon and asked for details. They open one up, the officer patiently explained; they grab a bunch of mail and go through it, looking for checks. Copy machines and scanners and software they got these days, bingo, they turn out stacks of your own personal checks. Exact duplicates. Signature and everything. They change the series numbers to avoid a conflict with the genuine article. They make them out like paychecks for day labor or house cleaning, stuff like that, and hand them off with a fake I.D. to professional accomplices who cash them all over town. Meanwhile the check they copied is carefully resealed in its envelope and sent on its way. Your bill or whatever gets paid so you're none the wiser until the bank starts bouncing your real checks because the fake ones have cleaned out your account. By that time—the officer snapped his fingers—the thieves and your money are long gone.

Well I'll be darned, Torvald said. He looked at Kerry's check, then back at the officer. That's awful.

The officer told Torvald that to be safe he should hand his mail over the counter to a live clerk at the post office. Then your checks have a chance to get where they're going without a nasty detour.

Torvald thanked the officer and said he certainly would do that. He hesitated. And what about this check?

The officer slowly shook his head. Mail it anyway, his partner suggested. It will be forwarded to the parents.

Her dotcom employer had called the police the morning of the second day she didn't show up for work or answer her cellphone. Her Jetta was parked on Broderick around the corner from her new building, an eight-unit student affair in the flatlands between the panhandle and Lone Mountain College. The Jetta was a convertible. Its top had been slit and some of Kerry's personal possessions—odd CDs, lingerie, sneakers, computer manuals and diskettes—were strewn up and down the block. Her previous address—Torvald's rental unit—had turned up when they ran a check of the car's license plate.

Her keys were found under the car; an oversight, no doubt, as anything else of value had presumably been stolen. A mountain bike and boxes containing the rest of her stuff were in her new apartment. But there was no stereo, for example. So the police were thinking along the lines of an opportunistic snatch. No body had been found, so her parents clung to the hope that the girl was still alive. Her dotcom had printed flyers and organized a search of the neighborhood and put up a website. On her chances for survival, the two officers offered no opinion. They had a look around the empty bungalow, thanked Torvald, and went away.

Should he mail the check?

Torvald realized that, if he continued to poach his own tenants —in fact, if he did it so much as one more time—the inevitable would happen sooner than later. This realization gave Torvald his first glimpse of the potential for control, even if it could only ever be partial control, over the inevitability factor.

Torvald mailed the check.

Sometimes, you have to invest in the future.

He came to think of his poaching a tenant and getting away with it as analogous to a man's managing to masturbate on a crowded subway car without being noticed. Everybody has masturbated on the subway—haven't they? No? People are so uptight! Plus they lie. The more Torvald elaborated this analogy, the more he liked it. One intriguing aspect was its built-in denial. You deny yourself the pleasure, and you deny yourself the pleasure, and you deny yourself the pleasure until, finally, you give in to it. Sensory fulfillment, spiced by sociopathy, trumps personal embarrassment and moral outrage. This denial and its prolongation can be many things but above all it's delicious. Inevitability figures into it, too. Sooner or later, if you masturbate in crowded subway cars, somebody's going to notice. If not, successful incidents accrue, and it's like hitting home runs. At a certain point you're batting for the record. But where baseball ends, the very personal nature of such crimes as interested Torvald begins. Right away, with such crimes, starting with the very first time, it's always a personal record. With each repetition, a new high is achieved. As the victories pile up. . . . It's harder to top and it's harder to stop.

As these two factors crescendo, the inevitability of getting caught envelops the mindscape like a storm, like. . . .

It's like watching a mountain in your windshield. At first it's so distant, as you drive toward it, as to be practically an abstraction. As you approach, however, the mountain grows larger. Details resolve. At some point you arrive at the mountain. You drive on. You ascend its flank. Now the mountain is everywhere. You're intimate with the mountain, so intimate that you can't really see it any more. Now, as you drive on, you become part of the mountain. . . .

As the rate of commission increases, it traces an asymptote to oblivion. The sensation is nothing short of sublime.

There are dirty aspects, too, pollutions of the purity. An ember of guilt. The desire for punishment. The need to be caught. The satiation of psychopathology has its drawbacks, but only if you fall short of apotheosis.

That's the risk, and that's the reward.

Torvald woke up an iBook that waited on a rosewood secretary adjacent the front door. It was not very often of late that a fit of lucidity came over him so thoroughly. He opened a password protected file, to which he added his thoughts from time to time, and began to make a few notes. He helped himself to a mint. He collected his thoughts as he sucked. He made more notes.

The image of the mountain intrigued him. Other similes had struck him, the baseball one for example. But hitting home runs hardly encompassed the scope of his endeavor: not to mention, hitting home runs had never been considered sociopathic—had it? In any case, it was a limited analogy.

But a mountain gave the scope to match a man's ambition. He fiddled with the keys, wrote a few lines. After a minute or two his typing trickled to desultory pecking, then stopped. Not unlike a slashed body running out of blood, he thought, and glanced at the two bodies on the living room floor. Had he ever enjoyed such a surfeit of victims? When the profilers speak of crescendo, they aren't kidding! In his mind's eye he surveyed the shelves of media lining the back of the control room, directly beneath him, one story down. He took another mint. He turned to take a look at the big monitor.

Angelica seemed to be asleep. So nice for her, that she can sleep in that throne of rough timber, which he'd purchased mail order from a catalogue of S&M accessories, using his former tenant Kerry's name and the address of his rental unit. She looked peaceful. Just as well. He turned back to his computer screen. He hadn't used a methamphetamine injection, yet. One shot for her, one shot for him. Separate needles, of course. Fair's fair, but a man has to be careful. She was frail, that one. Though hardly more than a child, she had been debilitated by years of booze and drugs, so far as he could tell. A pretty thing nonetheless. It's just amazing how youth insulates a body against self-abuse—or any kind of abuse. . . .

Three of them. Torvald rubbed his eyes. He'd gone over the top and let himself in for a lot of work. He'd let himself in for a lot of risk, too. All these young people were connected, somehow. Although, he glanced toward the body lying closer to the front door, some of them weren't so young.

He looked at the computer screen. Something about mountains and sublimity and oblivion and driving. . . .

Abruptly he closed the file. He sat for a few minutes, perfectly still. The battery conservation utility blanked the computer screen. The house was silent but, outside, the fog wind buffeted it. The twin junipers brushed against the house, actively defining its front door. The western of the two, closer to the sea, had sanded a six-inch swath of paint off the door casing, a vertical redwood 1x6 directly behind it. Years of unceasing effort. The neighborhood association had circulated a flyer indicating without naming names certain properties deemed to be suffering from 'substandard maintenance.' Torvald soundlessly chuffed the humorless laugh of the overtaxed homeowner, who knows in his heart who it was who, with his own hands, had wrested into reality a state-of-the-art secret beneath his house and beneath the very noses of his inquisitive neighbors. . . .

Substandard maintenance, indeed!

He could hear the labored breathing of the one closer to the doorway. Probably a crushed maxillary sinus. The other one, the girl, he'd stow below. Nice nautical sound to that. Stow her below, Bos'n. If only he had a Bos'n. Clap her in irons. Aye, Sir. Prepare the enema. Without delay, Skipper. Torvald giggled. Bread and water until I say gesundheit. Jolly good, Sir. And don't forget. Sir? The Bos'n pauses at the companionway, the girl dangling by her hair from his fist like a shotgunned duck. The annual novena for Malita. Not forgotten, Sir. Monsignor has been reminded? In writing, Sir, accompanied by a check. Away with you then. Very good, Sir.

One of the curious aspects of Torvald's madness was its hermeticism. Reality seeped in once in a while, like a shaft of late afternoon sunlight over the valence of a curtain. Take the two cops who had visited to inquire after Kerry, for example, three years before. Torvald's imaginative world had graciously accommodated them, yielding to their foray like a body of water yields to the bow of a ship, permitting, even abetting the ship's passage, marking it with a pretty wake, and, sooner than later, smoothing until not a trace of the incursion remains. Not a mark of the trowel, as it were. If flights of fancy occurred once in a while, well, perhaps they were . . . inevitable. His current fas-

173

cination with metaphor, for example. For a long time his lucidity had given him to think that a craving for power was at the root of his dominance over his victims. Their loudest scream and feeblest whimper nurtured this belief, both reflected and reinforced it. Certainly power, and gratification, and dominance, and sadism, not to mention blood lust, and, yes, the puerile craving to be the center of attention, all of these figured into the construction of the railroad that had conveyed Torvald from a quiet middle-class homeowner, mandatorily retired after seventeen years of supervising the flatness of floppy disks manufactured by a small plant in South San Francisco, all the way to what he had become today, which was . . . what? A purveyor of metaphor, who carried a certain meaning in his blood, much as others carry a virus? A connoisseur of simile, much like others cultivate the taste of Cuban cigars? An *eminence* of psycho-historic proportions? It all seemed too obvious, in retrospect. So . . . inevitable. Much as, a mere eighteen months after his retirement, Malita just had to go.

A killer with sand, as in mettle. His mind lingered over the volumes of cassettes, CDs, CD-ROMs and DVDs aligned along the walls of the subterranean control room. The net result would serve individual psyches in the way that war serves nations: it would make one or two and break the rest.

Not a killer, but one of the killers. Not an indefinite article, but the genuine article.

Torvald sighed. Given the times, seventeen people didn't seem like so many. The ways in which they expired, however, were systematic yet multifarious. These distinctions aggregated to his credit. And to his record of them.

The iBook had fallen asleep. Torvald frowned and keyed it awake. Bored, bitch? Typing key combinations as automatically as a doting mother dialing her son's telephone number, he started a slide show program which enabled him to select and organize, size and crop and rotate and view any number of

174

images he wanted. He could control gray scales, he could control gamma saturation, but most facilely he could manage the rate of presentation with a preset toggle or merely by touching the space bar, to pause or unpause an image or clip, to page or dawdle through the sequence of scenes, as he liked. Torvald had worked a long time at this particular edit. At fifteen seconds per exposure there were nearly two hours of viewing comprised of some four hundred and eighty images. As far as Torvald was concerned, this slide show documented the reinvention of his life. At first, when the number of images was limited, he'd intercut them with highlights from the first and only movie he'd shot on film, the black and white 16 millimeter documentary *Zero Tolerance: On Ensuring the Planar Regularity of Digital Storage Media*. But the result had proved too . . . successful. It was too affecting. Its platinum banality detracted from Torvald's real accomplishment. It was pornography with a plot, and its failure was precisely that.

He had cut the final product drastically. Every scene involving floppy disks was excised. A lot of work to undo. But now, after man-years of work, he was proud of the result. His achievement would stand for a long time, perhaps forever, as an aesthetically meticulous archive of his endowment to mankind, which, as he earnestly hoped, might stand as a clairvoyant metaphor for mankind's endowment to itself.

Many are the monsters of history. Torvald had made a study of them. He'd turned three walls of his basement control room into a floor-to-ceiling library, and the subjects of this library were the monsters and the monstrous acts of history, including himself and his own.

Among his favorites Torvald numbered Gilles de Rais. Gilles de Rais started out in history, and remains there, as one of Saint Jean d'Arc's staunchest supporters. But at some point he quit the young visionary and retired to his castle. There, over the next several years, he conducted human sacrifices, practiced cannibalism, and perpetrated heinous outrages upon his victims, torturing them to unconsciousness and reviving them only to torture them to death. Almost all of Gilles' victims were children. By the time a cardinal showed up at the head of an army to arrest him, it was said that the countryside surrounding Gilles de Rais' castle was bereft of children for fifty miles in any direction.

A full confession was tortured out of Gilles de Rais, and it makes for interesting reading. Torvald possessed a facsimile of the original as well as all translations into English he'd been able to find. He'd even commissioned his own translation. He had not permitted this particular interaction with a scholar of medieval French to become a reckless exposure, however; rather, that personage, long since terrorized by the horrors of the *Confessions*, had every potential to evolve into one of Torvald's most eccentric productions: Volume XII, "Freddy."

But the translation was so good, Torvald let Freddy live.

In the end, however, no matter what Gilles de Rais had achieved, it *wasn't on video*. There were *words* but there was no *footage*. Words have their place, but this is the twenty-first century. The word is kaput. Frames per second reign.

The reflected images cascaded over the features of Torvald's face. Occasionally he resisted the impulse to delete one. The edit had been locked and compressed. He had learned from experience that if he wanted to meddle with this carousel of images, he needed to save it under another name, leave the original intact, and tweak the copy. So meticulously had his work built up over the years that a whimsical cut or spontaneous rearrangement of its chronology would subsequently seem awkward. The concentration necessary to perform an edit at this advanced stage was enormous; at times he thought it might now be beyond his capacity to improve the current version. His energy was waning. He knew it. His bloodlust, while not sated, was losing its focus. This, too, he sensed as symptomatic of the yin and yang of inevitability.

Torvald keyed the space bar to accelerate the progression of images. When Kerry appeared he slowed the procession. What a beauty. . . . How she squealed and squirmed and wept. . . . So full of life. . . . So much energy. . . . She almost took his eye out with that kick. . . . And paid for it here. Click. Here. Click. And here. Click, click, click. . . .

Even so, Torvald's mind wandered. It was almost as if energy had its own life, as if its human form were merely borrowed. That Stepnowski, for example. Short work. A mere pistol—his own pistol. Yet the man shirked off his mortal coil—or vice versa —as if sick of it and good riddance, as if Torvald had shorn him, as it were, of his suffering rather than the gift of life. There'd been no time to convince him otherwise. In fact, there had been no time for the loppers. Then the truth would out. He'd found garden tools as effective as they are innocuous. The loppers, the hedge shears, the limb saw. Get it? Physically as well as psychologically, garden tools are so . . . hyperbolic. Grossly banal. But he'd had no time for the heinous hirsute beer belly on such a little man. Grotesque. What had his pulchritudinous wife seen in that swine of a husband? Torvald glanced over his shoulder. Still passed out. Boy, could he wake her up. Volume XIX, on the floor behind him, would watch Volume XVIII in production. There is no garden tool so tortuous as the imagination; of that, he had made a certainty. But even that, he'd been through. Been even there, done even that. Torvald suppressed the intimation of panic brought on by any hint of inadequacy. He glanced toward the body near the door. There had been a time, not so distant, when Torvald might have gotten aroused for a guy like that. Put him through his paces just to keep in shape. But six foot and two or three inches? With a shaved head? And the octopus?

Later.

Way later.

Torvald turned back to the computer screen. Idly, he took a mint. He looked at the slides without really seeing them. He turned around again.

177

It might make a good picture, he thought, as the blade goes in.

He tapped a thoughtful fingernail on the lid of his mint tin.

Multi-camera coverage, slow motion, sound of course.

He adjusted the crotch of his trousers.

Cameras on the floor, on the windowsill, on top of the TV. Every angle. Close. Zoom. Long.

He sucked on the mint. He repositioned his bridge with the tip of his tongue.

One foot on the head. The axe comes in . . . axially. Ha! Actually. . . . Axial Actualization: get it? This *ennui* comes in waves. Forgot the guy's name. Detail. The brother from Philadelphia. What did he take me for? I might have known he'd come back with her. Delicious, though. Worth the trouble. Let him remain anonymous. He'll be the interlude, an interregnum, between XVIII and XIX, the exception that proves the rule, with a music box playing Brahms' *Lullaby*. That's the stuff. Wait: *Cranial Croquet*. That waxes it; I'm a genius. Not losing the old touch. Not yet anyway. Not just yet. Far from it, one might say. My god, what a relief.

His spirit renewed, slaked at the well of creativity, he turned to watch the computer screen. Colors washed over his face. His jaw trembled. The images meant nothing and everything to him. His lower lip quivered. A tear coursed over his cheek.

Goddamn, goddamn, goddamn, Torvald thought, I might get it up after all. . . .

Seventeen

A few hours before daylight, almost any night, the Avenues of San Francisco are quiet. Sound is discrete. But fog manipulates sound deceptively.

That scratching is the junipers, flanking the front door.

That tapping is a computer keyboard. Unmistakable. In another part of the world, however, it might pass for the sound of quail pecking at seeds on the roof.

A steady sibilance, barely perceptible over the sound of the junipers abrading the facade of the house, might well have been a dry-cleaning plant, far down the block. But no; rather, it was the hiss of a forced-air respirator, breathing for someone who couldn't breathe on his own.

The bass moan would be the "moaner," a loud *basso profundo* foghorn, on the south tower of the Golden Gate Bridge.

The drool on the rug below a lower corner of the respirator's mask accrues in silence, tinged with blood.

Stuffed birds flew along the wall to the right of the front door, above the stationary heads of several cats and one dog.

A robin. A mockingbird. A pair of house finches, the male more rubicund than the female. Five pigeons. A golden crown sparrow. A vireo. One raven. Two crows.

There's something these birds are trying to tell me. What could it be? He adjusted the strap on the respirator mask and touched

179

the tip of the needle to a vein in the top of the hand. Answer, as the needle sank, They're all endemic to Golden Gate Park. A red contrail bloomed in the plastic barrel. Does that include the tomcat? He depressed the plunger. Yes, but that's no tomcat, son. That's a calico. Only the female occurs as calico.

Torvald's mind responded to itself, in an exaggerated falsetto, I didn't know that. Say, Uncle Torvald, are you boning me? How many times have I told you? Don't bone me. Wavering tone, there. Torvald sighed. He was too worn out to take it from the top. In the old days, he would have worked it until he got it perfect. But what difference could it make now? The castrato tittered. Why would I do that?

To . . . confuse me? Now the falsetto mocked itself. The Torvald tittered aloud and covered his mouth with his fingertips, a habit he'd developed after the flailing elbow of Vol. XIII knocked his front teeth out. Oh, we wouldn't want that. We find it's best when you know exactly what's going on. It's more . . . efficacious.

He unseated and reseated the bridge with the tip of his tongue. Efficacious. . . ?

For me, of course, he answered silently. Not for you, necessarily.

He stood behind Philadelphia, who lay on the floor facing away from him, feet toward the front door and head not a yard from the big television. Whatever it was about efficacious, it would be his, Torvald's, engineered efficacy. Not this kid's. Not by a long shot.

Torvald set the syringe on the rosewood secretary, alongside the iBook, and pulled up the chair. *How diverting it sometimes can be,* he typed into his computer journal, *when, in the attempt to forestall the inevitable, they bring all their intelligence to bear. It's too bad curare doesn't allow you to talk.*

". . .Is that a pit bull?" he said to the screen, as if trying out the line.

On the other hand, Torvald typed, *there are the ones who accept their*

180

fate without a word, as if they deserve it. Query. He paused. *Which is the more courageous?*

Staffordshire terrier?

"*Charmant,*" Torvald typed and said, as though responding to somebody who had spoken aloud.

Endemic to the park, too, I suppose.

Torvald stopped typing and said, "All predatory."

He looked to one side of the computer screen, "The pit bull preys on the cats," and looked to the other. "Correct." He looked up, "The cats prey on the songbirds," and down, using the falsetto: "Ditto."

"But the songbirds prey on. . . ?"

"Insects." He giggled. "Too tiny for taxidermy."

"Oh." After a pause, "And the crows? The ravens?"

"Garbage."

"But . . . the insects feed on garbage, too, don't they?"

"Garbage breeds them. Maggots, flies, even mosquitoes, happily enough." He cleared his throat.

"What about . . . the rats? Where do the rats come in?"

"There are at least three species of hawk that live in the park and prey on the rats that prey on the garbage. They are magnificent to observe, but hard to catch."

"Not impossible to catch?" queried the falsetto,

"Nothing," Torvald declared with an imperious roar, "is impossible to catch."

He added with a flourish, using the voice of Omniscient Narration, "And before the kid could point out the squirrel, his larynx seized."

Torvald laughed. He was enjoying himself. Sort of. In truth he felt awkward. This angered him. He beamed testily, though smug. The kid lives on, but quietly. Almost a minute passed, into the silence of which the greater silence of the Outer Richmond rushed like a tide. The junipers out front maintained their rhythmic sweeping of the little bungalow's façade. The breathing

181

of the woman on the video screen labored irregularly. Barely discernible, a sound separated its identity from the random noise. Gradually it took on a life of its own, as well as an identity. It was a siren. Far away. Torvald paused to listen. The wail increased in volume; its pitch waxed and waned. "That siren is coming this way," Torvald whispered.

There are three types of siren in San Francisco. One is common to ambulances, one to fire trucks, and one to police cars. Torvald listened. By its siren, this is a police car.

It was far away, but onward the siren came. The wail held its pitch for a moment, as if hesitating. It seemed that the siren had to have turned north on 32nd Avenue, which bounded the west side of George Washington High School, a mere four blocks east of Torvald's bungalow. And then, abruptly, the siren leapt a quantum in volume. Its vehicle had turned in front of the high school, which interrupted Anza for a block, and now it was on Anza Street. Heading west. It had to be. Towards me. Toward us. Towards the beach, too. But if it really wanted to get to the beach in a hurry it would stay on Fulton Street, with its synchronized lights and two lanes in each direction, three blocks south of Anza. But on it came, louder and louder, until all the other sounds were occluded by its ululation, until it virtually encompassed Torvald's doorstep, and careened past the pink concrete aprons and westward, towards the beach, diminishing.

The siren's pitch lowered, precisely according to the Doppler effect, as it sped away. The siren faded until, as if all too soon, reduced below a certain threshold, it was gone. He realized that, even though he was sitting down, most of his weight was on one foot.

Well, thought Torvald, redistributing his weight, that was a thrill. He cleared his throat. *Oh,* he typed, *to control and predict access to the thrill of fear. . . .*

From among the shadows cast by the flickering video onto the east wall of the living room, the snouts and beaks of Torvald's taxidermy overlooked the scene, like nocturnal forest creatures spying on a hiker transfixed by his campfire.

The insects and the garbage are your friends, Torvald typed. *The only creatures that will survive the human endowment to the planet. In that context of utter depredation, they will thrive. But what about machines or robots? Or clones?* he queried thoughtfully. *How about bad, self-replicating software? And nanobiobots?* He sniggered. After some consideration he dismissed these and wrote, *Artifacts of the human presence. Inanimate trash. Bad software destroys itself.*

"They're different from garbage?" he asked himself aloud.

Mere anomalies of the futurescape. Undefined bulges in the jungle, overgrown and forgotten, like temples of the Maya. Torvald pinched a mint out of the tin next to the syringe and typed authoritatively, *Garbage is* alive!

Tell him about it. Garbage is alive and paying property taxes in the Avenues. But now something was developing on the video feed. He turned to face the screen. The woman tied to the wooden chair in the cinderblock room had begun to wake up. Her labored breathing had become labored whimpering. She struggled against her bonds, which were a broad black belt with brass grommets in two parallel rows around her middle, from which two straps rose over her shoulders and buckled to the back of the chair. Except that it was leather, it might have been a safety harness—safely harnessed, hah hah! Each ankle had a smaller belt and buckle fastening it to a leg of the chair. A similar arrangement applied to each thigh and forearm.

Struggle as she might, she wasn't going anywhere. Having realized her predicament, the woman raised her head to look around.

Torvald's breath quickened. His face became brittle. He sucked the mint hard. He remembered the name.

Lavinia.

Her voice found no articulation. How could it? A harness of black straps, fitted over the top and back of her head, trapped a

183

bright crimson ball between her lips, half in and half out of her mouth. Cry out as she might, and now she tried, mere inarticulate whimpers would be audible, only. Mucus trickled over her upper lip; the exposed hemisphere glistened with it.

The woman's frightened eyes enlarged, revealing much white and their unusual color, violet, as they swiveled around the room. Up, down, left, right, she craned to look over her shoulder but the harness prevented this. It didn't make any difference. There was nothing back there but a sound baffle covered in a beige fabric that looked like corduroy.

"There's probably software out there," Torvald said quietly to the screen, "that would enable me to control your environment from this keyboard." He touched the computer behind him. "A fiber optic cable, an interface in the control room. . . . Unfortunately, I lack the time to research, let alone master, this technology."

He paused to gauge the crescendo of Lavinia's panic.

Let her macerate.

After a long minute, Torvald turned to the computer.

Strange to declare, but the time is nigh. I can feel it. True, I have more on my plate than I can reasonably handle. Foreboding but undeniable, as with "Angelica," I can evince none of the passion of yore, nor the resulting—and requisite—attention to detail. Am I so jaded? I don't think so. The simple truth is, I have explored these avenues before, and they have yielded up all the secrets they have to offer me. I know them well, too well, and the supply of energy for such explorations is too limited to repeat them unnecessarily. What is at work is mere habit, which manifests itself through lack of discipline. My plate is not only full but, by the virtue of the peccancy of gluttony, it is overflowing. The Virtue of Sin, surely someone must have written that book? Here on the heels of eighteen, Volume XVIII, yes, I burden myself with two more potential studies. It is too much. I fly, I faint, I fall. Simply put, I weary.

For the first time since the translation of The Confession *I have let slip the guise. Inconsequential as this may yet prove to be, I perceive it as erratic*

184

development, and I evaluate it not as lack of vigilance, but as stress fracture. The time has come to wrap up the field studies. Will I be afforded the energy, the time, the concentration necessary for a final cut? Time waits for no fiend. On the contrary, time copulates and breeds and feeds its own progeny to itself. The real-time of Lavinia ticks away, but her convulsive pules are less than heart-rending. What's that? The chair recognizes the floor.

Baldy tried to scream, the falsetto snitched, but his voice is a paper bag blowing across a deserted parking lot.

Torvald spoke to the computer screen. "You have merged with the floor; you have become seamlessly integral with it; it's as if the carpet sprouted from your head and died. Your mouth is filled with uncooked liver, formerly your tongue. Your interrogatives surf garbled saliva. Modulations from the thinnest string on the violin have become your inner voices. Content yourself with telepathic invective which, as you'll find, works much in the same way that prayer works. That is as much as to say, telepathic invective is futile."

Torvald rolled the syringe with a forefinger. "Tubucurarine chloride. . . . What? Do I roger your telepathic vilification?" He cocked his head as if listening for the siren. He aligned the syringe just so, equidistant between the iMac and the mint tin. "If you're a bear or an otter or even a human, it's a fine product. All your locomotor functions—arms, legs, voice—even your eyelids—are kaput. You can't even blink." Torvald shrugged modestly. "And anybody can buy it on the Internet."

He checked the gauge on the oxygen tank, on its own little handtruck by the window; he checked the transparent tubing for kinks; he snugged the straps on the mask. "A humanitarian would have some eyedrops to stave off desiccation." Torvald clasped his hands behind his back, leaned over Philadelphia, and smiled. "And, ultimately, blindness. *Nota bene.*" He opened his mouth and exhaled. "Spearmint. Like it? Doesn't it remind you of a leading brand of spermicide?" He stood again, beaming. "Yes, while you do not retain your sense of humor, kiddo, you do retain

185

your sense of smell. I chew these mints out of courtesy and precaution because, some years ago, I began to emanate a curious odor. People noticed it. The stench of evil." He laughed without mirth. "No doubt. When you think of it, however, Dorian Gray must have begun to smell strangely, most strangely, long before his decomposition became apparent to the outside world. Hmm? Rotted from within. Yes. Pheromones of decay. Those of fear, you know about. You generate them yourself. Mine are the reciprocal. Hah. Had I not sampled them with my own nose, I wouldn't have believed it."

Torvald withdrew a round brown bottle from the desk drawer and checked the level of its fluid against the light of the computer screen. "You'd think that by now the government would have stumbled across the idea of training dogs to sniff out evil." He unscrewed the rubber-bulbed top. "I'm serious. After a certain amount of time in this business, my personal odor changed. For the worse. If we had time, I'd prove it to you. Perhaps your girlfriend will describe for you how I proved it to her, when you meet in hell."

He leaned over and held the dropper about two feet above the upside eye, which bulged above the stitched hem of the respirator mask. A bead of clear fluid quivered at the tip of the pipette. Torvald paused. "The mind is not affected, either. It gets to wonder, is this battery acid?"

The drop enlarged. "Oh." The drop retreated. "Did I mention that you also retain your sense of pain?"

Torvald slowly squeezed the dropper's bulb until a single drop of fluid plummeted the two feet, directly into the right eye. The body twitched as if from an electric shock. Two additional drops followed, with commensurate twitches. "I'd do the other one, but it's too much trouble to roll you over. Besides, your witness shall be borne as lucidly with one eye as well as with two."

Torvald waited, as if expectently. "Well," he said, after a while, "I guess it's not battery acid."

186

He capped the vial and returned it to the drawer. "The police, having employed tubucurarine chloride to subdue their criminal, might read him his Miranda rights, and he would understand them. He would understand everything that was happening to him. His trial, even his execution. In your case," Torvald smiled and modestly flattened the fingers of one hand over his sternum, "your mind is actively reassuring itself that the stuff might not have been battery acid after all. Desperately, of course. It might have been battery acid, for all you know. Why not?" Torvald smiled. "It's not that I'm incapable of it."

On screen, "Lavinia" began to weep.

Ripening.

Let's see, Torvald thought. I think I can rig this up.

Torvald stepped back, chin in hand, and studied the situation. Let's call him Baldy. Philadelphia has too many syllables. Baldy lay on his side. After some consideration Torvald gripped Baldy's lapels and rotated his length some ninety degrees. Now Baldy could watch the monitor, which loomed mere feet away.

"Okay," Torvald said. From a drawer in the video cabinet he retrieved ping-pong ball-like gadgets with wires attached, three of his many cameras. He placed one on the rug between the body and the front door. He place a second camera on the floor, aimed directly at the top of the skull and about five feet away from it. He placed a third camera ball on the floor at the foot of the monitor cabinet, not two feet from Baldy's glistening eye and the rostrum of the respirator mask.

On the audio monitor, Lavinia was hyperventilating. While Torvald regretted the lack of a second DVD recorder, he unwrapped three fresh video cassettes and fed them into three decks in the stack of gear that lived in the cabinet below the wide screen, powered them up, and set them all to recording. One for each camera.

There was a panel of push button switches that controlled the inputs and outputs of his video and audio signals. Torvald toggled back and forth between the various cameras, each signal coming up on the big monitor as he adjusted for angle, placement, focus, "Happily absorbed in the minutiae of his craft," as he said aloud; and, delighting in the design of his next-to-last production, unpretentious parenthesis as it was, he almost laughed.

Interregnum. He tried its title aloud, "Cranial Croquet."

Torvald opened the front door. No doubt the breath of cool Pacific air bathed the bald dome on the living room floor, chilling the perspiration beaded on its stenciled tentacles, which quivered, no doubt, like a basket of augury entrails. With a proprietary glance up and down deserted Anza Street, Torvald set aside the left-hand 84" 1x6 board of the front door casing, just behind the sculpturally tapered juniper that chafed it, and removed an ax from the cavity. Within seconds the board was replaced and he was back inside with the dead bolt locked, his retrieval of the ax so smooth it might have been part of an ordinary urban routine, no more nor less normal than retrieving a morning *Chronicle* from the grasp of the shrubbery.

The bald head looked like a casaba melon, pale and damp in the gloom of a darkened supermarket, graced by the gentle mists which, perforce, bless all refrigerated produce. On the big screen, however, the head looked like the moon in a nightmare, ententacled, prolate, dead for aeons and, incongruously, runneled by brine.

Torvald decided to leave the monitor tuned to the camera shooting along the floor at the top of the head. The head lay on its left cheek, watched by the other two cameras, front and back, the head watching in turn its own image on the big screen. Torvald retrieved a large black plastic trash can liner from his pantry and carefully spread it on the floor beneath the head. All I'll have to do, he thought, stepping back to admire the setup, is turn it inside out around the mess, with no more bother than picking up ten pounds of dog shit.

"Okay," Torvald said, when he had tired of watching the

drugged eye struggling to search for itself on the screen. "Slate," and he sharply rapped the axe-head against the oxygen tank, which rang like a pick hitting rock. "Rolling ye *Interregnum*: Cranial Croquet." On the video screen a sensible wing-tip lowered itself onto the upper side of the lunar caustic. What's this going to look like? He breathed stertorously, excited by the prospect after all. An axe head lowered into the shot. He studied the screen, over his shoulder, and muttered, "No, no." He leaned down. A hand closed over the eye of the camera like a spider squatting on an egg. The little golf-ball-sized camera had a microphone too, and when the hand closed over it, the speakers yielded noises as of wind blowing umbrellas and lawn furniture off a terrace. When the picture came back, the angle of the shot had changed. Now the axe would come in obliquely, from the side of the frame, and thence, about two-thirds into the shot, it would sunder skull and brain. How deep the penetration after impact was not just anybody's guess. Not to worry. No. It was an *educated* guess. The cameras would record all. Later he would intercut the moment of contact with the reaction shot from the camera that looked directly into the eye: waiting, cringing aforetime, detecting, bulging with awareness, suffused by pain, dimming with the ebb of its life force, and fading in the end, like a slow-motion, blowing fuse, to black.

Slow motion would reveal the tiniest detail, like a high-speed mind reading the Bible.

Torvald toggled the monitor's three sources one last time. The face scrambled and resolved into the top of its own skull. There was some imperfection. The blows from the keyboard had done some damage. The face was caked with dried blood, the right cheek was deformed. The visible upside eye was discolored. It gleamed in the discolored face like a marble on a bed of caviar.

Torvald's wingtip lowered into the top of the frame, its shadow overhanging the face like a certain balcony overhangs a memory in Chekhov. "What would one think?" Torvald mused aloud.

He toggled to the axial shot, the top of the head: "Would one rather see it coming? Or. . . ?" He toggled the shot of the ruined face, huge in the monitor, its eyes as big as the camera balls: "Or would one prefer to see *oneself*, going? Hmm." He toggled back to the skull. "Blink once for the scythe," he toggled the eyes again, "twice for the flight of the soul." He sighed. "Blinkless. It's up to me. The lonely onus of the *auteur.*" He made slight adjustments to the cameras. He toggled the three shots—the top of the head, the back of the head, the eye—hesitated, and toggled them again. And a third time. "Okay." He made the decision. "Since I'm concentrating on a clean blow—for which," he added as an aside, "you should be grateful—I won't see either image until later. *Ultimately omniscient*, in a manner of speaking, I shall view these images at my leisure. I'll assume you're vain enough to have lingered over the image of your face in the mirror as you shaved this dome over the years," Torvald caressed the skull, "and *fingered your tentacles. . . ,*" with the edge of the blade; it grazed the top of the skull as if it were scratching a dog's head. "I think you'll watch your own eye at the moment of impact." He switched from the axial image to the shot of the eye. "First thought, best thought."

"Good thing I'm left-handed," Torvald muttered cheerfully, as he paused to roll up his sleeves. Then he wrapped his fingers around the hickory handle and waggled the axe head as if it were a niblick.

"Otherwise, we'd have to rearrange everything."

Eighteen

Prepare for calamari," Torvald advised, gauging the swing. He paused. "Although, come to think on it, calamari is squid. *Tako* is octopus." Torvald let the axe swing like a pendulum. "You wouldn't be HIV positive, by any chance? I'm nervous about the splash." He lowered the axe to the carpet, picked up his foot, and looked deeply into Baldy's upside eye. "No." He smiled and replaced the sole of his shoe on the side of the head. "Not a trace of the haunting. Not to mention," he gauged the swing of the axe, "I'm beyond caring."

A blast of fogwind buffeted the west side of the building. The drapes over the window stirred. Somewhere in the neighborhood, a bamboo wind chime clattered. The blade of the axe grazed the middle of the cranium. The edge slipped up an inch, down a half inch, and went away.

"You know," Torvald said dreamily, "when I was young, I wanted to be a musician."

The blade returned to leave an iron kiss. A polar touch. The trace of a frozen meridian. A molecular tingle.

"My mother sang in the choir at Old Saint Boniface in Fort Wayne."

The axe blade hung midair, a windless kite on a short string.

"I was an altar boy. Even as you teeter on the edge of the abyss, I can smell the incense, I can taste the sweet communion

191

wine, I can smell the starch in Monsignor's freshly laundered chasuble."

On the monitor, the axe head retreated through the right side of the frame.

"You probably won't feel a thing," Torvald said, as if speaking to the kid, but, strangely and obviously, addressing himself. "In the old days, old boy," he reversed the axe and let the flat of it nuzzle the top of the shaved skull, "you would have felt many things. Everything. By the time I was finished?" He clucked his tongue. "They begged for the sharp end." He sighed.

He recollected himself.

"The goldanged magic is gone."

He stared at nothing. "Mother made me take piano lessons. The teacher was very good. But, well, to speak plainly, the teacher was a pederast, too. Hmmmm. . . ."

Torvald's mind wasn't on his work, and he knew it. He stepped away from the skull, considered it without really seeing it, then bethought. He walked to the rosewood secretary, retrieved a bastard file from its drawer, and sat down in the chair with the axe across his lap. "Been a while since I brightened this edge." Torvald dragged the file over the blade. "Hey, Baldy," he continued conversationally, paying the while close attention to the task of honing, "ever heard that old saw —Hah! Get it?—about paper dulling a cutting edge faster than wood?" The file rang on the axe head. "Bone's worse. They say whale blubber's even tougher." Abruptly the filing stopped. "Mint?" Transferring the file to the same hand that held the axe, he let two fingers scuttle through the tin. "No, forget it." He transferred a mint. "You're beyond pensive suckling." He resumed filing. "Close enough, anyway. Two hairs from a freckle."

Torvald tested the burr with his thumb, eliciting a sound very like that of a distant doorbell; the old-fashioned kind, that rings as you twist its handle. "If I'd killed the Monsignor right off the bat or even right off the axe—hah—maybe I never would have graduated to mutilating surrogates." He tapped the axe head with a corner of the file. "Mere symbols," he muttered, abruptly humorless.

"That danged music teacher. I might have saved a lot of wide-eyed youth their precious traumas. And if I'd killed my mother right off the bat, with incredible violence of course, with a kitchen knife or broken mop handle and rage sufficient to slake my thirst for revenge, I might have been caught and sentenced immediately to an asylum for the criminally insane, which is where I belong: among my peers. There, like dear de Sade, I might have written to my heart's content, not to mention as my heart directed me to write, leaving the staff and ultimately society to find my musings invaluable if not key to their understanding of the deranged mind. And there too I might have studied music for real, with a teacher I could molest instead of the other way around, gleaning from her protestations—for a she it rightfully must be—inspiration for transcendent mad works, to be played in concert halls the world around for generations to come, or anyway for as long as mankind is willing to sit still for outbursts of genius."

He filed a few strokes. "By the clock you have, let's see, about two and a half hours of decrementing paralysis. By then however your energy will have been so sapped that it will be perhaps three or four hours later before you'll have the motor coordination to actually sit up. By that time, I assure you, you'll be bait in my feral pussy traps behind the gardener's shed west of Stowe Lake in Golden Gate Park. Where, it may be of some comfort for you to understand, you will be of more utility to the preservation of the songbird population than you were to anything at all in your present incarnation."

The honing started and stopped. Torvald raised his head until he was looking at the corner over the front door, where the wall met the ceiling.

"How the neighborhood has changed. When, as a new hire

193

at 2DMedia, walking to the bus stop of a crisp spring morning, I was acculturated to noticing syringes discarded in the gutter. Toward the end of my tenure, seventeen years later, I was counting golf tees instead. Is this an improvement?

"Hmmm." Torvald turned in his chair to ruminate on the bald head, without really seeing it. "Wait there." He stood the axe against the window sill and turned to the computer. "I must make a note."

Torvald laid the file carefully on the rosewood, parallel to the syringe, and clawed at his mints. After a moment of suckling introspection, he began to write.

. . .*Onerous,* Torvald typed. *Dismembering the corpse, feeding it piecemeal to the masticator, it takes all night, even saving out the choice bits for those nasty pussies, the liver and tongue they find so irresistible. . . . But what difference does it make? I'm not as young as I once was and it's a lot of work, but where is my enthusiasm?* Torvald cast a winsome look over his shoulder at the stuffed head of the pit bull. *It's not the same since Ted Bundy died.* He tapped idly back and forth between two keys, moving the cursor back one space or ahead one space. Then he wrote, *What a great name for a pit bull. Angelica, who expired so unexpectedly—* He stopped. He saved what he had written. The hard drive on the iBook had an annoying little whine. He saved again. Again the whine. He saved again. Whine. He sat for a long minute, his minted tongue clenched between his teeth. Behind him, the respirator hissed.

Outside the door in the night a car rolled up Anza, heading east. It barely paused for the stop sign at 36th Avenue, not fifty yards from Torvald's front door, turned, and drove on.

Torvald scrolled up a screen to read what he had typed. He pinched two mints out of the tin as he read, and laid one of them on his tongue. Enough of these, he thought ruefully, and all my problems will be solved. He dropped the second mint back into the tin. Except tooth decay. He resumed typing.

In the end ah the untimely end, "Angelica" was only good for terrorizing

194

"Lavinia." "Cranial Croquet," on the other hand, is proving good for less than nothing. I'm having trouble concentrating on him. I'm losing my touch. I foresaw a phase in which I gradually surrendered my integrity in exchange for closure, but I did not expect to simply drive off a cliff. I failed to anticipate the waning of my concentration, with which comes slipshod work, which, necessarily, will degrade into incompetence. It's the loneliness. It's the lack of recognition. In the beginning one expects to labor in the far reaches of isolation. It comes with the territory. It is the territory. One can't merely harvest greatness, let alone depend upon it, to find it awarded on a platter. One does, however, espy the threads of greatness woven into the sordid fabric of life. . . . But after years without recognition, which must perforce come only in its most blinding form, instantaneously, and with it an abrupt halt, and behold the overnight sensation so far as the rest of the world is concerned. But such success belies years, decades, perhaps a lifetime of concentration, training, and hard work. And I? I accomplished it in less than twelve years. Twelve years!

Nevertheless, and because of it, I am tired. I am near, but I am tired. My ambition and the scope of my accomplishment have perhaps outrun my capacity to achieve them. It is a narrow thing. So many details to coordinate, so many eyes to avoid, so great a burden to shoulder in solitude. Yet in solitude is greatness achieved. One imagines the geniuses of history—de Sade, Morgan, Gilles de Rais, John Wayne Gacy, Ted Bundy: ah the great, great Ted Bundy—men to match their deeds! Oh, that I might chat with giants over little white pleated paper cups heaped with colorful pharmaceuticals in a locked asylum! Not to discuss technique, certainly. Technique is merely a matter of daring; the rest is imagination.

And after? Feeble morality, mere criticism. Poetasters who demand the best seats based on articles they've written, talks they've given, round-table discussions dominated by belligerent narcissism, multiple appearances on television shows, the talking head surmounting a placard denoting 'Expert,' the charade reproduced endlessly on screens worldwide—I should mount one on my wall—

Torvald stopped typing. "Did you hear something?"

He listened.

195

The fog wind blustered against the house, sweeping the avenues of cigarette ends and plastic bags and cypress needles, blowing sand from the beach all the way downtown, scouring the asphalt and currying windrows of detritus along the north-facing curbstones.

He strained his ears until it seemed he could distinguish, beyond the hiss of the respirator, a diesel bus pulling away from the stop at Fulton and 32nd, a solid seven blocks away. A good fog and a twenty-five-knot wind make for whimsical acoustics; but it seemed almost capricious to hope that he could be deceived about anything at this point.

"Kid," Torvald said to the computer screen, "there's something I want you to know."

There came no response, of course. It had been a long time since somebody had fashioned for Torvald a coherent answer. But he said his piece anyway. "This isn't personal," he declared. "In all sincerity. I want you to believe that."

I'll bet you say that to all the slaughterees! he typed gleefully.

"Besides," Torvald added aloud, trying to sound serious, but immediately he began to type his words as he spoke them, *"Since you work for a music store, is it fair to assume that you, too, are a failed musician?"*

Torvald began to type furiously, as if receiving dictation from himself, a self become a high octane confessional machine. *"I realized that I was so afraid of my music teacher I literally couldn't hear him. I couldn't hear what he was saying, I couldn't hear what he was playing. If I couldn't hear him, you see, then I couldn't learn. If I couldn't learn, I would never play. The fear of my music teacher interdicted every possibility of achievement. Such potential as I possessed was obliterated. Canceled. Wiped out. Every time I sat down to the piano I froze. If my mother bought me a record, I broke it. If she bought me sheet music, I lost it, and once I even wiped my ass with it. Can you imagine the panic I experienced, when it wouldn't flush? Again and again, I waited for the tank to refill. Finally I— Ahem.*

"I could only think of what he had done to me, and that what he had done once he could and would repeat, and he would do it to me until I escaped. So I played wretchedly. My mother spanked me. I played worse. My father appeared only occasionally. Drunk? He was always drunk. He came home drunk and only to have sex with my mother. Afterwards he would beat her. Then he would litter the kitchen table with cash, always small bills, always a paltry amount, then he'd storm out. If I got in the way, my behind got kicked, too."

Leaving off typing Torvald said, "She liked the sex part of this . . . arrangement. . . ." His voice trailed off.

Silence.

"Did you hear something?"

Somewhere on the block the bamboo wind chime twisted and clacked. *She,* Torvald typed. He thoughtfully fingered another mint out of the tin, not looking at the tin but watching the cursor blink on the computer screen. He put out his tongue and placed the mint on it. The tongue retreated into the mouth.

"Mother liked the sex. The apartment was small, just three rooms. So when that man she called my father showed up to have sex with her, she would tell me that it was time for me to practice piano. This could be any hour of the day or night. She never knew when he would arrive. But he always came. And she always told me it was time to practice. Practice, practice, practice. Play loud. Play fast. They would laugh and open a bottle and take it into the bedroom, the bedroom she and I shared. Sometimes they would leave the door open, sometimes not. So I practiced. And practiced and practiced and practiced.

"I practiced scales, etudes, rondelles, folk songs, pastiche, atonality, the twelve-tone bash. . . . I never mastered bebop. I never mastered anything. The pain was too great. I banged away loudly and incompetently. Sometimes I sang lyrics. Sometimes I made them up. Sometimes I just yelled. And the more I played, the worse my playing got.

"Finally my 'father' came out of the bedroom with his galluses dangling, unshaven, in his undershirt, barefooted, reeking of whiskey and perspiration

197

and of something else I didn't want to think about. Knock it off, kid, he would say. Knock it off!"

Torvald stopped.

The respirator hissed.

He typed and spoke. *"Here's two bucks. Go to the movies."* He stopped. He started again. *"I hated him. I didn't want his money. But I took it—"*

Torvald stopped.

"Did you hear something?"

Silence.

Torvald tapped a key, then another, then the words rushed out as if borne along by the torrent of touch typing.

"I hated him and didn't want to take anything from him but I wanted out of the house worse. So I took his money and escaped. My 'father' would watch me go, but as I stepped off the front porch, I heard him say to my mother, That kid can't play worth a shit. I'm not paying no more fucking money for no more fucking music lessons. Call the leasing company and tell them to come get their damned piano."

Torvald broke down, face first into his keyboard, and snuffled. He sounded just like. . . .

He looked up.

He sounded *better* than "Angelica."

She should be punished for that.

But Angelica was gone.

He turned around.

On the screen was a bald head as big as a medicine ball.

Goddamn it, he thought wearily, this scene is going straight to hell.

He turned back to the computer. "That," Torvald said aloud. He sat up straight and looked for all the world as if he were about to begin a piano recital. He typed as he dictated, *"And that is how I stopped seeing my music teacher and began the long flight from my mother, which took many years, and why I never became a musician, why I could never listen to music, which is why I live out here,"* he banged the

198

keyboard, "*in the goddamned Outer Richmond, where it's* always *quiet . . . . Quiet. . . . Quiet!*"

The banging stopped.

Torvald wrote and said, "*Which is why it isn't personal, kid. You understand me? If you could talk I might even ask for your impersonal forgiveness. The kind God gives, you know? By His Grace. But since you can't talk, I'm going to make do with a little piece of advice.*"

And now, so abruptly that the room rather than Torvald seemed to move, Torvald sprang out of his chair and his own face materialized on the video screen, huge above Baldy's face, and the reek of not-quite-spearmint-blanketed civet musk descended with him until he had laid his cheek against the ruined cheek, and his eyes met the desiccating eyeball on the video screen. He caressed the damp skull and said to the televised orb, as if confidentially, "If you believe that nonsense about my father, let me tell you, boy," Torvald rapped the skull with the knuckles of his left hand, "you are going to wake up in hell a bigger sucker than you ever were in this life."

Perhaps it was this revelation, as much as any other, that forced an extra gout of red-threaded yellow mucus to seep under the lower seam of the respirator mask. Torvald laughed long and he laughed hard, and though his laughter was driven by many things and mirth was not one of them, his eyes never left the other eye on the screen. Abruptly he stopped laughing and sank his tongue into the upturned ear. Like a walking beam oil pump lifts its pitman arm in and out of the earth, he drove his tongue in and out of the ear, watching the scene on the screen. His tongue was thick and wet and minty and, when he finished, the ear was too, and his four-tooth bridge lay upturned on the rug.

He stood up clumsily, flushed, his breath whistling.

He retrieved his bridge from the floor, wiped it on his sleeve, and seated it against his palate.

Time to get down to business. Goddamn, it's time to get down to business.

199

He retrieved the axe.

The toe of his shoe lowered into the frame at the top of the video screen, like a remembered balcony in Chekhov. The flat of its sole arrived on the upturned side of the ruined face and cast a shadow over its eye. The edge of the blade touched the curve of the cranium, tangent to it, one penultimate time.

"So," Torvald whispered, "it's time to kiss your octopus goodbye." He smacked his lips. "The pathetic octopus of your existence."

The blade pulled out of the shot. Torvald's weight came down on the foot. He drew a breath.

He looked toward the desk.

Next to the computer, the tin waited.

He looked down.

The blade had a V-shaped notch in its edge.

For pulling nails. Nails incorrectly driven.

Why not.

The axe head, when new, had been painted red. But only the blunt end. Not the blade. It would take a lot more than filing to get all those other nicks out. Grinding, maybe.

Why not indeed, he thought to himself. "You never know," he said aloud. He smiled. "Why not." He unsmiled. "Let's roll the dice. Let's make it really interesting. Let's put it all on double zero." He stood away from the skull and leaned the axe handle against the window sill. "I was wondering when I'd figure this out. Wait here." He approached the antique secretary. "I'll be right back." He turned as he arrived at the desk. "Or I won't." He turned back to the desk. "Either way," he added quietly, "who knows? You might well have been driven mad already. You could be mad forever. You could be mad for just a few more minutes."

Torvald tilted the computer screen so he could reread the last page of text while two of his fingers prowled the open tin, which was nearly empty. Torvald smiled and read on. The dawdling

200

fingers selected a mint and carried it to his mouth. He frowned at the words "Outer Richmond." The mouth opened. The tongue came forward. Thumb and middle finger placed a mint on the tongue and the forefinger impressed it there, like a stack of chips. Tongue retreated into lair. Torvald tapped an arrow key and sucked. He blinked. He stopped sucking.

A smile opened his face like a zipper. Relief flooded his features. A cry caught in his throat. He brought a fist down to his thigh and struck it once, twice, thrice. By an act of will he swallowed the mint. His Adam's apple bulged around it. Peristalsis conveyed the mint to his stomach. His mind's eye followed the mint down like the crowd in Times Square follows the descent of the ball on New Year's Eve. The effects began almost at once.

With his middle finger he struck the return key. He coughed. Flecks of cupric blue foam speckled the liquid crystal display.

Torvald wrote.

At last. . . .

Nineteen

The paradiddles of Ivy Pruitt, conducted on his denim thighs by the palms of his hands, penetrated the narcoleptic mists shrouding an uncertain emergence.

"Wake up, Curly. Tell us how much fun it was."

My eyes wanted to remain closed. I was lying on my back. His hand jive was a visceral irritation. "Ivy Pruitt. Does it have to be you?"

"Welcome back to the animated portion of the program."

"Whence I can only regress. Go away."

"Come on, Curly, who else has visited you? Huh? Who? *Me,* that's who. I'm it."

My eyes allowed themselves to become slits. Separating them was like removing a depilation plaster.

In spite of translucent drapes drawn over the window behind Ivy, my eyes couldn't adjust to the light. His thinness emphasized his big ears; he looked like a numinous jug of olive oil. Newspapers littered the foot of the bed.

The eyes closed again. I experienced weightlessness. "Am I to be visited? Where?"

"Children's Hospital." Ivy chose a newspaper and put his feet up on the bed. The turning of pages couldn't have been more appalling if they had been the blades of a rotary lawn mower churning lengths of snake.

"Check this out: SEX SLAVE SAVED BY 'THE OCTOPUS'."

"That has to be the *Examiner.*"

"Don't you just love the new design? You're famous."

"It wasn't worth it."

"Sex slave. That'll be the day."

"Where is she?"

"Five floors up." The newspaper rattled. "In a private room with two windows and north light."

"She's alive?"

"Very."

I tried to blink. "This room's not private? Who wants to cohabit with The Octopus?"

"If you think about it, the answer's obvious."

I coaxed the eyelids open. The left eye was blurred. I closed it, raised my head, and used the other eye to inspect the room. Indeed there was another bed. It was surrounded by curtains. A gaggle of equipment clustered against the wall at the head of the bed was turned off.

Ivy let the *Examiner* fall to the floor. "The nurse says not to worry. They'll come get him when they have time, and he wasn't contagious."

I fell back on the pillow, exhausted.

Ivy explained, paging rapidly through the *Chronicle*, "A school bus has collided with a cable car. All hands to the ER."

I rubbed the left eye with the back of my right hand. An IV tree next to the bed rattled and tugged back. The wrist came away streaked with translucent jelly.

"What's her room number?"

"819."

"I can remember that. Add one to eight you get nine, subtract one from nine you get eight."

"You're a sick puppy," Ivy said to the newspaper.

We enjoyed silence for a minute or two until he read, "*New Life Form Found Living on Lobster Lips.*"

203

"Ivy. . . ."

"*Only the 36th known phylum of animals.* I'll be damned." He turned a page.

"Some biologist," I said, ten seconds later, "has never attended a big-band rehearsal."

Ivy said, from behind the paper, "That's funny."

Another minute passed. "Is she okay?"

"He cut her clothes off with garden shears." Ivy lowered the newspaper. "Showed her various foreign objects he threatened to penetrate her with. When she got good and hysterical, he threatened to shoot himself up with methamphetamine, then shoot her up with the same needle, while meticulously describing various symptoms of the highly communicable human immunodeficiency virus. The room was so cold she developed fluid on her lungs, which became bronchitis which somehow became pneumonia. I'm sure smoking tarball off aluminum foil several times a day for the last three years didn't help. Of course she jonesed while she was tied to that chair, but, still, she got off easy. She's alive and in one piece and on antibiotics, pain killers, and tranquilizers. Not that you can tell the difference."

"He didn't cut on her?"

"Only superficially."

Ivy folded the newspaper. "But the drummer's wife bled to death on the floor, right in front of her."

"Stepnowski's wife?"

"Carved up something terrible. That guy Torvald explained to Lavinia that she was watching her own future, and left her alone with it."

Ivy took up another paper while I dozed. I woke with a start and said, "Angelica."

The scatter of papers on the coverlet had gotten sparser.

"That was the name. Lavinia damn near hung herself trying to get out of that chair. Broke a wrist, screwed up her back."

"Can you blame her?"

204

"Nobody does. But her mother blames everybody."

This took a moment to sink in.

"Yes," Ivy said, "Lavinia was born of woman."

"Where?"

"Buffalo? Scranton? Someplace back east. Until the mother showed up, Lavinia was right down the hall. Then there was a lot of commotion and now it's a private room, a private doctor, a masseuse, and a nutritionist."

"No shrink?"

"Of course there's a shrink."

"He'll be fascinated."

"It's a she. There's a lawyer, too."

"Mom is suing a psychopath?"

"Almost. Mom is suing Sal Kramer."

"What? Ouch. Try not to startle me."

"Sorry," he lied.

"For what?" I asked. "Is she suing, I mean."

"Medical expenses. Mom's claim is that Lavinia got messed up while she was on the World of Sound's payroll. Sal maintains she was an independent contractor. Mom also claims, by the way, that she's not greedy."

"Sal had better settle."

"Sal doesn't think so. Mom also thinks Sal sent her little girl on a job she was over-qualified to perform." Ivy punched the fold out of a page. "She thinks that hardly any Vassar graduates do repo work. Sal claims to know better."

"Why not?" I squinted at the label on a nylon bracelet on my wrist. "The money's terrific."

"Hell, if I hadn't called the cops, Mom wouldn't have a daughter at all. Then Sal would really be in trouble."

The printing was upside down. "*You* called the cops?"

Ivy kept some newspaper between us. "Sal had given up on you guys. When I finally tracked him down, he was in a private booth in the back of the bar at Original Joe's with a hooker and a heat on."

"You needed money," I guessed.

"Business is business. I thought he was just being slow to pay me. But when Sal assured me he was still waiting for your call, I blew a gasket. It was more than a day later!"

"A day?"

"Sal coughed up some cop's pager number and I dropped the dime. I never called a cop in my life."

"Wow," I said. "It must have been hard for you."

"It turned out to be exactly the break this cop Garcia was waiting for. Something about cat blood giving insufficient probable cause. For you and Lavinia, though, he was able to get a warrant."

"Cat blood. Cat blood?"

"It still took four hours to get a judge to issue a warrant. Due process, and all that."

"What break?"

"Three years ago another tenant disappeared, a young woman. It was Garcia's first case since they took him off a beat, his first homicide, and he was the junior guy. His superior was a renowned detective, but the guy was burned out. Garcia worshiped him so it was a long time before he realized that the guy's sole interest in life at that point had nothing to do with solving murder cases. All he could think about was retirement with full disability. Plus a body was never found. So the case went nowhere.

"Stepnowski turned out to have the same landlord, and when it comes to murder, Garcia says, there are no coincidences. But Stepnowski's body was found on De Haro Street, and, what with the money left with the body and the missing wife, everything pointed to her. Garcia had to go the extra mile to disabuse himself, not to mention the D.A.'s office, of that theory. While the landlord gladly let the cops search Stepnowski's apartment, there wasn't sufficient cause or even sufficient suspicion to get a search warrant for the landlord's own place, even though it was right next door. But then you and Lavinia fell off the scope. By then Garcia had turned up the facts that not only had the landlord's wife disappeared without a trace almost twelve years ago, but his fucking next door neighbor had disappeared, too. So when I called, he was up to five missing persons with Torvald in common." Ivy snapped his fingers. "Bob's your uncle."

"Garcia solved his case."

Ivy shrugged. "In the interim, a whole bunch of people died. It haunts him."

My eyelids drooped. "A bunch. . . ?"

Ivy said a number. I didn't catch it.

After a while I woke up again. "So what's it been like, your brief visit to the right side of the law?"

"Hey," Ivy said cheerfully, "there's victimless crime, and there's the other kind." He cleared his throat. "Speaking of which. . . ." He fell silent.

My eyes narrowed. "Speaking of which?"

"That keyboard is too damaged for Sal to pay off on it, even if he ever gets it out of evidence."

The skin twitched over my crushed cheek.

"However," Ivy continued, "in the matter of Mom versus Kramer's World of Sound, Sal has retained me as a, uh, technical consultant."

"You're going to testify that under normal circumstances Lavinia could have blown that creep away?"

"Nah. I'm like the opposite of a character witness. Before Mom opens the can of worms she calls Lavinia, she needs to determine how widely she wants the can of worms she calls Lavinia broadcast."

"Gee. That sounds like legalized blackmail."

"Even Mom admits that Lavinia's next stop is detox. You'd think she'd let well enough alone."

"Mom doesn't need a lawyer. She needs a spin doctor."

"True story." Ivy gathered up the rest of the newspapers. "Gotta keep up appearances back east, I guess."

"In California, nobody can hear you care."

"The freeway's too loud. By the way, if you want to see Lavinia, you'd best crawl on up there. Mom's pressing for an early release. Fuckin' sports." Ivy threw the section to the floor. "Fuckin' business. Fuckin' food. Fuckin' home decoration. Fuckin' weekend." He dealt the last four sections to the floor. "First paper I've read in years. Nothing's changed. Waste of time." He settled back in his chair. "So, Curly, the King's retainer won't kick in until next week, after his lawyer deposes me."

"So?"

"So I need a hundred bucks."

"You're putting the bite on me in my own hospital bed?"

"Don't you think that's a personal problem?"

"Not only that, but where in hell would I get a hundred bucks?"

Ivy pointed at a little nightstand next to the bed. There were various medicine bottles with a *People* magazine and a *MacWarehouse* catalog on top of it, and a single drawer in its face.

I took a look around the room, stalling. Of the two doors one probably led to a bathroom, the other to a hall. Above the bathroom door hung two dark televisions, one aimed at each bed. "Did you turn those TVs off?"

Ivy sat back in his chair and tented his fingers. "It's a hell of a thing to come back from the other side, only to discover that your reward for staying alive is daytime television." He freed a finger from the tent and pointed. "That button at the end of that wire, draped over your left shoulder?"

I looked down my nose.

"Pure hospital M." Ivy spoke as if he were in church. "Damn near all you want. You've slept off the last dose. That's why you're so grouchy."

I felt as weak as a dandelion gone to seed. If someone puffed, all my anthers would blow away.

"Need a hand?"

A few minutes later a very big sleep was coming on, inevitable and unavoidable. I was very grateful. "What money?"

"Whatever was left."

"In the drawer?"

Ivy nodded.

I closed my eyes. "Why ask? Why don't you just take it?"

"What am I, some kind of thieving musician?"

"No," I smiled dreamily. "You're a drummer."

"It was the cat blood that tipped me."

Lieutenant Garcia sat by my bed, moving a stylus over the face of a palmtop computer. "On the warehouse floor."

"Cat blood," I repeated stupidly. "How did Torvald get him there in the first place?"

"A handtruck." The palmtop beeped. "We found it in the back of the cab-over van Stepnowski used to shuttle his band's equipment around, when he had a band. We found it abandoned in Bay View. We found his shoes, too, along with all of his other stuff. He really was moving to that warehouse. He had kicked off his shoes and was smoking a joint in an easy chair in the back of the van when Torvald shot him."

"Cat blood?"

"I was in the shower when I finally remembered the stuffed cats. I noticed Torvald's wall of taxidermy during my first interview with him, three years ago. Torvald did his own taxidermy, you know."

The morphine button was still in my hand. I pressed it.

"The interview was just routine. Landlord of a decedent. We always have too many missing people. Sometimes there are connections. You just have to see them. Then you have to prove

209

them. The cat blood made the connection. How could it not? It was deliberate. Boy, did it make a connection. Like a cold fish in the face." Garcia patted his cheek. "Torvald wanted us to net him, but who would believe me? I had already pulled out all the stops. The DNA test was routine, but I fast-tracked it. You never know. When the results came back cat blood, you could have knocked me over with a feather. But I didn't see the connection right away. The whole case hinged on the next time I took a shower. I get a lot of good ideas in the shower. You, too?"

"I forget. In the event, I don't often have them at all."

"Looking up into the spray, the story just clicked. It wasn't an hour later that Ivy Pruitt called. After that. . . ." Garcia snapped a fingernail at the palmtop. *"Roberto su tío."*

Once pressed, the morphine button takes a long time to come back up. You have to wait for it to come back up before you can press it again.

Garcia smiled. "They saved your eyes."

I blinked gratefully.

"The bad news is you can't afford to stay here. No insurance. Tsk."

The button came back up. I pressed it. "So Torvald did his own taxidermy."

"It was a near thing, though. By the time we got there, that oxygen tank was empty. Good thing the curare had almost worn off. Which reminds me. I'm supposed to tell you that you'll probably notice residual effects of the curare and of oxygen deprivation for a long time. Maybe a year."

"What sort of effects?"

Garcia read from the palmtop. "Erratic motor control. Apnea. Memory loss. Tinnitus. Trembling of the extremities."

"Why isn't a doctor explaining this?"

"He's too busy. Certain drugs will ameliorate your symptoms." He bit his lip. "But they're expensive."

"Hey, man," I told him, "you're good at this." The button had rebounded. I squeezed it again. The morphine machine, about the size of a taxi meter on a wheeled stand next to the bed, clicked reassuringly.

"I'm going to send in a friend of mine. She's a social worker." Garcia tapped his stylus. "You're probably eligible for vocational redirection. Computers, data-entry, automobile mechanics—"

"I could fix my car," I said weakly.

"She'll find a way to help you get back into the job force."

"I've got a few bucks." A little bell went off in my head, and I glanced toward the drawer in the bedside table. Was it six hundred dollars? Seven?

Garcia tapped his kneecap with the palmtop. "I smoothed that over with the D.A. He wanted to impound it. I pointed out that since you and your friends were indirectly responsible for stopping Torvald, who killed a lot more people than his own wife, his next door neighbor, and three of his tenants, the D.A. should cut you some slack. Think of the publicity."

"Lavinia and Ivy and I get a finder's fee?"

Garcia caught the laugh before it got away from him. "Torvald's suicide saved the state hundreds of thousands of dollars."

"He killed himself? In jail?"

"You don't know?"

"I don't remember. Should I?" Like a water moccasin just beneath the muddied surface of a stock pond, pain rippled beneath the thickness of morphine when I shook my head. It occurred to me that there are more people than not who think that a stock pond is some kind of office pool.

"Why, it's the only reason you and Ms. Hahn are still alive. Torvald killed himself right next to you, right there in his living room. It could just as easily have been you, or Ms. Hahn, or me, even. By that time he had gone random. He swallowed a cyanide tablet. We found another one mixed in with his breath mints. He was playing Russian roulette with them."

I found myself wondering, if he had taken the tablet beforehand, whether Torvald's poisoned tongue in my ear could have killed me, like Hamlet's father, whose name I could no longer remember. My mind seemed to be misfiring. Of all the questions I might have asked, appropriate or otherwise, I feebly inquired, "Where the hell did he get cyanide?"

"The internet, according to his journal. I believe him. You can get anything on the internet. Including," Garcia grimaced, "a full-length documentary of Torvald's career."

All I could think to say to this was, "Really?"

Garcia grimly shook his head. "Once something gets on the web, it never goes away. You can't get rid of it. It's out there forever."

"What was his . . . career, exactly?" The word sounded inadequate.

Garcia stared at his knee. "He kidnapped, tortured, and killed some seventeen people."

I had nothing to say. Two people, a man and a woman, came down the hall and passed the closed door to my room, in heated but indecipherable conversation. When their voices had faded, Garcia continued. "It hit the television news last night. The first call the D.A. got this morning was from the parents of the girl who disappeared from Torvald's rental unit three years ago."

"They've seen this movie?"

"No. Some *pendejo* left the URL on their answering machine." Garcia sighed raggedly. "The D.A.'s next call was to me, and we checked it out. It made me sick. Physically sick. Everybody who watched it puked."

I covered my eyes with the arm that wasn't attached to the IV tree.

After a moment Garcia continued quietly, "The provider will take the page down, but it won't do any good. If I'd known what that iBook was doing. . . . We just stood there like a bunch of idiots while it uploaded that filth." He stood and began to pace. "This guy Torvald was full of gimmicks. Apparently he would offer mints to anybody, indiscriminately, to himself, too, whenever the mood came upon him, blind. It's a miracle nobody else died. So far as we know, anyway. It's like a curse, sometimes, with these types of guys. The fix is in. No matter how they tempt fate, they don't go down until it's their time to go down. The tablets were about the same size as his mints, but the mints were white and the cyanide a pale blue. In the dark, or in choosing by touch, one might easily be mistaken for the other." Garcia shook his head. "We only caught the bastard because he was ready to be caught. With that cat blood he might as well have put a big neon arrow over his house. But first," he added morosely, "I had to take a goddamn shower."

He thumbed a key on his palmtop. "Our cyberexpert found a meticulous journal in Torvald's computer. It was encrypted but he'd left the file open, so our man was able to extract the text. Torvald was tired. He was bored and scared and defiant, too. He wanted to get it over with; he couldn't do it just like that. He needed to spice things up as much as possible. He bought a gallon jar of mints, wholesale at CostCo, and added four or five cyanide tablets to it. Even he wasn't sure how many. Then he scooped out his daily supply by the tinful, without looking at them. The medical examiner says even one of the cyanide tablets constitutes a massive overdose. As it happened, the tin Torvald left behind had one other tablet in it, so there were two cyanide tablets in it the day he kidnapped you and Ms Hahn."

"So somebody's number was up, and for once it happened to be Torvald's."

"It's damned hard to look at it another way. The dose barely gave him time to start uploading the movie virus. He had five to ten minutes of consciousness, maybe twenty minutes after that of vital signs. We missed him by many hours. By the time we got there, his mouth was full of blue foam and he was colder than a dry martini. That's if you don't count that damn iBook sitting there, uploading that movie to site after site, carrying on his evil

213

work for him." Garcia sat down again. "It would have been nice to watch him die."

The hospital morphine pump enables the patient to self-medicate up to a level preset by the attending physician. The dose for a broken cheekbone, a broken rib, a cracked vertebra, and a sutured skull is pretty high.

"I want to tell you something, Mr. Curly Watkins." Garcia squinted. "Are you awake?"

"Sure," I answered, but unconvincingly. My eyelids were on the way down.

"If you hadn't switched that video source, we might not have found Miss Hahn until it was way too late."

I didn't understand. "I thought you said he . . . he set it up that way."

"Angelica Stepnowski was supposed to have been his last victim. But when he first laid eyes on Miss Hahn, Torvald was smitten. Purely by chance, she got away. But then he figured out a way to get her to come back. You weren't supposed to be with her."

My eyes had sunk below half-mast.

"Are you awake?"

"I'm here. I just. . . . Resting. . . ."

Garcia cleared his throat and pressed on. "The stairs to his torture studio were accessed by a hatch under the refrigerator. It took us the rest of the night to find it. We would have looked eventually but if not for you we might have waited until daylight to initiate the search. You know, let the lab boys have the run of the place first. The procedure is to let them lift every print and hair before we tear apart the crime scene. Heck, by then Ms Hahn would have been looking at dehydration, kidney failure, internal bleeding. . . . Insanity, even. Death, very possibly."

"Dredth." I exhaled a long sigh.

"It was just a punch, a slap almost. We saw it. We all did. It was eerie. The doctor says he can't understand how you managed to overcome the paralysis sufficiently to do it, and the shock is going to cost you. But. . . ." Garcia paused. "You don't even remember doing that, do you?"

I lost consciousness.

I awoke to whispering shadows in a darkened room. The staff were removing the corpse from the adjacent bed. Whether I found this comforting or not, I fell asleep again. I awoke a second time to the sounds of a pillow being plumped. Comforting or not. . . . When I awoke a third time, two orderlies, supervised by a nurse, were transferring a groaning personage from a wheelchair to the empty bed. There was a lot of scuffling. I drifted off again. The next time I opened my eyes, it was night. Red numeric LEDs on the morphine machine blinked beside my bed. The room was illuminated by the flickering of a single silent television beaming its version of reality at my new roommate, who was snoring. The sound was off. Between our beds stood an empty wheelchair.

An orderly at the nurse's station in front of the eighth floor elevators didn't pay much attention to the specks of fresh blood inside the elbow of my nightie. He helpfully pointed my way, and I wheeled inexpertly down the hall.

I had the door pushed half open, using the wheelchair's footrests, when a woman, not much taller than me sitting down, pulled it wide. One look at me and she said, "This is the wrong room."

"Excuse me." I double-checked the numbered plaque. "Lavinia Hahn?"

"Who wants to know?"

The woman wore half-lens reading glasses from which dangled a rhinestone lanyard. The hand that held the door also held a copy of *Reader's Digest*, one finger keeping place. Her hair had

215

been cropped and tinted into a concept of eggplant severity that went with her rose fingernails and maroon pant-suit and rust-tinted blouse and American flag brooch. Whether paste or real its tiny colored stones and their gold setting twinkled on the slope of her bosom like the distant lights of a small mountain resort.

"Curly Watkins. I'm a friend."

"My daughter has no friends in San Francisco."

"Oh, hello, Mrs. Hahn. I'm pleased to meet you. I'm—"

"Threllgood. Hahn is her father's name. Not that it's any of your business, Mr. Watson."

"Watkins. Call me Curly."

She glowered at my discolored face and the two or three weeks' worth of cranial stubble that surrounded a shaved patch crosshatched by sutures that looked like a crop circle and she didn't call me anything. But I had been away from my warm bed and warmer morphine for half an hour already and was no more in the mood for false accommodation than she was.

"When my hair grows out, I'll look just like a stockbroker," I assured her.

Mrs. Threllgood expelled a snort of frank incredulity.

Beyond her I could see a small form curled in the hospital bed. Atop the standard issue bedclothes lay a mostly maroon patchwork quilt, sufficient to cover a child but too small to cover a supine adult. No doubt Lavinia herself had drawn the covers over her head to forestall confronting her indomitable mother. Ranked along a shelf over the headboard were a stuffed tiger, a Pooh bear, and a black-spotted purple dinosaur. All were threadbare. A pink, slightly deflated heart-shaped mylar balloon about eighteen inches across and bearing the word LOVE in letters of silver glitter drifted above the bed, tethered to the side rail of the bedstead by a spangled blue ribbon. A mild draft from an overhead heat vent caused the balloon to search one way and another, like an aquarium carp oscillating listlessly from one glass wall of its narrow tank to the next. Mrs. Threllgood backed me

216

into the hall and let the door close behind her. A cart clattered past, reeking of steamed food, pushed by a tired woman wearing green scrubs and white latex gloves. A speaker embedded in the hall ceiling paged a doctor. The hospital was beginning to wake up.

"How is Lavinia?" I asked the woman.

Having relocated her daughter's undesirable visitor into the neutral hallway, Mrs. Threllgood felt comfortable enough to say, "Recovering, no thanks to this place."

"I'm glad to hear it."

"A few weeks at a nice clinic will put her to rights." She sounded confident, but more likely she was resigned to being determinedly hopeful. Repetition of the mantra might make it come true. A word like "clinic" with respect to someone like Lavinia means sanatorium, that is to say, a detoxification facility. I wasn't certain as to how much her mother was admitting to herself about her daughter's addiction, but I was sure she saw no reason to be forthcoming with the likes of me. "Ah, yes," I said, as if wistfully. "A few weeks in the mountains. Fresh air, three square meals a day, badminton, a lap pool, massage, acupuncture and a fentanyl patch, far from the madding crowd's ignoble strife—" I stopped myself before I reminded her that the last phrase was plucked, long ago, from Gray's poem of the country churchyard. It seemed to portend a negative arc.

Mrs. Threllgood fixed the more obvious of my stigmata with eyes the color of anodized aluminum. "Some of us are beyond rehabilitation," she suggested pointedly.

Look to thine own tentacles, I might have said. But there was no reason not to endeavor to reassure the poor woman. If she cared at all, she had lost plenty of sleep over her daughter. "Lavinia will respond from day one. She'll be as good as new in no time. She has a lot of guts. I know her well." Her face darkened. I hastened to ask, "Would you have any idea as to when she might feel up to receiving a visitor?"

217

Mrs. Threllgood opened her mouth to say never, but thought better of it. A veil fell over her eyes, and wheels turned behind it. "Let me think." She enumerated her fingers with one end of the spine of her magazine. "The doctor will be making his rounds any time now. There's physical therapy, then lunch. A nap after lunch, a sponge bath after the nap. . . ." She pretended to cast her mind into the future. "Shall we say. . . ." She brightened, "Six-thirty this evening?"

"Fine," I said.

Her features relaxed, and she pointed the *Reader's Digest* at me. "Watson?"

"Watkins." I awkwardly rolled back and through a half turn. "I'd be obliged if you were to inform Lavinia that Curly wishes her a speedy recovery, and will pay his respects at six-thirty."

"Until this evening, then. Six-thirty. No earlier."

"So nice to have met you."

"Charmed, I'm sure."

"Curly," I reminded her, with a glance over my shoulder as I rolled away. Mrs. Threllgood didn't bother to conceal an expression she might normally have reserved for a piece of rotted salmon, as she transferred it from the meat drawer in her refrigerator to the trash caddy beneath the sink.

When I returned to the eighth floor at one o'clock, Lavinia and her mother were gone.

Twenty

The puncture contusions on my arms went well with the red-white-and-blue pineapple shirt Garcia's kindly social worker brought me from Goodwill, along with some cargo pants and a clean pair of hospital booties that passed for socks. My own boots were still wearable, but the rest of my clothing had been cut to ribbons by determined paramedics.

There's a bus that runs down Arguello from California until it takes a right on Fulton instead of going into the park, and only after it made the turn did I realize I was going west instead of east. I got off at the next stop and jay-limped across Fulton. I walked southeast through the park toward Stanyan, stopping more than once to rest in shady glades nestled behind the stone wall that isolates that corner of the park from the busy streets that border it. The sun photonated my narcotized eyeballs. The hangover from morphine and Torvald's curare had left me with the squinting stumbles. But I enjoyed the fresh air enough to persevere, on foot, to Haight Street. From there I caught a bus down to Octavia and walked halfway down the block and up three flights to my crib.

It looked just as I'd left it. The Gibson that belonged in the case with the bullet hole, now no doubt taking up space in some evidence locker, stood just inside the front door, next to the Mexican six-string. Clothes on the floor, dishes in the sink, dust on the furniture, mind on the blink. Make note for song. The back door must have been open since the night Lavinia stopped by. But the ersatz Picasso nailed over the window would stop any but the most single-minded burgling tweaker, and nothing obvious was missing. And anyway, excepting the two guitars, there wasn't much to miss. The B on the Mexican six-string had snapped in my absence. A change of temperature can do that. But a broken string on a guitar leaning in a dusty corner looks pretty forlorn, no two ways about it.

The glass I'd been drinking out of three weeks earlier stood in the sink. There was half an inch of vodka left in the half gallon jug, whose top was missing. I rinsed the glass, found one ice cube in the freezer, added the vodka, gave it a swirl, and downed half the dose. It tasted just like all the other medicines I'd been taking.

The pad was a riot of desuetude. I'd lived there for fifteen years and didn't want to be there anymore. In fact, however, I had no place else to go.

I emptied my pockets onto the kitchen table: a ring with three keys, a long printout from Children's Hospital, a wad of bills, mostly hundreds, and the cellphone.

The phone's digital window registered no calls. I shook it. Still no calls. I turned it on and listened: no dial tone. If you don't use it, a charge lasts a long time. But not three weeks. I plugged it in and set it aside.

I pulled up a chair and counted the cash. Six hundred and twelve dollars. I had maybe five hundred in the bank. If I took care of all my obligations—rent, the broken car, its registration, etc., I could spend it all before dark and still come up short.

Money. Goddamn money.

The key ring had the two keys to get into the building and the apartment, plus the mailbox key. Mail meant bills. To stave off that disappointment I restrung the guitar. I tuned it, too, but I didn't play it. I stood it against the wall behind the door and went downstairs to collect the mail.

There was a bill from the cell phone company: Forty-seven bucks. Peanuts. What that meant was few calls and even less business. There was the usual junk mail—two credit card offers, a postcard depicting a two-headed dog created by animal-abusing scientists in Russia, and a pink flier advertising a water-efficient toilet I could buy from the city for ten dollars in an Embarcadero warehouse two Saturdays ago. The eviction notice was *pro forma*. The lawyers that owned the building could double or even triple the rent if they managed to get me out of there. But I still had ten days to pay the overdue rent.

The only piece of mail that looked real was a lumpy envelope from Children's Hospital, hand-addressed to me.

I must have forgotten my worry beads.

I opened it. A car key on a ring with a Lexus alarm fetish fell onto the table. There was a letter, too, hand printed on three feet of toilet paper.

Curly Darling,

You should have let me take the gun, you stupid fuck.

Okay. I got that off my chest.

I didn't think I was going to get a chance to write. Mother's been watching me like a hawk. But right now she's down the hall arguing about what the insurance covers. My nurse said he'd see that this letter got stamped and mailed if I could get it to him by the end of his shift. It's a bitch with one wrist in a cast and oops the pen tears this paper but here goes.

Looks like this is the end for me and San Francisco, Curly. I didn't make much of a run at the old town either and anyway, it's more like the town has made a run at me. I'm done. Remember how we used to make fun of trust-fund kids from the East Coast? The ones who came west, kept you up all night talking about Art, took every drug, wrecked your car, broke up someone's marriage, starred in a porn film, and disappeared without a trace? Friend, lover, no matter, poof: Gone with not even an adiós. Years later one or

221

another of them would be spotted wearing a silly hat on a late-night TV commercial, insisting on the quality of the used cars vended by the dealership he'd inherited from his daddy in Buffalo. Now he's treasurer of the Rotarians, a member of his wife's church, he's got the golf game down to a six handicap whatever that means, there's one kid in college with two still in high school, and his cocaine consumption is confined to two binges a year at his beachfront timeshare in Belize.

Those guys. Remember them?

Well, Curly, brace yourself. Except for the used cars and the co-caine—I hope—c'est moi. I just held out longer than the rest of them, that's all. And it's not Buffalo, it's Pittsburgh.

I haven't seen Daddy in years and Mother's married to a man I can't stand but the fact is there are considerable assets that need looking after—they came to me from Grandmother—and I just can't pretend to manage them long-distance and strung out anymore. I see that now. A bank has been looking after them for years but it seems they've squandered and mismanaged and maybe even embezzled a meaningful portion of my nest egg and, as you musicians say, use it or lose it—right?

Not that I'll have to bite the bullet exactly. Mother's found a nice place in rural Pennsylvania where they ease you off whatever drug you're stuck on with a decreasing dose and a strict regime. Whatever it takes. You even get a personal trainer. The trust will pay for it so money's not a problem. In short—a new life!

Okay, Christopher just stuck his head in the door to say he's clocking out in five minutes.

I want you to have the Lexus. (As far as I know it's still parked around the corner from—ugh—you know where.) I'll mail you the title when I get out of detox, if I can find it. Meanwhile the registration is current until I think June. If Mother remembers the car at all I'll tell her I totaled it after I let the insurance lapse. By the way I was awake when she got rid of you this morning. Rightly or wrongly she associates you with Ivy and San Francisco and everything west of the Monongahela River, which is anathema to her, so I thought it best to 'let sleeping dogs lie'. Once Mother makes up her mind she is rather intransigent.

Here's Christopher.

I learned a lot from you Curly. Forget being a security guard, okay? Don't ever give up on your real talent. I'll be watching the bins for your records!

Love,
Lavinia

As regarded her daughter's recovery, it didn't look like Mrs. Threllgood was going to have much to worry about.

I was sitting with the keys in one hand and the thirty-inch tail of the letter in the other, thinking that the last time I missed a bus after a gig and had to walk home amounted to the last time I stayed up all night for art, when the cell phone rang. I jumped so hard, my cracked rib tweaked. It startled me. It really did.

"Mr. Curly Watkins, please."

"Padraic," I gasped, pressing the rib with the palm of my free hand, "is that really you?"

"Do people actually buy drugs from you?"

"Who, me? Never. I give them away."

"You don't sell them? Truly?"

"I promise."

"Good. I need a guitarist."

"You—?" I cleared my throat. "The rates you pay, I'm sure you do."

"I'm serious."

"So am I. But you fired me just. . . . When did you fire me?"

"Three, four weeks ago. Forget about that. The guys been coming through here, you wouldn't believe these guys. And they call themselves musicians?"

Three weeks? Four? It seemed like a year. "Did you advertise?"

"Advertising costs money. I put a notice in the window. Better I should put a sign on my back: KICK ME HARD. They are bad, these guys. Bad musicians!"

223

"What, no girls?"

"Oh, yeah, sure. Pretty girls, tall girls, three girls at once, even a pregnant girl. But they don't got . . . what you call it."

I shrugged. "Chutzpah?"

"Chutzpah, they got. What they don't have is songs. I mean knowledge. You know? What do you call it?"

Chops, I thought to myself. Aloud I said, "Repertoire?"

"That's it. Repertoire. How come this stuff is in French?"

"You mean how come it's not in Arabic?"

"It is in Arabic. But you don't speak Arabic."

"I don't speak French either."

"That's what I like about you, Curly. You are one hundred percent American."

I looked at the letter. It looked like toilet paper with writing on it. I wondered if it already came like that, by the roll, with the writing already on it. They could sell it in train stations. The wad of hundred dollar bills took on an abstract quality too, ruined and illegible like a waterlogged book. But somebody already makes toilet paper that looks like money. My eye fell on the Lexus key and I thought, I could drive to work.

"Same old job?"

"Yeah." Padraic said. "Sure."

I'd known Padraic Mousaief for a long time. In an environment designed to help his customers linger, he was convinced that just the right music would encourage them to linger longer. It had to do with money.

"Three sets? Forty-five minutes each? Forty-five bucks and dinner? A glass of wine after each set?"

"I was thinking maybe thirty-five bucks and an extra glass of wine, before you start—plus the one at the end," he hastily added.

"I like that extra glass of wine. Even your wine. But I gotta have the forty-five bucks. Isn't that what you meant when you said it was the same gig?"

224

Padraic hesitated. "Some people come in, they ask where are you."

"Make it sixty bucks. Dinner, sixty bucks, and four glasses of wine."

Silence on the line. I was certain I could hear the satellite whistling through the ionosphere. Finally Padraic said, "Okay. I accept."

"No, my friend, *I* accept."

"But you don't play loaded."

"Padraic," I said. "Have you ever known me to play loaded?"

He let that one go. "Six-thirty. We'll talk before you start at seven."

I grabbed a bus up Van Ness to Geary and maintained an uninterrupted train of thought about mostly nothing in the back of the nearly empty 39, even as it bored into a freezing wall of evening fog at Arguello. The bus and I stayed like that, cool and empty, all the way out Geary to 38th Avenue.

Walking downhill toward Anza the westerly nearly tore the gig bag off my back. I switched it to the windward shoulder. Better a guitar handcrafted in the mountains of Guerrero, whose luthier never imagined conditions such as these, than me. I wore a pea jacket, buttoned to my Adam's apple with the collar turned up, and a watch cap. The Navy wore such caps and jackets in the North Atlantic during World War II, but so what? A San Francisco fog penetrates them like gasoline wicks through cheesecloth.

The Lexus was parked where we'd left it, and its windshield wipers were festooned with parking tickets. They flapped in the breeze like a row of Tibetan prayer flags, each envelope a half-day or day more weather-beaten than the one succeeding it. The moment I swept them into the gutter, the car was mine. People had noticed that the back window was blown out and helped themselves to the CD player, the spare tire, and the jack. The

225

trunk, the driver's door, the glove box and the console lid were all open. Somebody had wiped their miserable ass with Lavinia's picnic blanket—that's what it looked like, anyway, from a discreet distance—and left it in the gutter. Insurance notices, maps, more parking tickets, and pages of the owner's manual were lifting and settling in windy eddies up and down the sidewalk.

Lids closed, blanket and tickets disposed of, this was still a nice car. But even blowfish, perfectly prepared, has its dark side. Somebody had been spending his nights in my back seat. The odor peculiar to an unwashed body suppurating badly metabolized wine from every pore clung tenaciously to the car's interior. Somebody had pissed back there, too. The more expensive the upholstery, the more difficult it is to get rid of such aromas. Ever notice that?

Somebody had knifed the leather upholstery and broken the steering lock, but nobody had bothered to steal the battery. The car started and purred, as silent and smooth as the odors from the back seat were loud and rough. All said and done, the Lexus might have the makings of a perfect street ride: trashed on the outside, mechanically sound on the inside. So what if the seats had been slashed? In such condition, people might leave it alone.

I powered down all the windows for the fresh air and made a U-turn out of the parking space. This put me on 38th looking south across Anza. I took a right, westbound, and immediately passed Torvald's adjacent houses. Both properties were garlanded with yellow Police Line, Do Not Cross, and Crime Scene tape, vibrating in the wind. A sheet of unpainted plywood was nailed over the front door of Torvald's home. Some lengths of tape had parted. The buildings with their trailing ribbons gave the impression of a grounded box kite, its two sections painted the same shade of an unadventurous gray.

226

Twenty-one

I drove the ten or twelve blocks out Fulton to the beach and parked there with the engine running. A sea was running too, much louder than the Lexus motor. Two surfers lingered astride their boards in the gloom of dusk, trying to make sense of water that boils at fifty-five degrees. A couple of dog walkers were way up the beach. Everything they had, hair, shirttails, pantlegs, parka hoods, and the mane of their golden retriever was blowing straight east. The Lexus engine was so quiet I could hear grains of sand ticking against the windshield. If I parked the car out there every night for a year, the glass would become opalescent.

Caffeine Machine held down the corner of Judah and 44th Avenue, a streetcar stop just a few blocks east of the Great Highway and Land's End. One thing about that address, there is always parking. Another thing is the streetcars that thunder by in two directions at all hours. Their rumble generally cancels out whatever guitar playing is going on inside the front window of the coffee house. But, hey, they say it rained at Woodstock.

Despite the freezing wind Padraic was pacing up and down the sidewalk out front, speaking Arabic into his cellphone and smoking a cigarette. He always sounded like he was arguing when he spoke Arabic; he sounded that way when he was speaking English, too. I didn't blame him. The son of a Palestinian professor of economics and an Irish relief worker, he grew up in Ramallah. When the Israelis nabbed a first cousin in an arms smuggling sting, they bulldozed every relative's home, and Padraic's side of the clan made its way to Jordan, where they languished in a refugee camp for two years before an uncle managed to land the three of them in San Francisco. That was a break, and Padraic was making the most of it. But, on the whole, Padraic Mousaief remained a naturally pissed-off guy.

Things hadn't changed inside the cafe, either. There were a vocal and guitar mike in the window to the right of the front door with a small wooden chair, very casual, to give the appearance that the entertainer had just taken a notion to get up there and play, inspired-like.

The rest of the place was equally stark and equally contrived. The floor was sanded maple with a hard finish. The walls had a nasturtium frieze in yellows, greens, and a loud orange, painted by an amateur for the price of the materials and a year of free coffee. The twelve-foot ceiling was high enough to hang art from the picture rail without its lower corners dangling in the soup or gouging customers in the back. There were always paintings or photographs on the walls, provided by a professional service that came around once a month to change them. All pictures were for sale. Padraic got a cut, the service got a cut, and, who knows, maybe the artist got a cut, too.

It had taken me a while to figure out what was going on in this place, but eventually I realized that Padraic had obtained all his chairs and all his tables from a day-care center that had gone out of business. That the price was right—get this stuff out of here and it's yours—went without saying; but having been constructed for children his tables and chairs could not comfortably accommodate an adult for any length of time. For some reason, rather than discouraging repeat business, the cramped seating increased it. My theory was that Padraic's customers were so wrapped up in their internal discomfort it never occurred to them that there could be an external, and simpler, cognate. The small furniture also explained why Padraic was able to jam fifty or so settings with a kitchen and a pastry counter into a thousand square feet.

One thing I never figured out was why, despite mediocre food and abysmal service provided by an ever-changing staff of clueless youth working for minimum wage plus tips, Caffeine Machine had lines for Sunday brunch. Lots of people hung around the rest of the time, too, drinking coffee, typing on their laptop computers, talking on their cellphones, and pushing feckless heaps of hashed brown potatoes around their plates while they discussed —what?

There was music playing almost all the time. Often I'd hear what has now become mainstream jazz—*Kind of Blue* Miles Davis and so forth—but most of the time Padraic let the kids working the tables play whatever they wanted to bring in, thus saving him the expense of purchasing CDs.

Often I wondered why Padraic wanted any live music in his place at all. But despite the canned art, the uncomfortable environment, and a decidedly unartistic clientele, they and Padraic too were acting out a nostalgia for a San Francisco they'd only heard about, a bohemian, poetry-spouting, Socialist, dues-paying, longshoreman, merchant-marine, two-fisted, labor-organizing, jazz-loving, jazz-playing, chain-smoking, hard-drinking, pot-growing, blue-collar milieu that is nothing if not ninety percent perished from the glorious island of prime real estate that retains the name of San Francisco. No daring thin ice for the cafe owner who hangs great art on the walls of his joint because his wife insists it's great; no clutch of credit chits under the tray in the cash register, the names on which can be found in almost equal number along the spines in the poetry room at City Lights Books; no pawned musical instruments in the back room, either; or forgotten dogeared underlined copies of Verlaine erotica or

Mingus charts. Me? I was there because my rent-controlled apartment allowed me to work in San Francisco for forty-five—make that sixty—dollars a night, supplemented by music lessons and royalties from songs I'd published fifteen years before. I entertained no illusions; Padraic retained my services as a nostalgia act, as vestigial to his Bohemian cafe as glass slippers on a two-toed amphiuma.

The door opened and closed behind me. "So you've come."

I had aged years since I'd last set foot in this cafe. The customers looked like kids. They looked naive, innocent, thin, prosperous, uninteresting, and let's don't forget ambitious. Hard by me sat a young woman reading a book called *How to Get Rich and Stay That Way—N.Y. Times National Best-Seller!*

"Yes, Padraic," I turned to face him, "I've come." Padraic wore a look of well-fed prosperity. A cookie-cutter version of this cafe half-way across town, Caffeine Machine No. 2, backed up this image with cash. No. 3 was in the works. He had the Mercedes SUV and three kids and a wife and a house in which to keep them all, too, but, no dummy, Padraic Mousaief bought his house in Hayward, across the Bay and twenty miles south on the freeway, where, they tell me, money still means something.

"Jesus Christ, Curly, what happened to your face?"

"I had an accident. But, don't worry. I feel . . . centered."

Padraic frowned. How can a shaved head with an octopus tattooed on it get any weirder? Well, start with a centipede of sutures, then add two black eyes. But I still had the watch cap on, so the face must have looked pretty bad.

Padraic overcame his misgivings enough to parry, "You should feel rested. A month without working? You sell a big song or something? Still, you look tired. How about a nice cup of coffee?" He clasped my arm and smiled. "On me."

"How about that first glass of wine instead?"

His smile faded.

"Red wine."

His eyes shifted. "While we're on the subject, there's one other thing."

Maybe I was tired. Usually I don't trust the minor details of wage-earning to the hands of the people I do business with, whether they're likable or not. "One other thing?"

The cashier was new but there was nothing new about that. Padraic beckoned, and she passed him a printout, which he turned over to me.

I had a look. "There seems to be a theme, here."

"How perceptive. The question is, do you know them?"

"Know them? You can't escape them."

"Excellent!" Padraic said. He clapped me on the shoulder, eliciting a wince. He noticed. He gingerly removed his hand and said, "You'll play them, then?"

"All of them?"

"If there's time. If you know them all. If not, you could repeat a few from set to set."

"But aren't these tunes a little . . . patriotic? That's the word."

"Of course they're patriotic. That's the idea." His cell phone began to chirp.

"Where the hell did you dig it up? The Library of Congress?"

"I took a poll." He swept his arm at the room as he unclipped the phone from his belt. "It's what they want. Hello."

I stared at the list. Padraic might not have been the first merchant in San Francisco to display a large American flag in the front window of his business after September 11, 2001, but he came close. Padraic's flag was up and showing no wrinkles before noon, Pacific Standard Time, and I can't say that I blame him. Three nights a week, until he took it down some three months later, I sat on a chair in front of that flag and played standards.

"Padraic. What about jazz, America's classical music?"

Padraic, listening to the cellphone clasped to his ear, raised a forefinger and wagged it right and left. I continued anyway.

"Couldn't we have more of a, I don't know, not a musical debate exactly but some variety, a sort of a musical dialogue, let's say?"

Agreeing with whomever he was talking to, Padraic wagged his finger back and forth and directed my attention to the front of the cafe. There the new cashier was helping a new waiter hang a new American flag in the alcove containing the mike stands. This flag was bigger than the earlier version. It would cover the entire window, like a curtain.

"How about," I said, "*Autumn in New York?* Or *Waltzing Matilda?* Those are . . . they're . . . relevant tunes. . . ?"

Padraic put his hand over the mouthpiece of his phone and quietly mouthed, *Too depressing*, in English. He removed his hand and began to disagree with the guy on the phone, too, only louder and in Arabic.

At that moment my own phone rang. Twice in one week? It had to be a wrong number. Since Padraic had interrupted our conversation to answer his phone, I interrupted it to answer mine.

The voice beamed down from the satellite, inviolate. "Curly baby, I am calling to rock your world."

"Oh, no. I only answered because I thought it was Carnegie Hall calling about my birthday tribute. Can't we talk tomorrow, Ivy? I'd rather have my world rocked after I've had a good night's sleep. It's not so hard on my kinesthesia."

"Sal 'The King' Kramer waits for no man nor no car sickness. Not only that but our quarry is scheduled to take the Midnight Flyer to L.A. tonight. You take possession of your new Lexus, yet?"

"How'd you know about the Lexus?"

"What, you think private hospital rooms come without telephones?"

"When did you talk to her?"

"Right before her mother pulled the plug. Is it gassed up?"

"Why?"

"The guy lives in Bolinas."

232

"So? What's that to me?"

"So come get me. Get a move on. Bolinas is a long way from Oakland."

I stalled. "You're nuts. What time is it?"

"It was my Daddy's watch," Ivy drawled. "I hated to pawn it."

A clock hung over the grill in the back of the cafe. "It's five minutes to seven."

"So?"

"So I'm to hell and gone at 44th and Judah. It'll take me at least an hour to get to you, fifteen minutes to gas up someplace along the way—"

Ivy laughed. "You know exactly where to gas up along the way."

"Another hour and a half puts us at nine-forty-five probably ten o'clock just to get to Bolinas, let alone find your . . . quarry."

"That's why we're taking the Lexus instead of your piece of shit Honda. It'll be faster."

Ivy knew I was stalling but I didn't care, for, just then, I bumped my teeth with the edge of the cellphone. Earlier, re-stringing the guitar, I'd noticed that my hands weren't as agile as they should have been. It was true I hadn't played in a month. But I'd been warned about the aftereffects of my recent drug experiences, and now reality dawned. No matter what I thought about Padraic Mousaief's patriotic playlist, it might be the only music I'd be capable of playing for a while. Maybe for a long while. Maybe—

"Curly? You there?"

"I'm here, Ivy."

"You sound depressed."

"Depressed? Why would I sound depressed?"

"If you're at 44th and Judah, you're about to kick off your first set in that shitbird cafe out there. Boring music for boring people in a boring place. Who wouldn't be depressed?"

"Listen, Ivy," I said sharply, "we can't all live the exciting life of a full-time junky."

"We can't all be full-time shitty guitarists, either," Ivy replied matter-of-factly.

"I can hardly believe I'm talking to the greatest jazz drummer ever to let me play with him," I shot back, "let alone the best player I ever knew to just plain hang it the fuck up."

"Listen to me carefully, Curly," Ivy said evenly, "while I set you straight on the one fact you need to know about life."

"Yeah? What fact is that?"

"The music business sucks."

Padraic clapped shut his cellphone and tapped one of its corners against the crystal of his watch.

The front door of the cafe opened and four or five people trailed in, talking excitedly. The lights of a streetcar skimmed over the street behind them, borne along by the thunder of rolling stock.

"Thirty-two hundred bucks," the phone said, the rumbling of the streetcar and the palaver of the crowd insufficient to drown the voice entirely. "Split two ways and I'll cover expenses. Plus," it added emphatically, "I'll hit you with that hundred bucks you were so kind as to front me in my hour of need."

I'd forgotten about that hundred bucks. But I said, "I'm losing you, Ivy."

Padraic tapped my shoulder.

"All the expenses," the phone continued. "Gasoline, bridge tolls, speedball, potato chips. . . ."

Padraic placed a tumbler of red wine in my free hand. "You can eat after the first set." He waved at a large slate that hung over the cash register, covered with menu items in colored chalk. "Anything you like."

"Curly?" the phone said. "You there?"

I held the phone away from my face.

"Well?" Padraic said.

"Curly. . . ?"

234

As before any gig, including yours, I powered down the phone and dropped it into my jacket pocket.

"Those two guys that just came in," Padraic said in a stage whisper, "with the three girls? They build web sites."

I swallowed half the tumbler of wine at a draught, took time to breathe, and downed the rest.

"They rent that storefront where the cabinetmaker used to be," he added significantly. "Right up the street."

"Try not to gloat." I wiped my lips with the back of my sleeve. "Out of all the grapes pressed in California, how do you manage to find such lousy wine?" I offered him the empty glass. "I'll have another."

"The neighborhood is changing," Padraic said significantly.

"Caesar salad with roasted chicken," I said, not glancing at the slate but watching Padraic. "And another glass of red."

Padraic glanced at the empty glass, then looked at me.

"I'd like the wine now," I said, "before I start."

He took the glass but I could see the outburst welling up. Before he could speak, I told him, "Charge me, Padraic. Run a tab." I held up my hands. "Look." They were shaking. Padraic frowned at them. Then he looked at me.

"Bring it."

Padraic handed the glass to the girl behind the counter. "Another cabernet."

I walked to the alcove next to the front door and hung my jacket on the back of the chair. I kept on the watch cap. Somebody turned off the CD player, leaving the room to its chatter. Nobody looked my way.

I stripped the gig bag off the guitar and sat down in the little wooden chair in front of the American flag. Two twenty-somethings at a little round table not three feet beyond the microphones looked at me uncomfortably. Without consulting one another they began to gather their things. I placed Padraic's list on the floor where I could see it and brought the guitar up to pitch in eight or ten strokes. By the time I'd improvised an introduction to the first tune on the list, the girls had moved to another table.